Before Senior Year

Paige Macfarlan

Contents

Chapter 1

My eyelids are torn from their closed position and it doesn't take me long to discover why. All I can hear is the brutal roaring of an engine. I sit up in my bed and push the curtains away from the window. It takes a minute for my eyes to adjust to the near-blinding sunlight and I look out towards the road and see what turned my peaceful cul-de-sac into a highway: a moving truck.

It is way too damn early for this.

I shove my black room darkening curtains back into place as I flop backwards and the back of my head reconnects with my pillow as a knock on my bedroom door arrives.

Now what?

"Alex! Are you awake?" my mother calls.

"How could I not be?" I yell back.

She nudges my door open and invites herself into my room. I can barely make out her shoulder-length blonde curls through the darkness.

"The new neighbors are moving in." She smiles.

"Yay," I say sarcastically and roll my eyes to prove my point.

"This is exciting." She sits on my bed and squeezes my leg. "We should go over and introduce ourselves."

"Mom, no, that's weird." I shake my head.

"It is not weird. It's nice."

"Okay, well, I will not be going over."

"Let's see what they look like." She reaches over me and opens my curtains.

"Mom, it's too bright!" I bring my hand up to cover my eyes.

She completely ignores me as she pulls the curtains open wider. "Oh, there's a little girl!"

"How little?" I ask through a yawn.

"Probably about four or five."

"Cute," I say.

"Looks like there's a son, too."

"Cute," I repeat.

"Yeah, he is." She smirks.

Oh no.

"What's that about?"

"He looks like he's about your age."

"Okay."

"Come look."

"Not interested."

"Alex."

"I have a boyfriend."

"Oh, please. Johnny is hardly a boyfriend. I give you two another month at most."

I roll my eyes.

"Just come look."

I sit up and join her at the window.

I take in the boy's short brown hair and tanned skin. He's gotta be at least six feet tall and it's easy to see he spends plenty of time working out.

He is pretty cute.

"What do you think?" She grins.

"I think I'm exhausted from their truck waking me."

"They gotta get their stuff to their new house somehow."

"Doesn't have to be this early."

"It's nine."

"Still early."

"Do you want them to move in the middle of the night?"

"That would be better than waking me up this early."

"Well, use it as a head start."

"For what?"

"Take a shower, do your hair and makeup, and get over there to introduce yourself."

"I am not doing that."

"He's cute, you should." She urges.

"I'm going back to bed."

She rises up from her spot on my mattress and I think I'm in the clear as she begins to move towards the doorway.

"I'll find out your future last name when I go over in a little bit."

Of course.

I lay in bed with my eyes closed and try to fall back asleep but the new people are very loudly unloading their moving truck. Metal is clanging against metal, things they don't need to move in first seem to be getting roughly tossed aside. I realize that my attempt at getting more sleep is useless so with one last yawn I roll out of bed. My feet land on my tan carpet and I walk across my room. The index finger of my right hand is slow to flick my light switch into the on position and the bright light reflects off my three white walls and nearly blinds me. The reflection of my room in my mirror shows that the pale blue of my freshly painted accent wall is even more beautiful than I anticipated.

Maybe I should paint the other three too.

A shower does seem nice right about now so I slide open my dresser drawers and grab a pair of dark blue denim shorts and a black tank top with silver buttons. I pull out a black strapless bra and a pair of black panties to match. My finger flicks the light off and I wander down the hallway.

I pull open the door to the linen closet and yank a green bath towel off one of the shelves. My hands struggle to hold everything as I close the closet door with my foot and enter the bathroom. I plop my supplies on the counter before shutting and locking the door and flipping on the three switches next to it. The lights flicker on and the fan grunts a few times before finding its strength.

I start the water for my shower and let it heat up while I undress. When I'm out of my pajamas, I stick my hand under the shower head to check the water temp. It feels perfect so I slide the floral shower curtain out of my way and step into the tub. My hair is the first thing I wet and I let the warm water dampen the rest of my body soon after. I pick up my bottle of pink, floral scented body wash and squirt a decent amount into the palm of my left hand. I coat my body with it and the liquid is cool against my skin. The foam slides between my fingers as I glide my hands over my body. Once my body is clean, I pick up my dark purple razor and shave my underarms and my legs. I cut my legs a few times and watch the dots of blood get slowly larger.

That's what I get for using an old razor.

I rinse the tiny spots of blood and leftover soap off my legs before squirting a bit of shampoo into the palm of my hand. I run it through my hair and let the water wash it out after a minute. My conditioner bottle doesn't let out any product when I pump the top so I pop it off and see the bottle is completely empty. I grab my mother's bottle of her conditioner and am thankful when I manage to get some out. I drag it through the ends of my hair and rinse it out before I turn off the water and step out of the tub.

My green towel waits for me and I can't pick it up and wrap it around myself fast enough. The goosebumps that cover my body give away how much I already miss the hot water from my shower. I hurry to dry myself off and I wrap my hair in my towel as I dress myself in the outfit I brought into the bathroom with me. I gather my pajamas and wet towel and my fingers flick the three switches to turn off the lights and the fan before I leave the bathroom.

I make it to my bedroom and toss my towel and pajamas into my hamper. The room darkening curtains are doing their job a little too well. My room is pitch black and I can't see shit. I grab my curtains and shove them to the sides of my window. The massive moving truck still hogs the whole dead end and the noise from their unloading is still just as loud.

I can't help but shake my head and walk away from my window toward my black wooden dresser. I pick up my stick of deodorant and apply some to my underarms. My blue hairbrush is the next thing I grab. Today's knots are something else and it takes me ten minutes to completely untangle my long blonde hair.

"Alex!" my mother calls. "I'm heading over to the neighbor's house in fifteen minutes! You're coming with me!"

"Okay!" I yell back.

Better not to argue with mom when I can't use my tiredness as an excuse anymore.

I consider leaving my face naked and not putting on even a drop of makeup and then I remember how hot the new neighbor is and decide I better show him what I'm capable of. My piles of makeup products have never seemed intimidating until now. I scan everything in front of me and start with my foundation and concealer.

Fifteen minutes is not enough time to choose and do decent eye makeup.

By the time I finish with my foundation and concealer, I've settled on a pretty pink eyeshadow. I pick up my brush and gather some product on it and apply it to my eyelids. Once I'm satisfied with my eyeshadow, I grab my mascara and give my lashes a few coats.

"I need lipstick," I say aloud.

I choose a light pink liquid lipstick and drag the applicator over my lips.

Perfect.

"Are you ready?" Mom asks, letting herself into my room.

"All set."

"Your makeup looks nice today."

"Just today?" I grab a pair of tan sandals with a black bow from my closet.

"You smartass."

I laugh as I slide my feet into my shoes.

"I made some cookies to bring over to them."

"What kind?"

"Chocolate chip." She leads us into the kitchen where she grabs the red round platter that's full of cookies.

"Save any for us?"

"Of course." She points to a bag on the white granite countertop on the opposite end of the kitchen. "You think I'm gonna take the time to make cookies and not keep any for me?"

"What the hell are you two still doing here?" Grandma enters the kitchen in her usual pale blue t-shirt and jeans. "You're supposed to be getting Alex a date with that new cutie next door."

"Grandma, you know I have a boyfriend." I roll my eyes.

"Johnny is not a real boyfriend."

"We're on our way now." My mom ends the conversation and slips on a pair of brown flip flops that match her shirt. "We'll be home soon, there's food in the fridge and the pantry that you can have for breakfast."

"Holy God, it's like I've never been home alone before." Grandma shrugs. "I'm seventy years old, I'm good. Go away."

I laugh and lead my mother down the stairs to the front door. Her hands are full with the cookies so I open the wooden door and let her out first so I can close it behind us.

"Make sure you smile, and no rude comments about the moving truck waking you this morning." She warns as we make our way down our sidewalk to our driveway.

I roll my eyes.

"And none of that either."

I follow her out of our driveway and take a handful of steps through the road, careful to stay out of the way of the movers carrying chairs and tables, until we make it to the new neighbors' driveway. My mom leads us up to the red front door that's propped open, letting anyone who pleases enter the tan raised ranch. I knock a few times before slowly beginning the walk up the set of wooden stairs on the right instead of down the ones on the left.

"Hello!" my mom calls out.

"Hello?" a woman answers. "Hello? Is someone here?"

"It's the next door neighbors, in the white house with the red shutters."

"Oh, yes, I'm in the kitchen!"

We make it to the top of the staircase and walk straight into the kitchen.

"Hello." A brown-haired woman with pale skin and glasses smiles. "I'm Maggie."

"I'm Tara," my mom says. "This is my daughter, Alex."

"Hi." I smile.

"We made cookies this morning and thought we'd bring some over. Figured you could use a snack." My mother hands

Maggie the platter and she sets it down on her laminate countertop.

"That's so thoughtful of you. It's so nice to meet you both. Alex, how old are you?"

"Seventeen."

"So is my son. Bryce, get out here! We have neighbors! He's just setting up his room a bit."

"Oh, of course." My mom smiles.

I hear footsteps and the teenage boy I saw before appears in the kitchen.

Don't get me wrong, he was attractive from a distance, but he could be an Abercrombie model when you see him up close.

"Bryce, this is Tara and her daughter, Alex. They live next door."

"What's up?" he asks.

"Hey." I smile.

"Where did you guys move from?" Mom questions.

"Maryland." Maggie smiles. "I got a job offer up here making double so I couldn't pass it up."

"That's great. I'm so glad we finally have good neighbors in this house. The last ones had a couple dogs that were always loose and super vicious."

"And the ones before them had a pet rooster that would screech all day." I add.

"Oh my gosh, that sounds like a circus." Maggie laughs. "Lucky for us, they left the place a wreck. It's the only way I could afford a house big enough for each of the kids to have their own room."

"Where is Layla, by the way?" Bryce asks.

"Your grandmother took her for a walk so I could get some stuff unpacked."

"And I wasn't invited?"

"You can unpack your own things and set up your own room. Layla is four."

"She's also spoiled as hell." He rolls his eyes.

"Alex, do you babysit?"

"Sure." I shrug.

"Why can't I be paid to watch Lay?" Bryce groans.

"Because you need a job and once you find one our work schedules will conflict."

"Okay so what about my days off?"

"Bryce, if I left you in charge for more than ten minutes the house would burn down around you and you wouldn't have a clue."

I can't help but laugh at how accurate that must be.

"Do you have a son?" Maggie asks my mom.

She shakes her head. "Alex is an only child."

Wasn't supposed to be.

"Consider yourself lucky, boys are a damn handful."

"Ma'am, where would you like this couch?" a mover asks.

I look over and see two men half inside the front door, each holding an end of a chocolate brown couch.

"Oh, that can go right downstairs. The room straight at the bottom of the staircase, up against the back wall if you don't mind. Thank you so much!"

I tune out of the conversation and take my first look around. Her countertops are clearly very old and in need of a good cleaning but she has decent appliances and her old black fridge is already in place and hooked up. There's an empty dining room that connects to the kitchen and I wonder if they've ever had a formal dining room table before. I look back at Bryce and he looks much better than his mother at the moment. His clothes fit him perfectly and look like they've only been worn a few times while Maggie's look like she's owned them forever. Bryce's shirt is still bright red and clean but Maggie's has stains scattered around and is a very faded blue. Her hair is up in a ponytail and she looks exhausted.

"Bryce, are you going to be a senior in the fall?" my mom asks him.

Please don't ask him on a date for me too.

"Yeah, I'm gonna be going to the public school, though, not private like most of the people in the area."

"You're coming to South Polk?"

"You go to South Polk?"

"You guys should exchange numbers." Maggie's face lights up. "It'll be nice to have someone you can contact who knows about this place."

"Okay." I nod. "I can show you around if you want."

"That'd be great, actually." Bryce answers.

"That's so sweet of you." Maggie smiles. "Speaking of sweet, they brought cookies."

I hand Bryce my phone and he types his number in before handing me his so I can do the same. Once we have our phones back I look over at his arms and see that his biceps are dangerously close to ripping his sleeves open.

"Like what you see?" Bryce asks as he catches me staring at him.

I blush and look away as his mom hands him a chocolate chip cookie and he takes a bite.

"Great cookies and a cute neighbor," Bryce says quietly for just me to hear as he winks in my direction. "This place might not be so bad."

Chapter 2

Mom and I are halfway through the dead end when I notice a red BMW parked in my driveway that stops me in my tracks.

"What's Johnny's car doing here?" my mom asks and I panic.

"Crap! We had breakfast plans, I totally forgot."

"I'm sure he won't be too mad."

"I was at our new neighbors' house where there is a very attractive seventeen year old boy."

"Okay, he'll be pissed."

Johnny gets out of his car and I look him up and down. His white t-shirt paired with blue jeans and his jet black hair and dark sunglasses has him looking like every girl's dream and my nightmare.

"I have to take your grandma to the doctor today, why don't you two talk?" My mom offers.

I nod and bite my lip as I walk over to Johnny and hug him. He's only three inches taller than me, standing at five-ten, so my head rests perfectly on his shoulder.

"I'm so sorry," I say. "We stopped in to meet the new neighbors and I lost track of time."

"And you didn't answer your phone because?"

I try to think of an excuse for not checking it all morning when I remember it's been on silent the whole time I was next door. "I didn't hear it go off. I'm so, so sorry."

"It's fine." He shakes his head.

"We can do something else."

"Like what?" he groans.

"My mom has to take my grandma to the doctor today."

"That's not much of a date, Alex."

"I wasn't inviting you to a doctor's office." I laugh. "I was inviting you to do something fun here while they're gone."

"What do you have in mind?"

"Whatever you want."

He wraps his arms around me and places his hands on my butt as he kisses me.

Disgusting.

"Let's go inside." I tilt my head up and kiss him again.

He nods so I grab his hand and lead him up the sidewalk. We walk inside and kick our shoes off by the front door before making our way up the stairs.

"Hello, Johnny." Grandma smiles.

"Hey, Maureen," he says and I lead him over to the black couch in the living room.

"We're leaving," my mom says. "We should be back in about three hours."

"Okay." I nod.

"Hey, kid, make sure you wear a condom." Grandma points at Johnny. "I don't want to be a great grandma until I'm dead."

"Would you stop?" Mom laughs. "They aren't having sex."

"They better not be." Grandma shakes her head and starts walking down the stairs.

My mom waves at me to get my attention and mouths the words 'be safe' before following my grandma down the stairs and out the front door.

I wait for the door to close and let out the laugh I've been holding in for the entirety of that situation.

"You told your mom we've had sex?"

"No, my doctor did." I roll my eyes. "She called with the results of the STD tests and since I'm a minor they don't need my permission to share it with my parents."

"That's fucked."

"At least she's fine with it."

"She can't really give you shit for it when she was doing the same thing."

"She just wants me to have an easier life than she did and for my future kids to have a better life than I do."

"Still, she had you when she was fifteen. We're already doing better."

"But we didn't start dating until we were sixteen."

"We've had a whole year to fuck it up, she should trust us by now without having to remind us to use condoms."

"Okay but to be fair, we don't use condoms anymore."

"But she should trust that we at least know that we should."

I laugh at the fact that he thinks that's a valid point. "Do you want to argue over whether or not my mother is handling this piece of information correctly or do you want to watch a movie?"

"I'd rather have sex."

"Well, I'm not in the mood so that's not an option."

"You're never in the mood anymore." He rolls his eyes.

"Sorry that girls need the emotional side of things to be good in order for the physical side to happen."

"That's such bullshit."

"It's not. You treat me like dirt eighty percent of the time."

"Seventy." He argues.

"Are you trying to say you treat me like dirt the majority of the time but arguing about exactly how much?"

"You're fucking exhausting. You always exaggerate. Everything is an overreaction with you."

I let out a sigh. "I'm not arguing with you today. Either knock it off or go home."

"Hey, you're the one who fucked up here. I was all ready to take you on that stupid breakfast date this morning. I did my part."

I don't say anything because he's right.

"You're pathetic."

"I'm sorry," I say quietly.

"Sorry isn't gonna cut it this time."

"Johnny."

"You always put every ounce of blame on me for everything. I'm sick of it, Alex. Nothing is ever gonna be your fault. You didn't answer your phone all morning and you weren't even here when I showed up for our date but I'm somehow still the asshole."

I look down at my hands in my lap and start picking at my nails.

"You have nothing to say to me?" he asks.

"You didn't want an apology." I shrug. "What do you want me to say?"

"Nothing." He shakes his head. "We're done."

"Johnny."

He ignores me and gets up from the couch. I grab his arm to stop him from leaving as I start to cry.

"Let go," he says.

"No. Don't go."

"We're a mess, Alex."

"So let's fix it."

"How?"

"I don't know."

"Well that's helpful."

"Johnny, please."

He lets out a sigh.

"Don't go."

"Why?"

"I want to fix this."

"Great."

"Please stay."

He sighs again and sits back down on the couch.

"Wanna watch a movie?" I offer.

"I don't care."

I take that as a yes so I grab the remote and start scanning the movie channels. After seeing a couple children's movies and some ones I've never heard of, I come to Johnny's favorite movie: A Bronx Tale.

"I'm gonna go make popcorn," he says as he gets up and walks into the kitchen.

"Wanna watch A Bronx Tale?" I ask when I see that it's just starting.

"Sure."

I put it on and turn the volume up a bit before pausing it so Johnny doesn't miss anything.

About a minute and a half later, the microwave beeps.

"Where the fuck is the popcorn bowl?" Johnny yells.

So he's still mad.

"It's above the fridge now."

"Why?" he groans.

"I don't know. That's just where my mom moved it to."

A few seconds pass and I hear him slam the cabinet door, the noise making me flinch. I get up and grab napkins from the dining room and bring them to the living room. I set them on the coffee table as Johnny returns from the kitchen with the large white bowl full of popcorn. He sits down next to me and puts the bowl down between us. I hit play on the movie and grab a few pieces of popcorn.

"Do you have any soda?" Johnny asks.

"Maybe. I can go check."

"Grab me a Coke if you have one."

I get up and walk down the stairs and head into the garage. I pull the fridge door open and scan the shelves for soda. My eyes finally spot a case of Sprite and a few cans of Coke. I grab one of each and close the fridge before going back upstairs.

"Find any?" Johnny asks.

I nod and hand him his Coke. "Here."

"Thanks."

I reach for another handful of popcorn and Johnny rolls his eyes. I decide to just ignore him and focus on the movie.

About half an hour into the movie, our popcorn bowl is empty so I pick it up off the couch and set it on the coffee table.

"Come here." Johnny pulls me closer to him and rests my legs on top of his. "I'm sorry."

"For what?" I ask.

How the hell can I make this less awkward?

I lay my head on his shoulder but it doesn't feel natural and instead makes this feel even more awkward.

"I'm sorry for being so quick to give up on us."

"I just don't get it. You cheated on me and wanted me to move past it immediately but then the smallest thing happens on my end and I'm suddenly not worth the trouble."

"You are worth it."

"Then what gives?"

"Life is stressful."

"We're seventeen." I roll my eyes. "If you can't be respectful and kind to your girlfriend just because you're stressed then what is this gonna be like when we're thirty? When we're working full time and there's kids involved?"

"I'll be better."

"How do you know that? How do you plan to be better?"

"I don't know. But I want to."

"Wanting to won't make this work. We both need to get our shit together."

"I know."

I let out a sigh.

"We're gonna fix this." He leans in and kisses me, giving my hand a tight squeeze as he does.

"I wish my mom could see this side of you," I say.

"What side?"

"Just the sweet side that cares about me and is considerate. All she really sees is the moody Johnny and the fighting Johnny and the angry texts from Johnny."

"Well, our relationship is between us. She doesn't have to see this side of me, you do."

"I guess." I shrug.

"She doesn't even need to see the bad stuff, but of course, you choose to tell her."

"I don't tell her." I defend. "She sees the texts on my phone and can tell when my mood changes and she can guess what caused it based on when you were over."

"Whatever."

We sit in silence and my mind wanders over to Bryce.

I wonder what he's doing right now. Is he still unpacking his stuff? Does he like it here? Is he thinking of me?

No.

I can't be thinking these thoughts.

I have a boyfriend and for all I know, Bryce could've just gotten out of a very serious relationship when he moved. He's probably not even looking for anything. His comment about me being cute was probably just him looking for a fling and I don't do flings. I do relationships. And I already have a relationship. It might be a work in progress, but it's still a relationship.

But Johnny's probably losing interest. He's been distant lately and we've been fighting more than ever. He's also really quick to put me down the second we aren't on good terms.

And the manipulation is nothing new, he tried to fake a suicide after he cheated on me. But if he's at the point of cheating again, we're doomed.

What if he is?

"Is there someone else?" I ask.

"No."

"Are you sure?"

"Where is this coming from? I thought we moved past all this."

"We did, it's just..." I don't bother finishing my sentence. He'll just dodge questions and get mad at me anyway.

"What?"

"Nothing."

He lets out a sigh.

"Do you ever wish I wasn't your first time?" I ask.

"What do you mean?"

"Do you wish you slept with someone other than just me?"

"I never really thought about it."

"Well, think about it."

"Why?"

"I just want to know."

He lets out a sigh. "I mean, it might be kind of nice to know what it's like with someone else."

"Oh," I say.

"Why do you do this?"

"Do what?"

"Ask questions you don't want to know the answers to?"

"I was hoping you'd care enough to lie to me." I admit.

"Last time I lied to you, it didn't exactly work out too well."

"That was different."

"How?"

"You kissed another girl and tried to hide it."

"Because I knew we could move past it."

"Whatever." I roll my eyes.

"Alex, don't be like this."

"I'm not being like anything."

"That's bullshit."

"Johnny."

"What about you, huh? Do you ever wish you'd slept with other guys?"

"No, I don't actually."

"That's more bullshit."

"It's not bullshit."

"I'm done with this conversation." He nudges me off of him and gets up.

"Johnny, don't go."

"Stop."

"Johnny."

"You do this every time we're together and things are going good. I don't know if you want there to be problems between us or what but it's exhausting."

"I'm sorry."

"I really don't think you are, Alex."

"Johnny."

"I have to work today, I can't stay anyway."

"Can I call you later?"

"I guess."

I nod and watch him get up.

"You're not gonna walk me out?"

"Every time I do, you get mad," I say.

"Awesome." He turns and walks toward the stairs.

I listen to his footsteps stomp down the stairs before the front door slams behind him.

How do I always manage to mess things up?

His car starts and taunts me as it roars up the road.

Ten minutes ago we were cuddling on the couch with a movie on and now we aren't speaking.

I grab my phone and check the time and see that it's now four in the afternoon which means it's already been two hours since my mom and grandma left. Multiple notifications from Johnny cover my screen and even though they're from this morning, I get excited and start reading them. Every single one is a nasty text laced with curse words and there's what I'm willing to bet is an even nastier voicemail from this morning too.

Fucking answer me or we're done.

I'm not messing around. Answer my texts you fucking bitch.

Quit whoring around and text your fucking boyfriend back.

Fuck you, I'm done.

Typical Johnny.

Even though those messages are from this morning, they still sting like hell. He's probably feeling the same way towards me right now. I decide I should delete the voicemail without listening to it and a tear rolls down my cheek as I do.

I should've checked my phone before we made up and then fought again.

Chapter 3

"**A**lex! Alex! Your phone! Alex!" Mom yells from across the house.

Only my mother treats a ringing phone like a bomb that needs to be diffused.

"I'm coming!" I yell back to her. I finally reach the kitchen and she's holding my phone in her right hand.

"It's Bryce." She smiles.

That's weird.

"Oh, okay." I take my phone from her and head back down the hall to my room. Once I'm far enough away from her, I answer the call. "Some people text, you know."

"Hello to you too." He laughs.

"What's up?" I ask with a smile.

"Do you have time to show me around today? My mom is up my ass about making friends and getting a job and I've found the mall but I don't know where else people here hang out."

"Yeah, I got you. When do you want to go?"

"Does now work?"

"Now?"

"We can go later if that works better."

"No, now is fine."

"Great."

"Great."

"I'll meet you outside in a couple minutes." He hangs up.

I wish I had time to straighten my hair but my blonde waves will just have to fall down to my waist. I check myself in my mirror and thankfully my makeup doesn't need to be touched up. My baby pink crop top matches my eyeshadow perfectly and I swear that should be an Olympic sport.

I grab my car keys and wallet off my nightstand and slip on a pair of black flip flops.

My mother appears in my doorway. "Where are you going?"

"Out with Bryce."

Why did I word it like that?

"Oh, a date already. It hasn't even been a week." She smirks.

"It's not a date." I roll my eyes. "I'm still with Johnny."

"For now."

"I gotta go." I push past her and down the hallway.

"Where are you going?" Grandma asks.

"Just out," I say and I run down the stairs and out the front door before I can be interrogated some more.

Bryce stands in the middle of the cul-de-sac and damn, he looks good. His black t-shirt is tight around his biceps just like his red one was the other day and I can't help but wonder if all his shirts fit like that. With biceps like his, they must.

"Hey," he says.

"Hey."

"I really appreciate you doing this."

"Yeah, of course. Are you trying to find anything specific or do you want to just drive around and get a sense of the area?"

"Kinda both."

"Okay. Let's go." I open the door to my Chevy.

"This is yours?" he asks.

"Yeah, why?" I hop in the driver's seat.

"I swear, everybody here has money." He gets in the passenger seat.

"My grandma has money, not my mom and I."

"What do you mean?"

"This is her house. My mom grew up here." I pull out of the driveway.

"Why do you live with her, if you don't mind my asking?"

"My mom was fifteen when she had me so she didn't get to go to college." I turn left off of Cedar and onto Cherry.

"Couldn't she have? You would've been three by the time she finished high school."

"It's complicated," I say, not wanting to talk about what happened her senior year.

"What do you mean?"

"That house is where Grandma Peggy lives." I ignore his question and point to a blue raised ranch with purple shutters.

"I thought you lived with your grandma."

"I do. Grandma Peggy isn't my grandma. Everyone here just calls this woman Grandma Peggy because she gets all of the neighborhood kids on the bus so their parents can get to work. She's kind of the neighborhood nanny."

"That's cute. So what did you mean by it's complicated?"

"It's a lot."

"I don't judge."

"See, everybody always says that, but then everybody always judges." I make a right turn onto Pine. "This road connects to more back roads that form a big loop. And my best friend growing up lived in that tan split level."

"You've got some good memories there, don't you?"

"Yeah." I smile. "Malayah. She has a twin brother, Eric, and his best friend and I would spend the night at the same time a lot, so the four of us got really close."

"Are you still close?"

"Funny story." I laugh. "Her brother's best friend, Damon, he actually got arrested in middle school for having naked pictures of girls on his phone and my mom never let me see him again."

"Damn, Damon started early." He laughs.

"Very. It sucks though, we were all so close. Everybody wanted the kind of friendship our group had. There was one winter, we had to be about nine years old. It had just snowed about a foot and a half so we were sleigh riding down their front yard. Malayah and I would go down on separate sleds side by side and Damon had this idea to stand about halfway down the hill with his legs wide apart for us to try to go through them."

"Oh, this is not gonna end well." He laughs.

"It didn't." I shake my head with a grin. "We each went right into one of his legs and he fell on top of us. Dislocated his left shoulder and had to spend the rest of the night in the house with an ice pack."

"Poor kid."

"We got it all on video too." I laugh.

"That could make you guys some good money if you send it into one of those shows."

"It really could." I agree.

"I wish I grew up in a neighborhood like this."

"You didn't have kids in your neighborhood?"

"I didn't have a neighborhood. I bounced around from one apartment to the next and the landlord basically raised me at each one. I never met my dad and my mom's love life is just a revolving door of jackasses so trust me when I say I'm in no position to judge your circumstances."

"Promise?"

"Pinky." He holds his pinky finger out to me.

As childish as it is, I wrap my pinky around his.

"Spill."

"My mom got pregnant again her senior year of high school. Same guy as with me, except he was abusive the whole time they dated and after I was born so my mom didn't want him around me anymore. And she really didn't want him around the second one. She tried to break up with him and he didn't take it very well." I stop at the stop sign and point up the hill straight ahead of us. "This is another small loop, we can drive it if you want."

"Sure."

I take my foot off the brake and head onto Oak to go up the hill. "So my sperm donor of a father attacked my mom while she was pregnant with my younger brother. The baby didn't survive and my mom almost didn't either."

"Damn, did they catch him?"

I nod. "He's currently serving thirty-five years."

"Wow. How long has it been so far?"

"With time served from waiting for the trial, about fourteen."

"Have you seen him since he's been in jail?"

I shake my head. "I've thought about it, but I wouldn't even know what to say to him."

"I get that. Do you think your mom would let you go see him?"

"I don't know." I shrug and point to a brown house on the right side of the road. "There's a trail in that backyard that leads to the soccer fields of the elementary school I went to. She would definitely want to keep me safe but at the same time I deserve to know my dad if I want to.""It's a hard situation, you can understand both sides."

"Exactly."

Why isn't it ever this easy to talk to Johnny?

"I'm sure she just wants you to be happy, whatever does that is what she'll think is best."

"I guess." I come to another stop sign and point out the hill we just drove up that's now on our left. "That's what we just went up." I point to the right. "That's where we came out before."

"Is everything here a loop?"

"Pretty much." I laugh. I continue straight onto Sycamore and go down the windy road that's dark from the trees on each side hanging over the pavement.

I reach the end and go left onto Willow next.

"I know this is gonna sound bizarre, considering we barely know each other, but if you ever want to visit him, I could go with you. Just so you aren't alone."

"That'd be nice actually." I smile. "This hill right here, we're gonna come down that in about four minutes."

"I wish I could say I'm surprised that there's another loop." He laughs.

"We've got plenty more."

"Jesus, who designed this neighborhood?"

"My best guess is a geometry teacher with a thing for circles."

He throws his head back with a laugh and nobody has ever liked my horrible jokes so much.

I continue on the road we're on until we come to our turn. "We go left here and that's where this girl Cassidy lives. She's a total bitch and probably dripping with STDs." I point to her house.

"Yeah, you definitely gotta let me know which girls are gonna give me something and which ones are safe to bang."

"Oh, ew."

He laughs and I point to the road on the right. "That's a dead end with a trail that leads to another neighborhood."

I drive down a hill and point to another right turn at the bottom. "That's another dead end with another trail that leads to a different neighborhood."

"There's trails everywhere here."

"Yeah, there's a lot." I drive up a hill and point to the left. "That's the hill I said we'd come down but we're gonna drive back here first."

"Another circle?"

"You catch on quick."

He laughs and I go left up the larger of the two hills.

"This area is really hilly."

"Yeah, but we have some great places to go hiking."

"We should go sometime, if your boyfriend would be okay with it."

Did he just pull the boyfriend line?

There's no way he knows about Johnny.

"He's actually pretty possessive," I say.

"That doesn't sound good."

"It's fine, really."

"You trying to convince me or yourself?"

Both.

"You."

"You gotta be careful with guys like that. I've seen girls get in some awful positions because of possessive guys." He runs his fingers through his brown hair and I wonder if he's talking about his mom.

"I'm good," I say.

"Does he have a dog in that stroller?" Bryce points to a guy walking up ahead.

"Oh, yeah. That's Tim." I laugh and wave out my window as we pass him. "He's always got his dog in a stroller for walks."

"Isn't the point of walking a dog to actually walk the dog?"

"You would think."

"This place is so weird."

I laugh and turn right. "Now we're going down the hill I've mentioned fifteen times."

"Finally. I was starting to think that hill was a tease."

I smile and drive down the hill and make a right. We reach the end and I go left onto Holly.

"We just came from the right, right?"

"Yes yes." I smirk.

"You're such a dork."

"You're hanging out with a dork, what does that say about you?"

"That I'm new."

"Ouch." I point to a house on a blind curve. "There's a girl who lives in that house who will do absolutely anything to sleep with every guy out there, do not let her talk you into it."

"Why? She got something?"

"Yeah, a kid. Three of them actually."

"Three? How old is she?"

"Eighteen. She lies and tells guys she's on the pill so she gets pregnant. She tries to trap them in a relationship and it never works. She just ends up with another baby."

"I think she needs a new method to get a guy."

"Definitely. That brick house on the right has a trail through the woods that connects to my backyard."

"Really?"

I nod.

"That's cool. Are your families friends?"

"We were when we were little but once we hit high school one of the girls made a nasty comment about my mom being a single mother and getting pregnant in high school."

"What the hell is wrong with people?"

"I've been asking that question for years. It's not all bad. When they're away on vacation we use that trail to sneak into their pool."

"Only way to do it." He laughs as I make a right turn onto Cedar.

"If you go straight there instead of turning where we did you'll hit the main road."

"Cool."

I make a left back onto Cherry. "You'd go right to get back home. Now that we're done with the neighborhood, what do you need to find?"

"Is there a drugstore near here?"

"Yeah, it's only about eight minutes away. It's by the mall actually."

"I must've missed it when I went out yesterday. I can go myself if you're tired of showing me around."

"No, it's okay. There's some other stuff I can show you that's up that way."

"Like what?"

"There's a really good smoothie place near there."

"You guys have everything that's so different so close together."

"Like what?"

"I saw a lingerie store next to a playground before."

"Oh, yeah, that placement was definitely an odd one." I laugh.

I head out to the main road and make a right. I come to a stoplight and get in the right lane to turn. "The drugstore is right on this road."

"Does that mean I went the long way to the mall?"

"Did you go straight at this light?"

"Yeah."

"Then, yeah. There's multiple ways to get everywhere, you'll figure out the fastest ones soon."

The light turns green so I make my turn and take the road about a quarter mile before turning left into the parking lot.

"I drove right past this lot probably four times."

"Nice sense of direction." I laugh as I pull into a parking space.

"I'll be right back."

"I'll go in with you."

"You don't have to."

"I need to grab vitamins, it's not a big deal." I open my door and get out and Bryce does the same.

"What are you looking for?" I ask.

"Just stuff."

"Stuff like?"

"I'll find it."

"You sure? You couldn't even find the store."

"Very funny. I got it covered."

"Okay." I turn and head over to the vitamins. It takes a couple minutes for me to find the brand I like and pick out the right dose of calcium. I head to the register and see Bryce paying for a box of condoms.

So that's why he was being weird.

I pretend I don't see him and wait in line for my turn to pay. Another register opens up and I'm the first customer called to it. I head over and pay for my vitamins before walking out.

Bryce is outside leaning up against the wall of the store on the phone with someone. He nods in my direction when he sees me and I unlock the car and we both climb in.

"I already told you my opinion on it, it's not going to change." He hangs up his phone and lets out a groan.

"Is everything okay?" I ask.

"My mom wants to get back together with jackass number three hundred thirty seven."

"And you hate him because?"

"He spanked Lay."

"He spanked her?"

"Hard. And just because she spilled a bowl of gummy bears."

"Jesus."

"She had a bruise halfway up her back for a week."

"That sounds awful."

"It was. And my mother wants to get back with him."

"That sucks."

"Yeah."

"Well, at least you got your condoms."

He looks like a deer in headlights.

"Relax." I laugh. "It's like you thought that I thought you were a virgin."

"Hey, at least I'm being safe so I don't get someone pregnant."

"You could just not have sex."

"Oh, good, you're one of those people."

"One of what people?" I ask.

"One of those people who are convinced that you can't have sex without getting a pregnancy out of it."

"That's not true." I laugh.

"Bullshit." He laughs.

"I've had sex before, I'm not pregnant, am I?"

"You could still be in the early weeks."

"Oh my gosh, shut up."

He laughs and I back out of the parking space. I make a left out of the lot and pull up to a red light.

"If you go straight here you'd hit the mall."

"Wow, I really went the long way." He laughs.

"You did."

The light turns green so I turn left and hop on the highway. We ride about a mile before we come to our light. I make a right to get off the highway and I make a left into the parking lot for the plaza the smoothie shop is in.

"And we're here," I say.

"What's good here?"

"I always get the strawberry banana."

"That sounds good."

We get out of the car and head into the store. A redhead girl I go to school with works the counter and she rolls her eyes when she sees me until she sees Bryce.

"Hi, I'm Natasha, what can I get for you today?"

"I'll have a small strawberry banana," I say.

"Make that two," Bryce says.

"Anything else?" Natasha puts on her most fake smile.

"That's it." I smile back and I want to knock her damn teeth out.

"Ten dollars please."

I pull out my wallet and Bryce stops me.

"I got it." He insists.

"It's okay, I can pay."

"Alex, you're driving me around all day, it's the least I can do."

I smile and let him pay for our smoothies.

Johnny never offers to pay for me.

Our smoothies are brought up in two red plastic cups and Bryce grabs them. I pick one of the empty wooden tables and lead him over to it.

"This has been a really fun day," I say.

"It has." He smiles.

"If you ever want to drive around again, just let me know."

"Yeah, definitely."

"You see the girl who helped us?"

"Yeah, Natasha?"

"Yeah. Avoid at all costs."

"Why's that?"

"She'll sleep with you and then your best friend two nights later."

"That's funny, that's usually my thing."

I roll my eyes. "I'm serious, Bryce. She's a new level."

"Sounds like a challenge."

I roll my eyes again.

"I'm kidding." He laughs. "I'll stay away from her."

"Good."

"Thanks for giving me a heads up about the girls here."

"Just don't want you to catch something else."

"Something else?"

"Well, I'm assuming you've already had at least one STD." I laugh.

"Hilarious." He rolls his eyes.

"How do you like it here? So far, I mean."

"It's okay. New York is a lot busier than Maryland."

"I bet."

"Are the people as rude as everyone says?"

"That's mainly the city. A lot of people do drugs up here, though."

"My mom would kill me if she ever caught me doing drugs."

"Same."

"So, how far are we from the city?"

"About two hours by train."

"We'd take the train?"

"It's way faster than driving from here."

"Damn."

"Welcome home." I laugh.

"Have you lived here your whole life?"

I nod and take another sip of my smoothie.

"It must have been so nice to not have to move around nonstop."

"Do you think you guys will stick around for a while?"

"That's what Mom says. I just hope she sticks to that."

"I'm sure she will. Moving around can't be easy with two kids. Do you have family here?"

"Yeah, my grandparents live up here and so does one of my mom's sisters."

"Well, that's a reason for her to want to stay, isn't it?"

"Let's hope."

I suck on my straw again and receive mostly air with the occasional drop of smoothie.

"All done?" he asks.

"Sadly." I laugh.

He sucks on his straw and gets the same contents I did. "Same."

We get up from our table and toss our cups in the garbage.

"Have a nice day!" Natasha calls.

We both ignore her as Bryce opens the door for us. I unlock the car and we hop in.

"Home now?" I ask.

"If I don't show my serial killer tendencies and take your head off first."

"Funny."

"I'm just saying, you got in the car with a guy you barely know."

"I think I'll be okay." I throw my car in reverse and see Natasha in my backup camera.

"Oh, why?" I groan.

Natasha walks up to my window so I roll it down.

"Hey, Alex." She grins.

"Hi."

"Just wondering, are you still with Johnny?"

"And how is that your business?" I ask.

"Well, I just think it's interesting that you're here with an-other guy. It'd be a real shame if Johnny found out."

"If he found out that she stopped for smoothies with her cousin?" Bryce raises his eyebrows.

"You-you're cousins?" Natasha stutters.

I nod.

She wordlessly turns around and heads back inside.

"Thank you," I say.

"Anytime."

I back out of my parking space and head for the highway but the light stays red for a few minutes.

"This is a really long light." Bryce points out.

"Most of the ones to get on the highway take forever."

We're finally given the green arrow so I make my left. I ride the right lane for a couple miles before making a right turn off the highway. We make it back to our neighborhood and I see Grandma Peggy outside.

"See that woman with the short gray hair?" I ask.

"Yeah."

"That's Grandma Peggy." I pull up in front of her driveway and roll my window down. "Hey, Grandma Peggy!"

"Alex, my dear! How are you?"

"I'm good."

She walks over to my car and sees Bryce. "And who is this handsome fella?"

"I'm Bryce." He smiles.

"His family just moved into the house next to mine."

"Oh, that's so nice. Welcome to the neighborhood. You got any younger siblings?"

"Yeah, I've got a little sister. Her name is Layla."

"How old is she?"

"Four."

"Oh, how wonderful! Tell your parents I get all the neighborhood kids on the bus, I'd be happy to get little Layla on next year if need be."

"I'll definitely let my mom know, thanks."

"Of course. Oh, look, it's Keith. Keith, come over here, we got a new guy in the neighborhood!"

I look in my mirror and see Keith wave and make his way over with a black covered stroller.

"Hey, Alex. Peggy." Keith smiles.

"This is Bryce, he just moved in next to Alex."

"Nice to meet you, Bryce."

"You too. Do you have a dog in your stroller too?" Bryce asks and I laugh.

"No, I have a baby." Keith laughs and pulls the cover to the side to show us his daughter. "There better not be a dog in here, my wife will kill me." He runs his fingers through his dark brown hair.

"I can't wait to get that angel on the bus one day." Grandma Peggy beams.

"She is gonna love you." Keith insists.

"What's her name?" Bryce asks.

"Bailey."

"She's gonna break a lot of hearts one day." Grandma Peggy shakes her head.

"She's six months old." I laugh.

"I said one day, not tomorrow, my gosh."

"Hey, are you done with school yet?" Keith asks me.

"Yeah, I finished last week."

"Lucky you. You willing to babysit a kid in diapers?"

"Of course, I love babies."

"I bet you're going to babysit little Layla, too, right?" Grandma Peggy asks.

"Yeah, if Bryce's mom needs."

"You've got a nice little gig, neighborhood babysitter." Keith laughs.

"It's definitely nice getting to play with kids and get paid for it."

"Well I gotta run. I'll see you tomorrow night." Keith smiles.

"What?" I ask confused.

"You're hosting tomorrow, Alex," Grandma Peggy says.

"I'm hosting? Hosting what?"

"Your mom didn't tell you?" Keith asks.

"I guess not." I laugh.

"You guys are having everybody over for a fire and s'mores."

"Great to know she keeps me in the loop." I laugh.

"It starts in at eight," Grandma Peggy says. "Since she doesn't fill you in."

"Yeah, apparently."

"Well, I'll see you tomorrow."

"See you tomorrow." I pull away and look over at Bryce. "Are you coming to that?"

"I have no idea. I'm assuming my mom will let me know."

"You guys should come."

"It sounds fun."

"I'm sure Layla will enjoy it."

"She definitely likes her s'mores."

I pull into my driveway and turn my car off. "I'll see you tomorrow then."

He smiles as he gets out.

"I'm serious, you better be there. I wanna meet Layla."

"I hear you."

"But will you listen?"

"I'll see you tomorrow."

"Expect fifty phone calls if you don't show."

He laughs and shakes his head.

"Bryce!" Maggie yells. "Is Alex out there?"

"Yeah, I'm here!" I yell back and start walking over.

"I need a favor so huge."

"What's up?"

"I got my dates mixed up and I have to go pick up a dresser now. Can you watch Layla?"

"Sure."

"I can watch her," Bryce says.

"I need your help with the dresser."

"I'm sure they have people there that can load it for you."

"But I need you to make sure the mirror doesn't slide around and end up breaking while I drive."

"Fine." He rolls his eyes.

"Alex, we'll be back in half an hour." Maggie smiles. "Thank you so much."

"Of course." I smile and head inside.

Chapter 4

I'm met with silence which isn't usually a good sign when there's a four-year-old in the house.

"Layla?" I call. "Layla!"

More silence.

Shit.

I walk up the stairs and see a light blue couch with a matching love seat in the living room. The hardwood floors are a little scratched but nothing too bad and there's a TV next to the fireplace that doesn't appear to be hooked up yet.

Focus, Alex. You have a child to find.

I peek into the kitchen and don't see her.

If I was a little kid all alone in an empty house, what would I do?

Personally, I'd try to find the cookies. Clearly Layla is much more sophisticated than I am.

"Layla!" I yell.

I'm an idiot.

She's four years old, by herself, and there's a weird girl she doesn't know in her house. She's probably hiding under a bed in a dark room.

I start walking down the hallway when one of the closet doors flings open and almost hits me.

"Boo!" a very tiny girl shouts with a laugh as she jumps out of the closet and gives me a heart attack.

"Oh my god!" I jump back and my hand reaches for my chest to make sure my heart is still beating.

"Did I scare you?" she asks as she tucks her light brown hair behind her ear.

Scared is an understatement.

"Yeah." I force a laugh. "Good job."

"Who are you?" she asks.

"I'm Alex," I say. "You must be Layla."

She nods.

"Hi."

"Hi." She waves to me.

"So what are you up to?"

"I don't know." She shrugs.

"Well, what do you want to do?"

"Can you read?"

"I can." I smile.

"Be right back!" She runs down the hall and into a room on the right.

Maggie must've been really desperate for a sitter to trust a girl she's only met once to watch her child, a child she hasn't even met yet. I think about how weird it is that Layla is so open to a stranger. Most little kids are super shy around new people. I wonder what kind of babysitters Layla had when they lived in Maryland. Were her babysitters even babysitters or were they just her mom's boyfriends? Is that how she was hit by the one her mom is considering getting back together with?

Layla returns with a stack of children's books. "Here."

I take the stack from her and she leads me to the couch.

"You sit here." She points to the cushion on the left.

"Okay." I take my assigned seat and she sits down next to me. "Which one do you want me to read first?"

She looks through the stack of books and pulls out the third one in the pile, a white cover with a large picture of a pink and purple butterfly on it. "This one."

"Okay." I put the rest of the books on the arm of the couch and start reading the one she picked out.

The book only takes five minutes to get through and even though the books are short and rarely have any depth to them, I'm still amazed that children's authors can pack an entire story into such a small amount of space and time.

I finish the stack of books just as the front door opens.

"Mommy!" Layla yells as she gets off the couch and runs toward the stairs.

"Nope. Just me," Bryce says. "Mom and I put the dresser and mirror in the garage for now but she's got more errands to run."

"Aw." Layla frowns.

"Well don't I feel special?" Bryce laughs. "Good job keeping the kid alive."

"I tried." I shrug. "Kinda felt like you guys wouldn't have cared either way so it didn't matter much. I like when there's no pressure like that."

"I like your sense of humor." He smirks as he pulls his phone out of his pocket. "Where did I put my laptop?"

"Girlfriend want to Skype?" I laugh.

Did I just pull the girlfriend line?

"Haven't had one of those in six months, easy." He shakes his head. "One of my friends wants to play video games and I need my laptop."

"Did you unpack it yet?"

"I have no idea. The contents of all those boxes kinda blurred together."

"I'm hungry," Layla says.

"Grab a snack," Bryce says.

"Where?"

"Come here." He leads her to the pantry and helps her pick out a granola bar before disappearing down the hall.

I walk into the kitchen and watch Layla eat her snack, always being cautious of choking when I'm watching a kid her age. By the time her granola bar is finished, Bryce is back with his laptop and headset.

And he called me a dork.

He parks himself on the couch, putting his legs up and taking up all three cushions, so Layla and I take the love seat. About forty seconds in, Bryce is clearly frustrated by something going on in his game.

"Shoot me one more time and you're gonna fu-"

"Okay!" I cut him off. "Layla, why don't you go color in the other room?"

"He always says bad words." She laughs. "I'm used to it."

"Fuck!" Bryce yells.

I toss a throw pillow at him and get him right in the back of the head.

"What was that for?" he asks annoyed as he pulls his headset off.

"Your sister is four."

"So?"

"Chill with the swear words."

"Oh, please, she curses more than I do."

"I do." She laughs. "Fuck."

"Layla!" My eyes widen and I try not to laugh.

"Relax." Bryce laughs. "You're not gonna get in trouble or anything. Mom taught her everything she knows."

Oh, good.

Bryce's headset goes back on and he turns his attention back to his game.

I gotta be honest, I did not have him pegged as a guy who still plays video games at seventeen.

My phone buzzes next to me and I flip it over to reveal a text from Johnny.

Wanna hang out?

I can't. I'm babysitting

Who is it this time?

The little girl next door. The new people

So you're over there again?

What do you mean?

The other day you missed our date because you were there and now you're bailing on me again today because you're there

I'm not bailing on you. We didn't have plans for today

They got a hot son or something?

Would you stop

I'm getting real tired of this

Tired of what? We didn't have plans

Whatever

I don't bother responding and stuff my phone into my pocket as I let out a sigh.

Bryce yells into his headset and I jump, causing Layla to laugh.

Just when I think things have settled down, Layla lets out a scream.

"Oh my gosh! What?" I ask.

"There's a bug!"

"Where?"

"The window." She points to the picture window and I see a brown stink bug crawling up the left side of it.

"Bryce," I say.

Nothing.

"Bryce!"

Still nothing.

Maggie wasn't kidding when she said the house could burn down around him and he wouldn't have a clue.

I roll my eyes as I get up and whack his arm.

"What the hell?" he groans as he pulls his headset off again.

"There's a stink bug on the window." I point to it. "Kill it for us."

"You kill it."

"I don't do stink bugs." I shake my head. "I'll grab you a napkin but you're killing him."

"What if it's a she?"

"Kill the bug." I roll my eyes.

"Get me a napkin."

I go into the kitchen and grab a napkin from the counter and bring it to Bryce. He kills the bug and Layla cheers as he does.

"Fuck you," he says to the balled up napkin with the bug contents in it before turning to me. "You're welcome."

"My hero." I bat my eyelashes and give him the world's fakest smile.

"Don't fall too hard. You might forget about that crappy boyfriend of yours."

I roll my eyes as the front door opens.

"Mommy!" Layla yells and runs over again.

"Hi, sweetie," Maggie says. "Did you have fun with Alex?"

"I scared her." She giggles.

"Oh my gosh, I'm sorry." Maggie laughs as she makes her way up the stairs. "I don't know how she's so outgoing with strangers, she's so shy with people she knows."

"You raised a weirdo." Bryce scoops Layla up sideways and throws her over his shoulder.

She laughs the whole way to the couch and I can't help but think about how lucky she is to have him as a big brother. He looks like a lot of fun and there's no doubt he'll kick the ass of any guy who hurts her ten years from now.

"Bryce, put her down!" Maggie laughs.

"What's the point of having a little sister if I can't throw her across the room and onto the couch?" He rolls his eyes as he drops her onto the couch.

"Here's some cash for you." Maggie holds out a ten.

"You don't have to pay me." I shake my head. "This was so quick and she was easy."

"No, please take it."

"No, really, it's okay. Just hire me back and I'll let you pay me for the next time."

"Thanks." She smiles. "Layla, go get shoes, we're going shopping. And make sure your shoes match."

"You're taking her shopping now?" Bryce raises his eyebrows once Layla is out of the room.

"She needs some new decorations for her bedroom."

"Do we have the money for that?"

"I'll make it work."

"How?"

"Bryce, you're seventeen. Money isn't your problem."

"It is when you buy shit we don't need and then I have to help with the bills for the shit we do need."

"I'm making it work. This conversation is over."

"What's your plan, Mom?"

"I have it handled."

"Whatever," he says as Layla returns with a pair of flip flops.

"Ready?" Maggie asks.

Layla nods.

"We'll be back in about an hour." Maggie smiles. "Alex, you're more than welcome to hang out here with Bryce while I'm gone."

"Thanks."

They head down the stairs and Bryce lets out a sigh the second the front door closes behind them.

"What's wrong?" I ask.

"She's delusional." He shakes his head. "She always thinks this is gonna be the month we get ahead so she splurges and then we get farther into the seemingly bottomless hole she's dug for us."

"Do you have to chip in to get bills paid often?"

"Only if you consider every month to be often."

"Jesus."

"That's why she's pushing me to find a job as fast as possible. She knows she'll need me to contribute. And if she keeps going overboard on buying shit for the house, I better start playing lotto and pray I hit the jackpot."

"I'm sorry."

"It is what it is. So when are you gonna leave that guy you're seeing?"

"Well that came straight out of left field." I laugh.

"You can't possibly be happy with him."

"What makes you say that?"

"The way you described him, the way you talk about him. Not to mention, the look on your face when he texted you while I was playing video games wasn't too indicative of a happy relationship."

"You don't know who was texting me."

"I've only ever seen that face on a girl when the guy she either liked or was dating was doing something shitty."

I shake my head.

"What'd he do?"

"It's no big deal."

"So why don't you tell me?"

I let out a sigh. "Fine. He wanted to hang out and I told him I couldn't because I was babysitting."

"And he was mad about that?"

"He was mad that I was here again."

"He knows you were here before?"

I nod. "I missed our date the day you guys moved in because I was here."

"So he's mad he's coming second to a family he's never met."

"He thinks I'm interested in you."

"He does?" He smirks.

"Wipe that stupid smirk off your face right now." I warn.

"You could come kiss it off."

"Pass."

"You're in denial."

"About?"

"It's clear I'm into you so-"

"You're into me?" I cut him off.

"You're playing dumb?" He laughs.

"You barely know me."

"I can still be interested in getting to know you better while also knowing I'm already a fan of what I've seen."

"It doesn't matter that you're a fan, I have a boyfriend."

"For now."

"Why does everyone say that?" I groan.

"So other people think so too." He smirks again.

I let out a sigh.

"The sooner you leave him, the better."

"You don't know anything about our relationship."

"I know it's clearly not going great and can't be healthy."

"And it's none of your business."

"I disagree."

"Why, Bryce? Please tell me how this is your business."

"Because the sooner you leave him, the sooner you're with me."

"I'm not gonna be with you."

"Wanna bet?"

I roll my eyes.

"We're gonna be married one day."

"No, we won't."

"Wanna bet on that too?"

I let out a sigh. "No, Bryce."

"I think you're interested in me."

Maybe. Very small chance.

"You just don't know it yet." He smiles.

Chapter 5

"**Y**ou didn't tell me we were hosting tonight," I say.

"It's on the calendar, I didn't think I needed to tell you." My mom points to today's box on the calendar on the countertop.

As I suspected, the box is empty.

"If it weren't for Grandma Peggy telling me, I still wouldn't know." I laugh.

"When did you see Grandma Peggy?"

"Yesterday, when I was with Bryce."

"Oh, speaking of Bryce, I talked to Maggie today. The three of them are planning on coming tonight."

"Oh, good."

"I forgot to tell them to wear pajamas though, could you text Bryce and let them know?"

"Sure." I pull my phone from my back pocket and go into my conversation with Bryce.

About tonight, wear pajamas. It's a thing

I send my message and his reply is quick.

Uh, okay

Mom turns to face me. "Could you grab the Adirondack chairs off the deck and bring them down to the lawn and set them up around the fire pit? Make sure they're far enough away that the smoke won't get in people's eyes but close enough that everyone can still reach the fire to toast their marshmallows. And leave some room for blankets for the kids."

"Got it." I grab a rag and open the sliding glass door and head onto the deck.

The dark blue Adirondack chairs are stacked up in the corner against the house so I pull the first one off the top of the pile and wipe it down. Since we use them pretty often, a dry rag is enough to do the trick. I do the same with the rest of the chairs and start bringing them down to the fire pit. Once I get the chairs set up, I head back in for the blankets. I make my way to the linen closet and grab some of our old blankets off the bottom shelf.

"Is four enough?" I shout to Mom.

"Should be! We can always grab more if we need to!"

I grab the stack and carry the blankets down toward the fire pit and drop them onto the ground with a satisfying plop. The purple square one is on top so I reach for that one first. I spread it out next to one of the chairs and decide it's a little too close to the cement blocks that make up the fire pit so I pull it back a bit and adjust the sides. A blue fuzzy blanket is now on the top of the stack so I grab that one next. I spread it out next to the purple one before grabbing the green one. It's a bit smaller than I thought it would be but I lay it down anyway. The last blanket is a black, fuzzy, rectangular one. I spread it out behind the other three and leave room for a fifth in case we need it. Once they're all spread out, I head back inside.

"Blankets are down," I say.

"Great. I've got a bunch of baskets with s'mores stuff we can bring out."

"Okay."

"Why don't you go put on pajamas first and then we can take care of the baskets?"

"Sure." I head to my room.

Okay, Bryce is coming tonight so I have to look decent.

Why does that make me want to look decent?

I slide open my pajama drawer and pull out a pair of gray sweatpants that are tight in my butt and thighs but flare out at the knees. My hands dig for a shirt and I settle on a pink high school football t-shirt from one of the team's many breast cancer fundraisers.

Perfect.

My blue crop top and black denim shorts come off and I change into a light purple and gray thong to avoid Bryce seeing any underwear lines when he inevitably checks me out later. I pull my sweatpants on and take a look at my butt in the mirror. I'm happy with how the bottoms look on me so I put on the t-shirt too. I look good but not like I'm trying to look good.

I hope.

I turn off my light and head back to the kitchen.

"All set?" Mom asks.

"Think so." I nod.

"Oh, by the way, I invited Johnny."

Her words make me panic instantly. "What? Why?"

"I saw him at the grocery store when I was buying some last minute things and since he's your boyfriend, I asked if he'd like to come."

"And?"

"And he said he'd drop by."

"You didn't tell him I was with Bryce yesterday, did you?"

"Of course not. He's the type to shoot the messenger."

"Thank God."

"If you have to hide your guy friends from your boyfriend, you probably shouldn't be with your boyfriend."

"It's fine."

A knock on the front door interrupts us.

Please don't let this be Johnny already.

"I'll get it," I say.

I sprint down the stairs and open the front door to see Maggie with Bryce and Layla.

Thank God.

"Hi," I say.

"Hey," Bryce says.

"Hi, Layla." I smile at the little girl whose hair matches Bryce's.

She hides behind Maggie's leg and Bryce laughs.

"She's feeling kinda shy tonight." He explains. "Parties aren't really her thing."

I look them up and down and Maggie and Layla are in matching red and black footed pajamas. Bryce is in gray sweats and a black hoodie.

"You didn't want to match with them?" I ask Bryce.

"Can you blame me?"

"He's such a teenager." Maggie shakes her head.

"Alex, who is it?" Mom calls.

"Bryce and his family!" I yell back.

"Hey, Tara!" Maggie calls.

I lead them up the stairs and into the kitchen.

"Look at you two matching." My mom smiles.

"It was Layla's idea." Maggie grins.

"It's very cute."

"It is." I agree.

"We thought we'd come by early to see if you guys needed help with anything," Maggie says.

"Oh, you didn't have to do that." My mom smiles.

"We don't mind." Bryce chimes in.

"What can we do?" Maggie asks.

"I have these baskets that can go out." My mom points to the baskets on the counter. "You can just set them on one of the blankets that are out there if you don't mind."

"Not at all." Maggie smiles. "Layla, you want to take the one with the marshmallows?"

Layla nods and Maggie hands her the basket.

"Too heavy, Mommy," Layla says.

"Do you want me to help you?" I offer. "We can carry it together."

Layla hesitates and looks to Maggie for an answer.

After the way she tried to give me a heart attack yesterday, her shyness tonight is baffling.

"Go ahead, let Alex help you."

Layla smiles and nods and I wrap my right hand around the handle. She wraps her tiny fingers around the wicker and I lead her down to the fire pit. Maggie and Bryce follow us with the baskets of chocolate, graham crackers, and wet wipes and napkins.

"This can be the snack blanket." I point to the green one since it's the smallest of the four blankets and Layla and I set down our basket of marshmallows. Bryce and Maggie do the same with the other three.

"This is a really cute setup." Maggie smiles.

"Thanks," I say.

We head back toward the house and I grab Bryce's arm.

"What?" he asks.

"Can we talk?" I whisper.

"I guess. Is everything okay?"

I nod and follow Maggie and Layla up the steps to the deck and in through the sliding glass door to the house. A warm smell of cinnamon and chocolate fills the air.

"Is that hot chocolate?" Maggie asks.

"Yeah, could you actually grab a thermos from that cabinet? Or three?" Mom asks with a laugh as she points to the cabinet above the fridge.

"Of course."

"Come here." I grab Bryce's sleeve and pull him out of the kitchen while our moms are occupied. I lead him down the hall and into my room and I close the door behind us.

"Is this the part where the other girls pop out and I get gang raped?"

"Funny." I roll my eyes.

He laughs and I shake my head.

"Johnny's coming tonight."

"That your boyfriend?"

I nod. "Please don't tell him I was running errands with you yesterday."

"I won't, but what exactly would happen if I did?"

"Bryce, I'm serious!"

"I promise, I won't tell him. I'm just curious."

"He'd flip out and probably try to fight you and he'd definitely dump me for it."

"Alex, why are you with him?"

I don't say anything.

"Do you not know why?"

I shrug.

"He doesn't hit you, does he?"

"God, no."

"Alex, I'll kill him if he ever lays a finger on you."

"He doesn't."

"It needs to stay that way."

"We better head back before our moms notice we're gone," I say.

He nods but I can tell he doesn't want this conversation to end just yet.

We make our way back to the kitchen and I see that every thermos has been filled with hot chocolate and is ready to go out.

"There you two are." My mom points out.

"Alex, Layla has something she wants to tell you." Maggie smiles.

"Okay." I smile and bend down to her level.

"You're really pretty," she says quietly.

"So are you." I grin.

There's something about a little kid calling you pretty that makes it feel like a higher compliment than when it comes from an adult or even someone your own age.

"Do you want me to get the fire started?" Bryce offers.

"That'd be really helpful." My mom smiles. "The wood is next to the shed, and the lighter is in that drawer next to the stove. There's fire starters in a box behind the end table to the right of the couch if you need them."

Bryce grabs his supplies and I follow him down to the fire pit.

"Thanks for doing this," I say.

"No problem." He tosses a fire starter and some wood into the ring of cement blocks.

"Can I ask you something?"

"You just did."

I laugh and shake my head. "Have you ever had a serious girlfriend?"

"Yup. Never doing that again."

"What happened?"

"She cheated."

"Is that the last girl you dated?"

He nods.

"Is that why you're just looking for girls to hook up with here? You're afraid of being hurt again?"

"Alex, you're getting way too deep with this. I'm a guy. I'm horny. Hookups let me have sex without having drama. It's got nothing to do with pain."

"Not all girls are gonna bring you drama."

"Does Johnny bring you drama?"

"Johnny's not a girl."

"That wasn't my question."

"He's harmless." I roll my eyes.

"I guess I'll find out for myself tonight."

Smoke rises and a flame pops up.

"Nice job," I say.

"Thanks." He picks up the lighter and we go back to the house.

"That was quick," Maggie comments.

"Your son is creepily good at starting fires." I laugh.

"Would you stop?" Mom shakes her head and chuckles.

"Do we need still need to bring out skewers to toast the marshmallows with?" Bryce asks.

"I totally forgot about those." I nod and head over to the cabinet in the dining room that holds the metal skewers and grab a bunch. "Got 'em."

"I'm gonna bring out the hot chocolate. Could someone just grab that last thermos?" Mom asks.

"I got it." Bryce picks it up off the counter and we head back out.

"How long do these get-togethers usually last?" Maggie asks.

"Couple hours." Mom answers. "The families with small kids usually leave after about an hour which is why we start before sunset. More people show up once it gets dark."

"Are there any kids around Layla's age?" Bryce asks.

"Yeah, but they're pretty shy," I say.

"It'll probably take a couple of these things for them to warm up to each other." My mom shrugs.

"Do these little neighborhood events happen often?" Maggie asks.

"All the time." I nod. "Sometimes it's a fire pit, other times it's a bonfire with music and alcohol, sometimes it's a pool party."

"This neighborhood seems so nice."

"So we're gonna stay here for a while?" Bryce asks.

Maggie hesitates before answering. "I'd like to."

"Do you move around a lot?" Mom asks.

"Life's been complicated." Maggie explains. "I've never been able to afford a house until I took this job which is ironic since New York is one of the most expensive states to live in."

"How much did you get the house for, if you don't mind my asking?" Mom questions.

"Forty grand."

"Wow," I say.

"It was a foreclosure and a dump to begin with. It took a lot of cleaning up before we could move in."

"We noticed some vans there the last few weeks," Mom says. "We wondered what was going on."

"That was the cleaning crew my parents found for us." Maggie explains. "This place wasn't livable before."

"We got really lucky when we found it." Bryce laughs.

"When you found it." Maggie corrects him.

"You picked out the house?" I ask.

"I was tired of moving from one crappy apartment to the next and she said the only way we'd stay put is if we had a house." He shrugs. "And then the issue became the cost so I looked online until I found one we could afford that was close enough to the new job she was offered."

"That's really great."

"Hello, everyone!" Grandma Peggy calls.

I look over to the left of the house and can see Grandma Peggy's big, bright smile from here. She's got her three grandkids with her and I see a couple other families walking up behind her.

"Alex!" Emmy, one of Grandma Peggy's granddaughters, yells and starts running toward me.

"Hi, cutie." I smile and scoop her up.

"I missed you." She lays her head on my shoulder and her curly red hair tickles my neck.

"I missed you too."

"Hi, Alex," Brandon, Grandma Peggy's grandson, says and hugs my legs.

"Hey."

"They just love you so much." Maggie smiles.

"Alex here used to babysit all of them when I'd go out with their parents." Grandma Peggy explains. "She was the only one who could handle all three of them together."

"Speaking of babysitting, I meant to ask you, Alex, would you be able to watch Layla for me tomorrow?" Maggie asks. "I have to work and Bryce is helping his grandfather take down a shed."

"Of course." I nod. "What time should I come over?"

"Is five okay?"

"Perfect."

"Alex is the best in the neighborhood; Layla certainly won't be bored." Grandma Peggy beams.

"The party has arrived!" Johnny's voice booms.

Along with his big personality.

Fuck. Me.

Chapter 6

I turn and see Johnny walking down the yard in a gray long sleeve shirt and black sweatpants.

Be nice. Don't give him a reason to flip out in front of everyone, he'll find that on his own.

"Hey, you." I fake a smile and hug him.

"Hey, babe. You wanna introduce me to them?" he asks as he gestures to Bryce's family.

"This is Bryce and his mom, Maggie. And this is Layla. This is my boyfriend, Johnny."

"It's nice to meet you." Maggie smiles and extends her hand out to him. "We just moved in next door."

Johnny doesn't reach to shake her hand and I have to try not to gag.

"So you guys are the new neighbors she's been hanging out with." He looks them up and down

"I guess." Maggie smiles as she retracts her hand.

"That's right." Bryce nods and I swear he stands up straighter now than he did before Johnny got here.

"Who wants to make the first s'more?" Mom asks, sensing things going down a bad path.

Thank God.

"Layla, you want to make the first one?" I ask her. "I can help you toast it."

She looks to Maggie who nods with a smile.

Layla nods so I grab a bag of marshmallows from the basket and rip it open.

"Could you pass me a skewer?" I ask Bryce.

"I got it." Johnny snaps and grabs one and something tells me he shouldn't be trusted with sharp objects right now.

I quickly accept the skewer from him and guide Layla's hand as she slides the marshmallow on so she doesn't poke herself.

"Do you like it toasted a lot or just a little bit?" I ask Layla.

"A lot. On fire."

"You like it on fire?" I laugh.

"She does, she's crazy." Bryce shakes his head.

"Then on fire, it shall be." I wrap my hands around Layla's and we hold the marshmallow in the flames.

"Is your grandma coming down?" Johnny asks.

I shake my head. "She's got bingo tonight and then she's grabbing a bite with friends."

"It's on fire, mommy." Layla laughs.

"Good job. Take it out now and blow it out." Maggie smiles.

We pull our skewer back and Bryce holds Layla's hair so it won't touch the flame as she blows her marshmallow out. I'm pretty sure she killed the flame with her spit and not with her breath.

"Grab a graham cracker," I say.

"I got one." Bryce hands one that he broke in half to Layla and I hold her skewer.

"Put the chocolate on one." Maggie hands Layla a piece of a chocolate bar.

Her face lights up at the mention of chocolate.

"Now put the cracker with the chocolate under the marshmallow and the other on top of the marshmallow."

She does as I say and I put my right hand over hers as I use the crackers to slide the marshmallow off the skewer.

"There you go." I smile and hand her the s'more.

"What do you say?" Maggie grins.

"Thank you," Layla mumbles through her first bite.

"Who's next?" Mom asks.

All of Grandma Peggy's grandkids start fighting over who gets to be next as if we don't have at least a dozen skewers as a few more families arrive.

"Who are all these people?" Bryce asks me.

"Why do you give a shit?" Johnny rolls his eyes.

"Hey," I say. "Let's not start something out of nothing. There's kids around. Bryce lives here now so it's a good idea for him to figure out who everyone is."

"I don't give a fuck! I saw the way he's been looking at you the whole fucking night!"

"Johnny, you're making a scene out of nothing," I say quietly. "He hasn't been looking at me."

"I don't want your girlfriend, relax." Bryce shakes his head.

"I'm not fucking talking to you." Johnny stands up.

"You're talking about me." Bryce does the same.

"Boys, hey! Knock it off!" Mom gets between them. "Johnny, I think it's time for you to head out."

"Are you kidding me?" he groans. "You're making me leave?"

"You're the one causing a scene." She defends.

He shakes his head. "Whatever."

I watch him walk away and a tear rolls down my cheek.

"Alex, could you go inside and grab one more bag of marshmallows?" Mom asks. "They're on the top shelf of the pantry, you might need the step stool."

I nod.

"I can go with you," Bryce says. "In case you can't reach them."

I wordlessly start the trek back to the house and Bryce follows. My phone buzzes from its spot in the waistband of my sweatpants so I grab it and see a text from my mom.

We don't need marshmallows, just thought you needed a minute.

I lock my phone without responding and I ascend the steps to the deck. Bryce opens the gate for me and I quietly thank him. I open the sliding glass door and let us in.

"You okay?" he asks.

I nod and head to my room and of course, he follows me.

"Alex?"

"What?" I ask as I sit down on my bed.

"You can talk to me." He takes a seat next to me.

"He always does this."

"Does what?"

"He thinks he's defending me and then it gets bad. I wish he could defend me without being the one starting something. You defended me without dropping a single curse word and you did it without being the one to cause a scene."

"Why are you with him?"

"I don't know." I admit out of frustration. "He wasn't always like this. He wasn't always manipulative and dramatic and downright mean."

"So leave him."

"I can't."

"He's not gonna go back to how he was before."

"You don't know that."

"I do."

I shake my head.

"Alex, leave him. You could do so much better."

"Like who? You?"

"If you want."

"What happened to no more relationships?"

"Dump him and find out."

"Bryce."

"Come on, Alex. You know that's not a healthy relation-ship."

"You know nothing about our relationship."

"I've seen enough."

"You haven't."

"So fill me in."

"I just don't understand why he has to start fights all the time!" I groan. "It's like no guy can just be friends with me, he always thinks there's something more. And then he had to accuse you of looking at me a certain way."

"I mean, I kinda was." He admits.

"You-what?"

"I was looking at you like he said, Alex."

"Why are you telling me this? You're saying he was right to throw a fit."

"I'm not saying he was right to throw a fit, I'm just saying he was right."

"Bryce."

"You're beautiful, Alex. I'd be crazy not to look at you."

I look down at the floor and his index and middle fingers of one hand find their way under my chin and he tilts my head up.

"Look at me," he says. "You're beautiful."

I look in his eyes and then glance down at his mouth.

"Alex, I know you're dating Johnny, but-"

I cut him off. "Just kiss me before I change my mind or remember my crappy boyfriend is still a boyfriend."

He obeys and connects his lips with mine. I run my fingers through his hair and am not the least bit surprised by how soft it is. His hands hold my waist and he leans in closer.

Kisses with Johnny never feel like this. Kisses with Johnny always have to lead to sex or happen before a goodbye.

Kissing Bryce feels innocent. This won't lead to sex and it's not a goodbye. It's just a kiss.

I pull away and whisper his name, "Bryce."

"I know, I'm sorry. You're with Johnny."

"It's not about Johnny."

"Then what is it?"

"You shouldn't have to share a girl."

"I'm not sharing."

"Bryce."

"Leave him."

"I can't."

"Alex, you deserve better than him."

"What happened to not wanting a relationship? And don't tell me to leave him and find out."

"I want you."

"Bryce."

"You know I can treat you better than he does."

"I'm not saying you wouldn't."

"Then what's the problem?"

"He might be a crappy boyfriend, but he's still my boyfriend."

"Why do you think you have to stay with him?"

"I don't like giving up on people."

He shakes his head. "You're giving up on yourself by staying with someone who treats you like that."

"Bryce."

"I think I'm just gonna head out."

"Please don't go."

"You don't want to leave him. I'm not gonna be with someone who has a boyfriend just because she can't leave a toxic piece of shit. If you're one of those girls who's afraid to be single, you won't be. I'm not saying this so you'll leave him and then I'll walk out, I'm here, Alex."

"Bryce."

"I gotta go."

He gets up and leaves my room and I don't try to stop him. I take a minute to collect myself before going back outside. As I walk toward the fire pit, I see Bryce sitting on a blanket next to Layla. I take the seat I was in before which happens to be right next to their blanket and he gives me a small smile when he sees me.

"I thought you were going home," I say quietly.

"I changed my mind." He shrugs.

"What made that happen?"

"Just want to be here in case he comes back."

"So, Alex," Grandma Peggy says, "you're still with Johnny because?"

"I don't want to talk about him." I shake my head.

"His behavior was just a little concerning is all." She shrugs. "I mean, there's kids around, after all."

"It was a little scary," Keith says. "He got heated pretty quick."

"I don't think it's a good idea for him to come to these anymore." Grandma Peggy shakes her head. "That could've turned violent."

"Bryce got heated." I point out. "Nobody wants him to leave."

"I got heated because Johnny got heated. He was one step away from accusing us of being together." Bryce rolls his eyes. "Besides, he was defensive the second he saw me."

"He's always defensive when there's another guy around," Mom says.

"Mom!"

"I'm just saying. He's very jealous and insecure."

"It's pretty bad that I can tell how awful he treats you and I met him once." Bryce shrugs. "But that's just my opinion."

"I'm with Bryce," Keith says. "Remember when the Donovans' son would come to these?"

"Oh, and Johnny would make Alex sit as far away from him as possible." Grandma Peggy nods. "The two of them got into physical fights a few times."

"I remember that." Mom nods. "That was scary."

"It was." Grandma Peggy agrees.

"So this is a pattern with him?" Bryce asks.

"Oh, yeah. I'm surprised he left without us having to call the police." Keith nods.

"You said he wasn't violent," Bryce says to me.

"I said he doesn't put his hands on me, which he doesn't."

"So that makes all this okay?" Maggie asks.

"I didn't say that. Why is everybody ganging up on me?"

"Nobody's ganging up on you." Mom squeezes my hand. "We're just concerned."

"I really think you should consider leaving him," Grandma Peggy says.

"I agree." Maggie nods.

"So do I," Mom says. "I've told you that before. And I said it again after what happened when you found out he kissed another girl."

"What happened?" Grandma Peggy asks.

"He faked a suicide attempt."

"How?"

"Flushed some pills, staged the empty pill bottle, and let his mom think she was finding him so she called an ambulance, called Alex, and boom, he was forgiven and fine."

"And you stayed after that?" Bryce asks.

"I'm going inside." I get up from my chair.

"Don't go, we're just worried about you." Grandma Peggy frowns. "We care about you and your safety."

"I'm cold, I need to grab a hoodie."

"You can wear mine." Bryce pulls off his hoodie.

My eyes move to stare at his abs peeking out from beneath the fabric as he does so and it takes everything in me to pull them away from the view.

"Thanks." I try not to roll my eyes or sound sarcastic as he hands it to me.

Getting away from this conversation for the two minutes it would've taken me to grab a hoodie would've been just enough time for the subject to change.

I slip on Bryce's hoodie and can't help but notice how good it smells. Unlike Johnny's hoodies, it doesn't reek of cologne.

"I'm having a pool party in a couple weeks," Grandma Peggy says. "Everyone is invited. There will be snacks and soda and juice and alcohol for the grown-ups of course."

The pot-stirrer in me wants to ask if I can bring Johnny but I know that's not the best idea.

"That sounds so fun." Mom smiles.

"And there will be plenty of kids to play with Layla," she says to Maggie.

"We're out of cups," Mom says. "Alex, could you grab some more?"

"Sure. Where are they?"

"The cabinet to the left of the microwave."

"Okay." I get up and start heading up the lawn.

"I'll go with you." Bryce starts following me.

"I can get cups by myself."

"I know you can," he says as he catches up to me. "But you shouldn't have to."

"It's just cups."

"But you're gonna check your phone in there and I'm willing to bet there's a nasty text or two from your tool of a boyfriend and I'm not gonna let that ruin your night even more."

I roll my eyes and head inside.

"What's going through your head after that conversation out there?" he asks.

"People need to mind their business."

"Everyone was kind of on the same page out there. You really don't think that's a red flag?"

"They don't know him like I do."

"Yeah, that's the issue. He's like that in public so what the hell is he like when no one is around and it's just the two of you behind closed doors?"

"He's fine."

"I don't believe that." He shakes his head. "You really think everyone else in the world is wrong about him and he's just misunderstood and you're the only person who knows the real him?"

I want to say yes but even I can tell how pathetic that sounds right now.

"Pull out your phone."

"Why?"

"I know he's texted you and said something you don't deserve."

"I don't care."

"I do."

I roll my eyes and pull out my phone. "No texts."

"Bull."

"It's not." I turn my phone around for him to see.

"Who's the missed call from?"

Shit. I hadn't noticed that.

He takes my phone and pulls up my call history. "He left you a voicemail."

"I don't want to listen to it. I usually delete them without listening to them anyway."

"Why?"

"Because he doesn't mean the things he says when he's mad."

"You're making way too many excuses for this guy." He shakes his head and presses my phone to his ear.

"What are you doing?"

"Relax, I'm not calling him. Just listening to what he doesn't mean."

I grab the cups and when I turn back around Bryce's arms are crossed over his plain white t-shirt.

"Alex, I'm asking you right now to leave him and let me take you on a date."

"Bryce."

"You'd really rather be with him than see where things could go with me? You know I won't treat you like he does."

"I can't leave him."

"That's great, Alex. Enjoy being with the guy who leaves you a voicemail so nasty that him calling you a lying whore is the nicest part." He leaves the kitchen and walks out the front door.

I look down at my phone on the counter and delete the voicemail without listening to the other curse words and insults that I'm sure are thrown into it.

Maybe I should leave him.

Chapter 7

My feet hit the welcome mat on Maggie's front steps and I take a deep breath.

Relax, Alex. Bryce isn't even here.

I ring the doorbell and it only takes a second for Maggie to answer.

"Thank you so much for doing this on such short notice."

"Of course," I smile.

Maggie leads me up the stairs and I see Layla sitting on the couch playing on a tablet.

"Layla, that's enough with the tablet for today." Maggie warns.

Layla whines but listens to her mother.

"I should be home around eleven, is that too late?" Maggie asks.

"Not at all." I shake my head.

"Layla's bedtime is eight. She's already had dinner but she may get hungry for a snack around seven. She can have some fruit or a yogurt, or there's granola bars in the pantry she can have, she knows which ones are hers."

"Does she have any food allergies or anything I should be aware of?"

"No, nothing like that. I'm not sure what time Bryce will be home from his grandparents' house but he'll definitely beat me home."

I feel my face get warm at the mention of him.

"Okay."

"I think that's everything. You can help yourself to what's in the fridge. I'll see you later. Layla, I gotta head out now."

Layla scurries over to Maggie who bends down to give her a big hug. I drop my bag down next to the love seat while they say their goodbye.

"I'll see you in the morning, okay?" Maggie smiles.

Layla nods. "I love you, mommy."

"I love you too. Be good for Alex."

Layla nods and I'm amazed how well Layla handles Maggie leaving. Most of the little girls I babysit hate watching their mom leave.

The door closes behind Maggie and I'm ready for a sudden screaming fit but it doesn't come.

"Can we play a game?" Layla asks.

"Of course." I smile. "What do you have in mind?"

She shrugs and I laugh.

"Where do you keep the games?" I ask.

"The closet."

I follow her into the hallway and she opens the door she jumped out of the other day and points upward.

"Up there."

I read some of the names to her and it doesn't take long for one to get her attention.

"Sorry!" she cheers. "I want Sorry!"

I grab the box and pull it off the shelf. Layla leads me to the dining room where there's an old card table set up with some folding chairs around it instead of a formal table.

I take the seat next to Layla. "What color do you want to be?"

"Red." She smiles.

"Okay, I'll be blue." I set the box down and open it up.

Layla grabs the board and clumsily unfolds it, whacking herself in the face with it a few times.

"Careful." I laugh.

She finally gets it open and lays it down on the table. I spin it so the red start position is in front of her. She puts our pieces where they belong while I get the cards organized and set up. I let her go first and she's ecstatic.

Our game takes about an hour and Layla is thrilled to beat me.

Four-year-olds really don't know when you let them win.

We clean up our game and I put the box back on the shelf in the hall closet.

"Can we play UNO?" Layla asks.

"Of course." I grab UNO off the shelf and hand her the pack of cards.

Her tiny feet thud on the hardwood floor as she races back to the beige dining room.

I close the closet door and meet Layla back at the table where she already has the cards out of the box and scattered around.

"How many cards do we each get?" I ask.

"Seven."

"Okay." I pick up the cards and shuffle them a bit before dealing us each seven cards.

I let Layla go first again and she doesn't hesitate to make me draw two.

If I weren't so nice, she'd be drawing four.

We play a few rounds and I let her win all of them.

Better to deal with some bragging than a temper tantrum.

Layla hands me some of the cards to put away and they're all facing different directions. I get them organized before sliding them back into the box and putting the box back onto its shelf.

"Alex, I'm hungry."

I look at the clock and read the numbers: 7:01.

Impeccable timing.

"Would you like a snack? Your mom said there's fruit or yogurt or granola bars."

"Yogurt."

"Okay." I open the fridge and see multiple flavors. "Do you want blueberry, strawberry, peach, or vanilla?"

"Strawberry."

I grab one of the red containers and I peel it open for her. She grabs her own spoon which I'm thankful for because I don't know where any of their stuff is in this kitchen.

Layla takes her yogurt over to the table that's so far been used for games and eating and I can't help but wonder what else it functions as.

Is this where Bryce will do his homework when school starts in the fall? Is Bryce even the kind of guy who does his homework? Does Layla do crafts here while Maggie cooks dinner? Does Layla even do crafts? Is Maggie even the kind of mom who cooks dinner?

I look Layla over and her clothes are cute but seem like they may have been handed down from someone older than her. Her long brown hair falls in curls and I wonder if they're natural or if she braided her hair after a shower. I hadn't noticed her eyes before but they're a nice light brown and fit her face well.

She hops up from her seat.

"All done?" I ask.

She nods and tosses her empty yogurt cup into the over-flowing garbage can and adds her spoon to the pile of dirty dishes in the sink.

By now it's almost a quarter past seven and she yawns.

"Getting tired?" I ask.

She nods.

"You should go put on pajamas and get comfy."

"Okay." She goes down the hall and into her room. "Alex!"

"Yes?" I yell back.

"I need help!"

"Okay!" I walk down the hall and into her room.

The walls are a bright pink and the comforter on her bed has pink and purple mermaids. Pictures on the walls keep the theme and even the knobs on her closet doors are pink and glittery.

Now I see what parents mean when they say they put their kids first.

"I like your room," I say.

"Thanks."

"What do you need help with?"

"I can't reach my pajamas."

"Where do you keep them?"

"In the top." She points to the top drawer of her wooden dresser.

I pull it open and peek in. "What do you want to wear?"

She shrugs.

"Do you want me to pick you up so you can see what you have?" I offer.

She nods so I pick her up and rest her on my hip so she can pick out her pajamas. Her tiny hands pick up a pair of tiny black shorts and I see that the tag says 3T. Considering she's four, she's tiny for her age. She pulls out a light pink tank top next and I close the drawer and set her down.

"Thank you." She says quietly and I close her door as I leave her room so she can change.

Quite a few minutes pass before she emerges in her pajamas.

"Let's get your teeth brushed," I say and lead her into the bathroom. There's a plain red toothbrush next to a pink one with mermaids and I think I can guess which one is hers.

"I need my step stool." She pulls open the cabinet and takes out a yellow plastic step stool and hops up. She picks up the mermaid toothbrush and a tube of pink, bubblegum flavored toothpaste. I help her squeeze some onto the bristles and watch her brush to make sure she doesn't swallow any of the toothpaste.

By the time Layla finishes brushing her teeth, it's five to eight.

"Ready for bed?" I ask.

She nods so I lead her down the hall and she hops into bed.

"Do you want your blanket on or is it too hot?" I ask.

"Blanket. But put the fan on." She points to an old box fan on the floor by the closet.

"Okay." I pull her blanket over her and flick the fan on.

"Mommy puts it in the door."

I pick up the fan and stand it in the doorway. "Here?"
She nods.

"Do you want me to turn off the light on your nightstand?"

"No! That stays on."

"Okay." I smile. "Is that everything?"

"Yes." She nods.

"Okay," I say. "Goodnight, Layla."

"Goodnight, Alex."

I leave her bedroom and go into the living room. My bag is still next to the love seat so I pick it up and take a seat. The gray cloth is soft and the couch and matching love seat are definitely new.

I wonder if Maggie's ordered a formal dining room table and it just hasn't come in yet or if she only had the money to buy a new living room set.

I open my bag and pull out a brand new book. It's a new thriller, a massive change from the romance novels I usually read, but everyone's been raving about it so I figured it's worth a shot.

I read sixty pages when I hear the lock on the front door turn followed by bodies clumsily bumping into the wall as the door closes. I look over the railing at the foyer and see Bryce with none other than Jessica Myers, the girl Johnny kissed at that party.

Bryce looks phenomenal in his black and white joggers and black short sleeve shirt. Jessica, on the other hand, couldn't look any cheesier in her tight denim skirt and red tube top.

Why does this girl keep taking guys from me?

I have to remind myself that Bryce isn't mine and I clear my throat loudly enough for them to hear me and stop.

"Your mom is gonna be home in three minutes," I say. "So unless you're capable of getting this done rather quickly, you might want to reschedule."

"Alex." Jessica glares at me.

"Jessica." I roll my eyes.

She flips her fake red hair over her shoulder and grabs Bryce's arm.

"You're down to two minutes," I say.

"I'll see you later, Jess." Bryce opens the door for her and she steps through.

"You should be careful with her," I say. "She's kind of a snake."

"I can make my own choices about who I sleep with."

I roll my eyes as I shake my head and I take my seat.

Bryce stomps down the stairs and I close my eyes but a tear wiggles its way out anyway.

A few minutes pass and Bryce angrily makes his way upstairs. "What happened to my mom being home in three minutes?"

"Did I say three minutes? Huh, I meant two hours."

He shakes his head.

"I don't want to hear you have sex, Bryce."

"Sucks."

I roll my eyes.

"What's your deal?"

"My deal?"

"Yeah, Alex, your deal."

"My deal, Bryce, is that I like you. Okay? And I want to fucking be with you."

"If you wanted to be with me that bad, you would."

"What's that supposed to mean?"

"You know what it means, Alex."

"No, Bryce, I don't."

"If you wanted to be with me, you'd drop Johnny. It's that fucking simple."

"It's not simple." I shake my head.

"Alex, I swore off relationships and changing that decision was real fucking easy when I met you. If you wanted me, you'd leave Johnny."

"And if you wanted me, you wouldn't fuck Jessica Fucking Myers."

"I want you, Alex. But I'm not gonna sit around waiting for you to get your shit together and leave the guy who makes you feel so fucking horrible all the damn time."

"My shit is together, thank you very much."

"We both know you're not stupid enough to believe that."

"Bryce."

"Forget it. I'm making popcorn, do you want any?"

I shake my head and he disappears into the kitchen.

I hear angry crinkling of the plastic bag the kernels come in and the microwave door slams shut.

"Could you try to be quieter?" I ask. "Layla's sleeping."

"She sleeps like she's dead, she'll be fine."

I keep my mouth shut and read a few more pages while his popcorn pops.

He exits the kitchen and sits on the couch, much calmer now. "Mind if I put a movie on?"

"Go ahead." I shrug.

He grabs the remote and puts on a horror movie. I try to ignore it so I can keep reading my book but it catches my attention after just ten minutes.

"I bet she's gonna die," I say.

"No way. She's one of the main characters."

"Doesn't matter. She's gonna be the first to go."

He laughs and shakes his head and I hope he's as done being mad at me as he seems because his popcorn smells amazing.

"You getting scared yet?" he asks.

"I don't get scared," I say and realize I should've said yes. "But maybe you should come sit by me in case."

He smirks and gets up and joins me on the love seat. I steal a piece of popcorn from his clear plastic bowl and he glances over and smiles at me. My eyes connect with the screen just in time to see our girl get killed.

"I told you." I smile.

"They can't kill her."

"They just did."

"She's a main character."

"Not anymore." I laugh.

"That's fucked."

I laugh and steal some more of his popcorn.

"I bet her boyfriend is the killer."

"No, it's definitely the ex." I shake my head.

"Oh, well, since you said it, it must be right."

"Obviously."

We finish the movie and of course I was right and her ex was the psycho killer.

"How do you do that?" he asks. "You predicted the entire movie, plot twists and everything."

"It comes naturally." I laugh and I pick my legs up and lay them on his lap without even thinking about it.

Nothing ever comes this naturally with Johnny.

Bryce shakes his head and exits out of our movie before placing the popcorn bowl on the floor.

"Can I ask you something?" I ask.

"You just did."

I give him a look.

"Go ahead."

"Why her?"

"Why who?"

"Jessica Myers. Of all the girls here, why her?"

"She's hot." He sighs. "That's the only answer I have right now."

"Johnny kissed her at a party this one night."

"While you two were a couple?"

I nod.

"I'm sorry."

"For what?"

"I didn't bring her here to sleep with her just because she's hot."

"What do you mean? Are you two a couple? Are you dating her?"

"God, Alex, no. I knew you were babysitting tonight and I wanted to make you jealous."

"So you brought her here to hurt me?"

"Alex, no!" His left hand lays on my legs. "I didn't know there was history there. I just wanted you to feel what I feel every time I have to see you with Johnny."

I shake my head.

"Alex, why are you with him?"

"I don't want to talk about him."

"Then what do you want to talk about? You're the one who started this conversation."

"I don't want to talk anymore."

"Alex, look at me."

I turn my head and we make eye contact.

"You know you're way too good for him."

I shake my head and start to look away when he grabs my chin and tilts my head back to face him.

"Look at me when I'm talking to you." He orders.

"What?"

"Alex."

"Bryce."

"Alex."

"Bryce."

"Alex."

"If you're planning on kissing me again, now would be a good time. Because if you don't do it soon, I might remember I have a boyfriend."

He pulls me into him and kisses me. His right hand reaches for my waist and his left hand tangles itself in my hair.

He lets out a short breath against my lips and pulls me onto his lap.

I hear the front door open and I freeze when I hear Maggie's voice. "I'm home."

Chapter 8

I can't believe I did that last night. I was babysitting Layla and I made out with Bryce. I'm dating Johnny and I made out with Bryce.

A knock on my door pulls me out of my thoughts.

"Come in!" I call.

My door opens and I peek over the top of my laptop and see Bryce.

I sit up immediately. "What are you doing here?"

"I needed to see you after last night."

"Bryce."

"Alex, I want you."

"I'm dating Johnny."

"That doesn't stop you from making out with me."

"It should."

"Yeah, you're right, it should. But it doesn't. You aren't in love with Johnny and you know you aren't."

"I'm not in love with you either, Bryce."

"You don't have to be in love with me, I'm not your boyfriend."

"Bryce."

"Friends with benefits."

"What?"

"At the very least, let's be friends with benefits."

"I have a boyfriend."

"Alex, we've already been through the 'that doesn't stop you' part of this conversation, do we really need to do it again?"

I shake my head.

"Let me ask you one thing."

"What?"

"Have you ever wondered what it would be like?"

"What what would be like?"

"Being with me." He takes a step closer to me. "Going on dates with me." Another step. "Kissing me whenever you want." And another. Until he's standing right in front of me.

"Bryce."

"Have you?"

"You know I have." I admit.

"See? We both want to be with each other."

"That doesn't mean we should do it."

"I won't tell Johnny if you won't."

"Bryce."

"Alex, come on."

"Why do you want this so bad?"

"Because I want you so bad, Alex. I want to be with you."

I let out a sigh.

"Alex, come on. Go on a date with me."

"Bryce, no!"

My eyes open and I look around my room. Bryce is nowhere to be found.

Did I really dream up that whole conversation?

I grab my phone off my nightstand and check the time and see that it's half past eight.

Bryce might be awake.

I unlock my phone and pull up our conversation.

I can't believe I'm doing this.

I type a quick message and hit send.

Me: Are you awake?

Bryce: No

Me: Funny. Can I come over in a bit?

Bryce: Sure

I hop out of bed and take a quick shower.

My towel works on drying my hair while I pick out my clothes for the day. I pull open the drawer that holds my shorts and slip into a pair of black denim ones that just barely cover my ass. I pull on a black tank top and don't put any makeup on today. I take the towel off my hair and carefully brush the knots out.

Perfect.

I slip on a pair of black and tan sandals and head out the door.

My knuckles tap Bryce's front door a few times and it only takes a second for him to answer and let me in.

"Hey," he says.

"Hey."

"What's up?"

"Can we just talk for a sec?"

"Sure."

"Is anyone home?"

He shakes his head. "You wanna go to my room?"

"Okay."

I follow him down the stairs and into a doorway on the left. A bed is in the corner and much to my surprise, the blue comforter isn't a mess on the floor.

"A boy who makes his bed." I laugh. "Rare."

He smiles and sits down on the corner of his bed. "What's going on, Alex?"

"I want you. I want to be with you. In a perfect world, Johnny wouldn't exist."

"Alex, he doesn't have to be an issue. You can break up with him and if you start dating me, I'll keep him away from you."

"You don't understand." I shake my head. "I've tried to break up with him in the past and it didn't go well. He goes insane, okay? He stages an entire suicide. He doesn't take anything but it's staged well enough to need a hospital and scare me into staying."

"Was this after he kissed that girl at the party?"

I nod. "Jessica Myers. Or Jess, as you call her."

"I already apologized for that one but, Alex, that's insane, it's abusive. You need to break up with him and tell him to go to counseling."

"What I need to do is get him into counseling now so I can break up with him without him wasting valuable hospital resources that could go towards saving a life that's actually in danger."

He shakes his head.

"Bryce, I want to talk about us."

"There isn't an us, you made that clear."

"There's not an us yet. But maybe one day, hopefully soon."

He's silent.

"But for now, can we maybe-"

"Can we what?"

"You deserve better than a girl you have to share."

"What are you trying to say, Alex?"

"I want to be more than friends but less than a couple."

"So what is that?"

"I don't know." I admit. "We can go on dates and kiss but we can't be public about it."

He thinks for a second. "Okay."

"Okay?"

"On one condition."

"What is it?"

"You have to break up with Johnny within two months of us starting this."

"Okay."

"Okay?"

"I'll find a way."

"I'm serious, Alex. I'm not gonna wait for you to leave him forever. That two month mark is it. That means by August tenth he needs to be out of the picture."

"Okay."

"So we're doing this?"

"We're doing this."

He shakes his head again.

"What?" I laugh.

"This is crazy."

"Most good things are." I walk over to him and sit on his lap, wrapping my legs around him. My head rests on his shoulder and he wraps his arms around me.

"You look really good in black."

"Yeah?" I ask as I lean in and kiss him.

"Yeah." He nods against my lips.

I will never understand how that conversation led to this.

"So that happened," Bryce says.

"I guess so."

"Are you okay with that?"

I think for a second and turn to face him as I nod.

He reaches over and sets his hand down on my bare stomach, his thumb drawing tiny circles on my skin. "Good."

"Are you?"

He nods. "Yeah."

I lean in and kiss him and he slides closer to me, wrapping his arms around me.

"What are you doing?" I ask.

"Cuddling with you."

"Isn't the girl usually the one to want to cuddle?"

"Yeah, just the like the guy is usually the one doing the cheating."

"You didn't have to go there." I laugh.

"Just cuddle with me."

I lean in close and lay my head on his chest. He kisses my forehead and a smile spreads across my face.

This feels normal. It feels right.

I don't want this feeling with anyone else.

But what if he does?

"Are you gonna hook up with other girls?" I ask.

"What?"

"I'm not saying you can't, I have a boyfriend so that would make me a really big hypocrite. I'm just curious."

"I wasn't planning on it."

"Oh."

"I want you, Alex. I don't need to have sex with someone who isn't you just because you're having sex with someone who isn't me."

I nod.

"Come here." He lifts my chin and kisses me.

"What's gonna happen if Johnny finds out about this?"

"He won't find out."

"What if he does?"

"He's not gonna."

"Bryce."

"Alex, I promise you. We'll find a way to keep this between us."

"How?"

"How about you tell me when you're gonna be with him so I know not to text you?"

"Okay, that works."

"Even if he were to find out, which he won't, I would handle it.

"Why you?"

"He can hit me all he wants but he's not gonna touch you and he's not gonna have another excuse to call you shitty names. Besides, you're not gonna be with him two months from now anyway so I don't need to stay on his good side."

"I hope I'm not with him two days from now."

"Really?"

I nod. "I thought about it and after the way he flipped out the other night, in front of kids, I don't want to be with him. How could I want to stay with someone like that."

"I don't blame you. He's an idiot for not doing everything possible to make you happy."

I can't help but smile at that.

"I'm serious." He kisses my forehead. "I feel like the luckiest guy in the world to be laying next to you right now, naked or not."

I press my lips against his and smile.

"You know, I can't help but stare at you sometimes."

"Like when?"

"Well, the fire pit the other night. You might be the only girl who can make sweatpants look good."

I laugh and hope he can't see me blushing.

"What are you thinking about?" he asks.

"I don't know." I roll over and lay on top of his chest.

He wraps his arms around me and one of his hands rub my back while the other brushes my hair out of my face.

"This is weird," I say.

"Good weird or bad weird?"

"Good weird."

"Good. What's weird about it?"

"Well, for starters, I barely know you."

"I think you know me a little better now." He laughs.

"I'm serious." I smile. "I never do this. I've never slept with someone I wasn't in a relationship with."

"We'll be together soon."

I smile and kiss him.

"What else is weird about this?"

"I know you don't want to hear about Johnny, but I could never do this with him."

"Do what?"

"This. Talk and cuddle. Just enjoy being together. All we do after we have sex is fight."

"Over what?"

"Anything you could imagine."

"That's not healthy."

"I know."

"All I want to do right now is hold you so for him to be anything other than happy after sleeping with you is a reflection of him."

"I can't even let myself be in the moment with you because I'm stressing out over him."

"I think I can help you be in the moment." He leans in and kisses me softly.

I kiss him back before laying my head on his shoulder. "I could lay here forever."

"I'm not stopping you," he says and kisses my forehead.

I wrap my hands around one of his biceps and he starts to rub my back again.

Laying in bed with him makes me feel so safe. I don't have to worry about him blowing up over nothing, I don't have to worry about him leaving or kicking me out, I don't have to worry about him starting an argument and getting mad at me. I don't have to worry about anything.

I hear my phone start to ring and can't figure out where it's coming from when Bryce finally points to it on the floor. "There."

He rushes to pick it up and hands it to me.

I see Johnny's name on the screen and instantly panic. "Oh my God! Do you think he knows?"

"There's no way he knows, Alex."

"But what if he does?"

"Well, he might get a little suspicious if you don't answer his phone call."

I quickly answer it and try to sound as normal as possible. "Hi, hey, what's up?"

Because that's so normal.

"Uh, hey. I'm at your house and you're not."

"You're at my house right now?" I panic.

"Yeah. So where are you?"

"I'm actually next door."

Why did I tell him that?

"You're with that guy?"

"No, not like that! I babysat his little sister last night and she wasn't having a very easy time leaving her mom so we thought it'd be best if she spent time with me while her mom was home." I reach for my clothes and slipping them on. "I'll be home in two minutes though."

"Okay. I'll be here, I guess." He hangs up the phone and I'm grateful to be able to breathe again.

"That was very smooth." Bryce laughs.

"I have to go," I say.

"I heard."

"I'm so sorry."

"I'm not mad at you."

"I know you're not, but I'm still sorry. Where's my shirt?" He smirks.

"Give me my shirt."

"What's the magic word?"

"Alex will never see you, talk to you, kiss you, or sleep with you ever again."

"Fuck, good guess." He pulls my shirt out from behind his back and hands it to me.

I slip it on and Bryce walks over and wraps his arms around me.

"I don't have time for this," I say.

"I'll be quick." He leans in and kisses me.

Johnny never kisses me after sex unless he thinks it'll get him more sex.

Bryce is nothing like Johnny.

I smile and I finish getting dressed.

"Your hair needs some attention." Bryce points out.

"Fuck!" I groan and run my fingers through it.

"You're gonna have to put it up."

"I know," I whine and toss my hair into the world's messiest bun. "He's gonna flip."

"If he does, you call me."

I nod.

"I mean it."

"I know."

"Hey," Bryce says as I turn to leave.

"Yeah?"

"You still look beautiful."

Chapter 9

Johnny's car is waiting in my driveway and Johnny's on the front steps with a bouquet of flowers.

That's new.

I walk up the sidewalk and stand in front of him. "Hi."

"Hi."

"What are you doing here?"

"I wanted to take you on a date."

"You never take me on dates."

"I know." He runs his free hand through his hair. "But I messed up the other night."

"Yeah. You did."

"I know. And I'm really sorry."

"You tried to start a physical fight with kids around."

"I know."

I look down at the ground for a second and he wraps his arms around me.

"I'm sorry. I know I really hurt you."

"And you did it anyway."

"In the moment I was just so heated, I wasn't thinking straight. Seeing another guy look at you like he was." He shakes his head.

"Bryce is just a friend."

With benefits.

"I know that's all it is on your end, but his might be a different story."

I shake my head.

"Alex." He reaches out and grabs my hand. "I'm sorry."

"Let's go inside." I open the front door and let us in.

"Are you gonna take your flowers?"

"When we get inside you can trim the stems and put them in a vase for me." I joke.

"Oh, I can do it?"

"Yeah, you can do it."

"You're lucky you're cute."

"I know." I grin and lead him into the kitchen.

He sets the bouquet of red roses on the counter and grabs the scissors from the wooden butcher block while I grab a glass vase out of the cabinet above the fridge. I place the vase on the counter and start filling a glass with water.

"Is this a good height?" Johnny asks and I look over to see him holding a flower next to the vase.

"That's perfect." I dump the glass of water into the vase and he drops the first flower in. I set the glass on the counter by the sink and stand behind Johnny. I wrap my arms around his torso and rest my cheek against the back of his shoulder.

"What are your mom and grandma doing today?"

"I think they're out shopping."

"Why didn't you go with them?"

"Well, I was still sleeping when they left. But either way, I had to go next door."

"Right. How's she doing?"

"She's okay." I slide my right hand down his stomach and it settles on his hip.

"Babe."

"Yes, babe?"

"I'm holding scissors."

"So?"

"So you probably shouldn't put your hand near my dick."

"That's boring."

"It's distracting."

"I think you'll live."

"I might lose a finger." He laughs.

"Then maybe you should hurry up and finish with my flowers so we can get to the fun part."

He shakes his head and I'm sure he's got a smirk on his face.

The last few stems are cut and the flowers are placed in the vase. Johnny dumps the packet of flower food in as I pour in some more water. He discards of the plastic the bouquet was wrapped in and grabs my hand.

I stand back and admire the vibrant roses. The bright red petals compliment the bold green stems and I hug Johnny.

"What are you doing?" he asks with a laugh.

"Thank you."

"For what?"

"Making it right when you fucked up."

"Don't get used to it."

I wasn't planning on it.

I roll my eyes and kiss him.

"Hey," he says. "I love you."

"I love you too."

His hands grab my ass and I'm certain he's forgotten all about his intention of taking me out on a date today. We kiss for a few more moments before he lifts me onto the countertop. I lay my right hand on the back of his neck as his fingers pull on the fabric of my black tank top and he yanks it over my head just before he freezes.

"What's wrong?" I ask.

"I think I heard a car door."

And as soon as the words leave his lips, the front door opens.

"Fuck," I whisper. I rush to turn my shirt right side out while Johnny fixes my shorts that I hadn't realized he unbuttoned. The fabric of my tank top barely covers my skin as I hop down from the counter just in time.

"Hey, guys." Mom smiles from behind her collection of shopping bags.

"Hi," Johnny says.

"Where's Grandma?" I ask.

"She's outside talking to Grandma Peggy."

"And she left you with the bags?" I laugh.

"Typical Grandma." She rolls her eyes.

"What are they talking about?" I ask.

"So nosy." Johnny laughs.

"Isn't she always?" Mom agrees. "Your grandma wants to seal the driveway and Grandma Peggy just had hers done so she's asking her who she used for hers."

"And I'm the nosy one." I laugh.

The front door opens again and Grandma comes into my view.

"Did you get the name of the company?" Mom asks.

"Oh, we're not using them. She said they had to come back a second time because they messed it up the first. Kids today, you guys are so stupid you wouldn't know your ass from a hole in the ground." Grandma shakes her head.

I want to laugh at her word choice but I hold it in so I don't piss her off even further. Johnny, apparently, doesn't get the memo.

"Hey, you're included in that group." Grandma points at him.

"At least I'm a stupid kid and not an old person starting to lose it." He shrugs.

"Johnny!" I whack his arm.

"You better watch it, kid." She warns.

"Why don't the two of you go do something fun? Out of the house." Mom suggests.

"Good idea. Let's go." I grab Johnny's wrist and pull him out of the kitchen and down the stairs before pulling him out the front door and slamming it shut behind us. "What the hell was that?"

"What?" he asks.

"Could you have been any more disrespectful?"

"I could've, actually."

"Johnny!"

"What?"

"You're unbelievable."

"Thanks, babe." He winks at me.

"You should go."

"Are you serious?"

"Yeah, I am. Go."

"Unbelievable."

"Believe it." I cross my arms.

"What about our date?"

"I'm not going on a date with you."

"Fuck you, Alex."

"Fuck you too, Johnny."

He gets in his car and I see Bryce standing in his driveway. Johnny pulls out of the driveway and takes off up the road.

Tears form in my eyes and I try to blink them away but they escape down my cheeks. I sit on the steps and bury my face in my knees. After a few seconds, arms wrap around me and a small part of me hopes it's Johnny here to apologize. I look up and see Bryce.

"I'm not gonna tell you you should be with me, but you shouldn't be with him." He kisses my forehead and I lay my head on his shoulder.

"What did I do to deserve a guy like him?"

"You didn't do anything. Alex, the sooner you break up with him, the sooner you'll feel better."

"I can't believe he showed up with flowers and I actually thought things could be different now. God, I'm so stupid."

"You're not stupid. He's manipulative and the flowers were just a tactic."

I pick my head up and see that my tears have turned tiny patches of his baby blue shirt a dark navy. "Sorry for crying on you."

"Don't apologize. I want to be there when you need me."

"Do you want to come inside?" I ask.

"Sure."

He stands up and holds his hand out for me. I take it and he helps me up before I open the door to let us in.

"Back already?" Mom asks. "There better be an apology for that outburst."

"I'm not with Johnny." I climb up the stairs. "Bryce is here."

"Oh, perfect. The two of you should come sit so we can have a chat."

Does she know about us? She couldn't.

I lead Bryce into the dining room where my mom and grandma are sitting at the table together.

"What is this, an intervention?" I laugh.

"Actually, yeah." Mom nods.

"What? Did you know about this?" I ask Bryce.

He silently nods and looks down to avoid my glare.

"I talked to him when I got home and he seemed to agree with my thoughts."

"Your thoughts on what?"

"Why don't you sit down?" Mom points to the chair across from her.

"If I have to sit, so do you." I order Bryce and he sits down with me.

"We wanted to have this conversation with Johnny here but after his attitude, we're just going to do it now."

"Do what?"

"Alex." Mom starts. "After what happened the other night, we don't think you should be with Johnny anymore. And today solidified those feelings."

"What exactly happened today?" Bryce asks.

"The little punk wanted to talk back to me and suffer no consequences." Grandma shakes her head.

"He was downright rude." Mom agrees.

"And I made him leave instead of hanging out with him today." I point out.

"Oh, big deal. Tomorrow you'll be right back to kissing his ass." Grandma scowls.

"I don't kiss his ass, but if he apologizes, then yes, I will accept it and be nice to him." I roll my eyes.

"He's not gonna apologize, Alex." Mom shakes her head.

"He apologized for being a jerk the other night. He got me flowers too."

"Oh, tell him to go shit in his hat and punch it." Grandma slaps her hand down on the table.

"Do you not believe that you deserve better?" Mom asks.

"You know what happens when I try to break up with him." I remind her of his suicide attempts.

"Yeah, I do. And that's even more of a reason for you to break up with him. That's manipulative. He's toxic and mentally, emotionally, and verbally abusive."

I don't say anything because defending Johnny in front of Bryce would just mess up what we have.

"You could do so much better, Alex," Bryce says.

"See? Right here? Why can't you date Bryce?" Mom asks.

"Excuse me?"

"Johnny wasn't wrong about the way Bryce looks at you." She shrugs. "He'd treat you a hundred times better too."

I shake my head. "You're insane. You barely know him."

"Why are you so damn stubborn?" Grandma asks.

"Because I can be." I deadpan.

Bryce laughs.

"And he thinks you're funny." Mom raises her eyebrows. "He's already doing much better than Johnny."

"You guys are so weird." I roll my eyes.

"Just hang out with him." Mom persists. "You're not busy today, are you, Bryce?"

"Not at all." He shakes his head.

"Fantastic. Go do something fun."

"Are you serious?" I ask.

"Yes, I'm serious. Go."

"Why can't you encourage me to hang out with Cassie or another one of my girl friends?"

"Cassie's on vacation but good try. Go."

I roll my eyes and get up from my chair.

"Have fun, you two." Mom smirks.

I grab my keys and lead Bryce outside.

"Are we really gonna go hang out?" he asks.

"Do you want to deal with another one of those?"

"Not particularly."

"Then, yeah, we're gonna go hang out."

"What are we gonna do?"

"Ever played with cows?" I ask.

"There's cows everywhere back home, you see them at every street corner."

"But have you ever played with them?"

He thinks for a minute. "Actually, no."

"Then I'll bring you to play with the cows."

"Sounds good."

We get in my car and I pull out of the driveway.

I exit the neighborhood and head down the main road.

"Are we almost there?" he asks.

"Excited to see some farm animals?" I laugh.

"A little, yeah."

"Well, we're not even halfway there."

We get to the end of the road where we meet a green light so I go straight to go across the highway. I stay straight for a few miles and finally see the wooden fence of the farm.

"Is this it?" Bryce asks.

"This is it." I pull into the parking lot and pick a space by the barn.

"Do you come here a lot?"

"Over the summer, yeah."

We climb out of my SUV and head into the big red barn first.

"Sheep are this way." I point to the left.

"There's sheep too?"

"There's also chickens and pigs and back outside there are bees."

"Oh, wow."

I lead him to the area where the sheep are usually kept.

"It's empty."

"Give it a minute. Randy will bring them in."

"Randy?"

"The owner. He knows my car so he knows to bring them in when he sees me."

"Wow, you do come here a lot."

About twenty sheep come running into the barn, including a couple babies.

"Holy crap." Bryce laughs. "This is insane."

"Hi, baby." I bend down and reach through the fence to pet the first one that runs to me. I reach into the wheelbarrow of hay and pull out a handful to feed her.

"We're allowed to feed them?" he asks.

"Yeah, Randy leaves this here every week. Sometimes there's just hay, sometimes there's carrot tops. People can bring things in and as long as they're approved by Randy, they're added to the wheelbarrow for people to give the animals."

"That's awesome."

"Grab a handful."

He reaches in and pulls out a carrot top and the sheep I was feeding leaves me and runs to him.

"You stole my sheep!" I laugh.

"He likes me better."

"She."

"She? How do you know?"

One of the lambs runs over to her and starts to nurse.

"That's how."

"Hey there, Alex." Randy smiles.

"Hey! This is Bryce. His family just moved into the house next to mine. Bryce, this is Randy."

"Welcome to your new home." Randy reaches out and shakes Bryce's hand.

"Nice to meet you."

"Stick with Alex, and you'll be here quite a bit this summer."

"That doesn't sound too bad." He smirks in my direction and I feel myself blush.

"Hey, have you seen the bees yet?" Randy asks.

"Not yet." Bryce shakes his head.

"Oh, you gotta see the bees. Let's head over."

We follow Randy outside and through the garden to the bee yard.

"What are these things?" Bryce points to the wooden boxes covered with bees.

"It's called an apiary." Randy explains. "This is where I harvest the honey."

"That's really cool."

"It is." I agree. "The honey always tastes great. And that's coming from someone who hates honey."

"I'll have a batch ready tomorrow, I could drop some off if you'd like." Randy offers.

"That'd be great, we're getting low."

"I can bring a jar for your family too, Bryce."

"Yeah, we'd really appreciate that."

"Why don't you two go see the rest of the animals? The cows are in the field, you can let yourself in."

"Do they need to be brushed?" I ask.

"Yeah, Benny does. Thanks."

"No problem, I'll catch up with you later." I smile and without thinking I grab Bryce's hand. "Cows are this way."

"Okay." He smiles and he doesn't try to pull his hand away.

I lead him to the field and I open the gate to let us in.

"Where are they?" Bryce asks.

"They're usually on the other side of the hill. It's just a short walk." I grab the brush off the hook.

We make our way through the grass and reach the top of the hill. Four cows stand about halfway down and a smile spreads across my face.

"Ready to go pet some cows?" I ask.

He smiles and we walk down to them.

"Here." I hand him the brush.

"What do I do with this?"

"You brush them."

"I have no idea how to brush a cow."

I take the brush back from him and brush Benny a few times. "Like this." I hand the brush back and he takes over.

"So, you do this a lot?"

"All the time."

"You ever bring that boyfriend of yours?"

"This isn't really his thing."

"What do you mean?"

"Dirt."

"Oh, so you're dating a princess."

I laugh until I realize how different Johnny and I really are.

"You okay?" Bryce asks.

I nod.

"Hey, what's wrong?"

"Nothing. I'm good."

"Alex."

"Bryce."

"You can talk to me."

"It's just, Johnny and I don't even have anything in common. If I were to meet him today, I don't think I'd have any interest in him."

"You can leave him, Alex. I'll come here with you every day. I'll let you show me all your favorite places and I bet I'll love them, too. You don't have to stay with Johnny."

I let out a sigh.

"Alex, I'll treat you how he should've been treating you this whole time." He inches closer to me and begins to lean in. I do the same and our lips are just centimeters apart when Benny lets out his loudest moo.

Chapter 10

My phone buzzes on my nightstand and I pick it up and see a text from Johnny: Nobody's home. Come over?

I roll my eyes at his horrible attempt at being subtle and text him back: Can't. Time of the month

His reply is quick and exactly what I expected from him: Gross. See you whenever that ends

I put my phone down and let out a groan. He always disappears when I have my period.

I venture out into the living room and see Grandma on the couch.

"You break up with Johnny yet?" she asks.

"No. I'm gonna do it in person one day next week."

"You say that now."

"He's a psychopath, okay? I have to be careful with how I go about this."

"You should just do it fast and get it over with."

"That's not how Johnny works. Fast to him means impulsive. He needs to know that I thought it over and that it's what I want and there's no changing my mind."

"He'll know it's what you want if you start dating someone new right after."

"I don't want him to know when I move on. That would just hurt him and make him spiral again."

"He's gonna spiral anyway."

"He might." I admit. "But at least this way, he can't question what I want."

"He'll still question it."

I let out a sigh and shrug. "Probably. Where's mom?"

"How the hell should I know?"

"No need for the attitude." I laugh.

I make my way back to my room and see a text from Bryce as I flop down onto my bed.

Come over?

What is with both of the boys in my life wanting a booty call today?

I text him back quickly. Can't today sorry :(

Are you with Johnny?

I roll my eyes as I type my reply. No

His response is fast and only mildly pisses me off. Then what gives?

I groan as I text him back. I just can't

My phone buzzes and I roll my eyes as I read his response. But why? Alex, what's going on?

I scream inside as I press send. If you must know, I have my period.

His text back makes up for all the frustration his previous ones caused: Can I bring you anything?

Oh, I'm gonna have fun with this.

I smile as I text him back. Brownies would be nice

His response makes me smile. Do you want me to make them for you or bring over a box of brownie mix and we can make them together?

I text him back with the biggest smile still on my face. Second option please

You got it, babe

I set my phone down and roll over in my bed. A few minutes go by before a knock on the front door finally comes. I jump up and lay my comforter over my bed to make it look a bit neater before heading to the front door to let Bryce in. I stop at the top of the stairs when I notice Grandma sitting on the couch.

"You weren't gonna get that?" I ask.

"Do I look like I was gonna get that?"

I laugh and head down the stairs. My fingers grab the cool metal of the doorknob and I open the door to let Bryce in. "Hey." I smile.

"Hi." He pulls me in for a hug. "How are you feeling? Do you have cramps or anything?"

"Not really." I shake my head and notice the box of brownie mix in his hands. "You're the best."

He smiles and takes his shoes off and I lead him up the stairs to the kitchen.

"What do we need for those? Just an egg?" I ask.

"And oil."

"Can you grab the oil from that cabinet?" I point to the cabinet next to the fridge.

"Sure." Bryce grabs the oil while I grab an egg.

I open the cabinet above the fridge so I can grab the glass pan but I don't see it. "Where did it go?"

"Where did what go?" Bryce asks.

"The glass square pan I always use for brownies." I open the next cabinet, above the pantry, and don't see it there either. "Grandma, do you know where the glass pan for brownies is?"

"Nope."

"You don't?"

"Nope."

"But you know where everything is."

"Nope."

"Grandma!"

"What?"

"Where is the pan?"

"I don't know."

"Do you actually not know?" I ask.

"Why does it matter?"

"Well, are you losing it or do you just not give a shit?"

"I just don't give a shit." She laughs.

I shake my head with a smile.

"I think I found it!" Bryce calls from the kitchen.

I walk in and see him holding it.

"Where was it?" I ask.

"That cabinet." He points to the cabinet across from the fridge. "This is it?"

"Yeah."

He sets the pan on the counter and wraps his arms around me.

"What?" I ask.

"Nothing. I just like holding you."

Johnny never holds me like this.

I smile and pull away. "Should we start baking?" I don't wait for an answer before I grab the mixing bowl. "Could you preheat the oven to three hundred?"

"Sure." He walks over to the oven and presses a few buttons while I open the box of brownie mix.

I dump the mix in the bowl and unscrew the cap on the bottle of oil. Bryce cracks the egg and drops it in the bowl while I fill the tablespoon measure with oil. I dump it in while he throws out the shell and washes his hands.

Bryce mixes everything together and pours it into the pan as the oven beeps to let us know it's up to temperature. I go to grab the pan but he stops me.

"I got it," he says and picks up the pan. "I don't want you to risk burning your hand putting it into the hot oven."

That's actually kind of sweet.

I smile as I set the timer. "Want to go watch a movie in my room?"

"Sure."

I lead him to my room and sit on the edge of my bed and grab the remote.

"What kind of movies do you like?" he asks.

"Anything scary."

"Had you pegged as a romance fan." He smiles.

"I'm dating Johnny." I laugh with an eye roll.

"For now." He bends down and kisses my forehead. "Pretty soon you'll know what it's like to have a real boyfriend who values you."

I can't wait.

"You okay with watching something scary?" I ask.

"Yeah, put on whatever you want to watch."

Johnny rarely lets me pick and when he does, I still have to run it by him.

I put on a horror movie and set my remote on my night-stand before laying down. "Come lay with me."

He smiles and climbs into bed with me. I lay my right arm over his chest and rest my head on his shoulder. We make it about three minutes into the movie when my phone goes off.

"Your mom texted me. She wants me to babysit next week-end."

"What day?"

"Saturday."

"Great. Date night." He rolls his eyes.

"Don't like this one?"

"It's a new one. She dropped that last bum."

"That's rough. Where are you gonna be Saturday?"

"I got a job, so working."

"You got a job?"

"Gotta make money to take my future girl on cute dates."

I can't help but smile. "Where do you work?"

"JT's autobody shop."

"Oh boy."

"What?"

"Johnny's dad owns that place."

"Are you fucking kidding me?"

"I wish."

"Fuck."

"Johnny never goes there, it'll be fine."

"Alex, I will hit him with somebody's car if he shows up."

"I don't doubt that." I laugh.

"Of all the fucking places I could've gotten hired." He rolls his eyes.

"It'll be fine."

"Yeah, I'm sure." He rolls his eyes. "What time are you babysitting Lay?"

"Your mom asked me to be over at seven. What time are you working until?"

"Eight. We can hang out when I get home."

"Sounds perfect."

The timer we set for the brownies goes off so I pause the movie we're barely watching and climb over Bryce to get up.

"You could've let me get up first." He laughs.

"And where's the fun in that?" I grab his hand and yank him up and lead him to the kitchen. I see Grandma sitting on the couch. "Were you gonna turn the timer off?"

"It's not my timer." She shrugs.

"Were you gonna tell me it went off or were you just gonna let it beep?"

"You heard it, why would I have told you?"

Attitude.

I hit the button on the microwave to silence the timer's perpetual beeps.

Bryce grabs the red oven mitt off its hook and slides it onto his right hand as he opens the door to the oven with his left. He pulls the brownies out as I open the cabinet next to the microwave and pull out a toothpick to stick into them. I push the toothpick in and pull it out and inspect it for any batter.

"Perfect," I say.

Bryce sets the brownies on the stove top as I turn off the oven.

"Can you grab a knife out of that drawer?" I point to the drawer beside the sink.

"Sure." He opens the drawer and grabs a knife as I slide the oven mitt off of his hand and onto my left hand.

I take the knife from him and hold the glass pan still with my left hand as I cut into the brownies.

The smell of brownies must finally reach Grandma's nose as she comes into the kitchen and goes right to the pan.

"Need a taste tester?" she asks.

"Sure." I use the knife to lift the first brownie from the pan and I set it on a napkin for her.

She picks the brownie up and brings it to her mouth. After a few seconds of chewing she finally

smiles. "These are great! Could you make some for me to bring to poker next week?"

"I thought you played bingo." Bryce chimes in.

"Only when Tara makes me." She rolls her eyes. "Now that I'm not allowed to play darts anymore."

"You used to play darts?"

I take one look at Bryce's face and can't help but laugh.

"You didn't mention that your grandma used to play darts?" he asks me.

"I didn't think you'd believe me."

"Well, if you told me, probably not. But hearing it from her?"

"Why are you surprised that I used to play darts?"

"My grandma sits at home baking cookies all day, not playing darts or poker."

"Or pool." I add.

"You play pool too?"

"We've got a pool table downstairs, wanna watch me kick your next girlfriend's ass?"

"Grandma!"

"Oh, I'm sorry, sweetie. Did you not want me to tell him you stink at pool?"

"Yeah, that's the part of that sentence I'm correcting you on." I roll my eyes.

"We all know you're gonna date him after you finally dump Johnny."

"And what makes you think Bryce even has feelings for me?"

"Why don't you ask me yourself?" Bryce laughs.

"No. We are not having this conversation with my grandmother."

"Alex, you're a damn moron." Grandma shakes her head.

"Thank you," I say.

"You are dating a piece of crap boy, putting up with way less than what you deserve, when you could be dating Bryce."

"You're getting in my business again."

"Somebody has to, you can't figure it out for yourself."

"Thank you, Grandma. Here's another brownie, go enjoy it in the living room." I hand her the napkin with another brownie on it.

"You can give me all the brownies you want, I'm still right." She exits the kitchen.

I wordlessly set brownies for me and Bryce on napkins and hand him his. We eat them in silence and I consider asking him to go home.

"Do you want to go back to your room?" he asks.

"Sure." I throw away our napkins and press the lid onto the brownie pan.

Bryce grabs my hand and leads me down the hall. I follow him into my room and he stops in the middle of my floor.

"What?" I ask.

He places a hand on each of my cheeks and leans in and kisses me. I kiss him back for a few seconds before I pull away.

"Bryce."

"You okay?"

"I just..." I let out a sigh.

"What is it?"

"I didn't want to catch feelings for you yet."

"Yet?"

"Well, I knew I was going to. I just figured it could wait until I was single."

"Alex, I'm not Johnny. I get he's gone crazy when you've dumped him in the past, but at some point you have to realize that what he does isn't your problem."

"Even though I'd rather be with you, I still care about him. I don't want him to hurt himself, especially over me."

"He doesn't hurt himself, he pretends."

"And what if that changes over me?"

"Alex, it wouldn't be over you. He has issues he needs to work out and it's not your job to make him see that. You say you know you deserve better and you can have it."

"I can't leave him until I know he's gonna be okay."

"The only way he'd be okay would be if he left you."

I look down because I know he's right. "Can you and me just focus on you and me?"

"Sure." He nods. "Let's finish our movie."

I take his hand and lead him back into my bed. Once we're settled I hit the play button on the remote and lay my head back on his chest. He runs his fingers through my hair and I want to stay here forever.

Being in Bryce's arms feels so safe. I don't have to worry about a random fight starting, or about him being rude to my family.

"Bryce?"

"Yeah?"

"I want to be with you."

"I know."

My phone buzzes on my nightstand and Bryce grabs it for me. "It's Johnny."

I force a small smile and answer the call. "Hey."

"Guess what I just did," he says and slurs his words.

"Johnny, have you been drinking?" I ask.

"Just a tiny bit."

"You're drunk."

"No, you are!"

"Okay, I'm gonna go."

"No, you didn't guess yet."

"Guess what?" I ask.

"You need to guess what I just did."

"Jesus, Johnny, I don't know."

"I just had the best sex of my life with Jessica Myers."

My stomach turns and my heart drops.

"Did you hear me? Best sex ever!" he yells.

"I heard," I whisper as a tear falls down my cheek. "Please don't ever call me again. We're done."

I hang up my phone and toss it onto the floor.

"What happened?" Bryce asks. "You okay?"

"He was drunk."

"I got that much, but what's wrong?" Bryce gets up and picks my phone up, setting it on my nightstand.

"He cheated on me. Again. Worse this time."

"He what? Alex, are you okay? I never liked him. I know you've heard it from me enough, but I never liked him."

"I know," I whisper.

"What did he do? Did he get caught on a date or kissing someone?"

"He fucked a girl. Jessica Myers, remember her?"

"Shit. Alex, I'm sorry."

"She's got a real talent for getting with the guys in my life. She'd probably ride my dad if he weren't locked up."

"I'm sorry."

"I'm so angry."

"He's fucking garbage, Alex. He's worse than garbage."

I grab a tissue and wipe my eyes as Bryce pulls me in for a hug.

"It's okay."

"I can't even be mad at him because I'm doing the same thing but worse. Imagine how he'd feel if he found out. Imagine what he'd do."

"Alex, this is just more of a reason to leave. He doesn't have to know about us, he doesn't have to even be told you lost feelings. You can just blame it all on him cheating and then he'll only be mad at himself."

"I can't blame him, he'll hurt himself."

"Alex, you can't stay with him after this."

"I need to know that he'll be okay after a breakup. I'm just gonna take a few days to not talk to him and then I'll reach out and if he's fine, I'll leave."

"Alex."

"Please drop it."

"Do you at least know you deserve better?"

I nod.

"Okay." He kisses the top of my head. "It'll be okay."

My attempts at watching the movie are futile and the way Bryce keeps rubbing my back tells me he can sense that.

"You can go home, if you're bored," I say.

"I'm not bored."

"Are you sure? Because if you trace the alphabet on my back one more time we might both go crazy."

"I'm just worried about you. I figured distracting you from the movie you aren't watching would be a good thing." My phone goes off again and Bryce grabs it. "Johnny."

"I don't want to talk to him right now."

"Okay." He sends it to voicemail so it stops ringing.

At some point during the movie that I'm barely acknowledging as background noise, my eyes close and I fall asleep.

"Alex," Bryce says and gently shakes my shoulder to wake me. "Your mom is calling you."

I yawn and hold my hand out for him and he places my phone in it for me. I answer the call and put it on speaker. "What?"

"Hello, to you too." She laughs.

"What do you want, Mom?"

"What's wrong?"

"Johnny. Why'd you call?"

"Your grandmother told me Bryce is over, I'm ordering a pizza for dinner if you want to ask him to stay."

"Wanna stay?" I ask Bryce.

"Sure."

"He'll stay."

"Okay. Now what happened with Johnny?"

As if on cue, he starts beeping in. I send him to voicemail before filling my mother in.

"Oh my gosh. Are you okay?" she asks.

I let out a sigh.

"I know. At least it's over now and you can move on."

I don't say anything.

"Oh, Alex, you have to leave him. You're both clearly inter-ested in other people. You can both go and be happy now."

"I don't want to talk about this." I hang up and reach over Bryce to put my phone on my nightstand.

"Come here," he says and pulls me down onto his chest.

"Bryce?"

"Yeah?"

"I want to be with you."

"You can have me whenever you want."

"Now?"

"Do you want me now?"

"I always wanted you. But Johnny messed up and that's on him. So he can't be mad that he lost me."

"So you really want to do this?"

I take a deep breath and nod.

"Okay. Then it's official."

"It's not official until you ask me to be your girlfriend."

"I don't know, you sound a bit high maintenance. I might want to rethink this."

"Shut up!" I laugh.

"Well, I can't ask you to be my girlfriend if I have to shut up."

"Okay, I take it back. Don't shut up."

He leans in and kisses me. "You wanna be my girlfriend?"

"That'd be nice." I smile.

He kisses me again and I pull away and yawn.

"Still tired?" he asks.

I nod.

"You can go back to sleep and if you're not awake by the time we have pizza I can wake you."

"Are you sure?"

"Yeah. Aren't girls usually more tired when they have their period anyway?"

"How do you know that?"

"I did some research during your first nap."

Johnny would never.

"What else did you find out?"

"That you're superhuman."

I laugh and kiss his cheek. "Remember that."

"Of course, babe."

I lay my head on his shoulder and kiss his neck.

"I can't believe this is finally happening."

"What? A relationship?" I ask.

"A relationship with you."

I smile and close my eyes.

"Alex," Bryce says and wakes me. "Your mom is home with pizza."

"How long did I sleep?"

"Couple hours."

"Sorry."

"Don't be."

My phone starts vibrating on my nightstand again and Bryce grabs it for me.

"Who's Carla?" he asks.

"Johnny's mom." I roll my eyes and take my phone from Bryce's hand. "Hi, Carla."

She's in tears and I can barely understand a word she's saying.

"Carla, slow down. Take a deep breath, I can't understand you."

"It's Johnny. He's in the hospital."

My heart pounds in my chest and I forget to breathe for a moment.

"He tried to kill himself."

Again. Except he didn't.

"What hospital is he at?"

"Saint Mary's."

"I'll be there in twenty."

Chapter 11

The double doors slide on their track and I take a deep breath. My right foot shakes along with the rest of my body as I take my first step onto the white ceramic tile of the hospital lobby. I walk to the desk where a brown haired woman sits in a black chair and peeks out from behind a computer screen.

"Hello, can I help you find something?" she asks.

"My boy-" I stop myself. "My friend. Just a friend."

"Name?"

"Johnny Tate. Johnathan Tate."

She types for a second before making a few clicks. "I'm sorry, he's currently being moved out of the emergency room and into a private room. You're gonna have to wait a few minutes."

"Do you know what room?"

"Not yet." She shakes her head and tucks her hair behind her ear. "If you want to take a seat I can keep his page up and let you know when it's updated."

"Thank you." I turn around and look at the empty chairs and couches in the lobby. My feet take me to a wooden chair with a bright green cushion and I sit down.

My phone is going off with texts from Cassie.

Girl, are the rumors true? Did Johnny hook up with that skank again?

Why aren't you answering???

Alex

Talk to me

Bro wtf

Are you okay? I'm getting worried

Alex

I text a quick reply. It's true. Can't talk

My phone buzzes with her reply and I don't turn my phone over to look at it.

I take a deep breath.

I should turn my phone off, shouldn't I?

It would look awful if Bryce called or texted me while I'm with Johnny.

I flip my phone over just in time to see Bryce calling.

Definitely turn the phone off. Right after this.

I tap the green button to answer his call. "Hi."

"Hi."

"Hi."

"How's it going?"

"I'm still in the lobby. They're moving him from the ER to a room."

"Is that a good sign?"

"I guess."

"What are you gonna do when you get in there?"

I let out a sigh. "I don't know."

"You should work on getting him into therapy."

"He doesn't have a choice now. Therapy is mandated after, you know."

"I know. It's gonna be okay."

"What if he actually did something this time?"

The lady at the desk waves me over before he can answer.

"I gotta go, babe."

"Wait, we're still a couple?"

"Yeah," I whisper. "I gotta go." I hang up my phone and rise from my seat.

"He's got a room now," the receptionist says. "He's in 403. Take the elevator up and when you get out make a right. When you reach the end of that hall take another right and his room will be about three quarters of the way down on the left."

"Thanks."

She smiles and I turn toward the elevator.

I walk slowly over to it and my right hand shakes as I hit the button with the arrow pointing upwards.

The elevator arrives and the doors open to let me in. I step in and there's a man inside already.

"What floor?" he asks.

"Four, please."

He presses the button for me and I thank him.

I take a look at his brown tweed jacket and gray slacks.

Someone's in the wrong century.

"I'm visiting my mom. She's finishing chemo today. We're very excited."

"Good for her."

"Who are you visiting?"

"A friend." I roll my eyes.

"Celebrating? Do they get to leave soon too?"

"I'm not sure."

"What are they here for?"

The elevator dings and the doors open at the fourth floor.

"Suicide attempt." I smile at the man's nerdy black glasses with white tape in the middle and step off the elevator.

I follow the directions from the woman in the lobby and find Johnny's room. I take a deep breath and peek into the room but I can't see much. I knock on the open door. "It's Alex."

"Oh, come in," Clara says.

I slowly walk in and see Clara pushing the tan curtain aside to reveal the bed.

"He's asleep."

I look at Johnny laying there with his eyes closed.

So far it's the same old routine. The second Clara steps out, his eyes will open and he'll miraculously stop wanting to die.

"What did he do?" I ask.

"Pills. Same as last time."

And the three before that.

"How has he been?"

"Quiet. He had done some drinking today so they need to watch for interactions. I think he feels a little scared."

I nod.

"I'll give you a minute with him." She tucks her red hair behind her ear and gets up from her chair. "I think I'm gonna grab a drink from the cafeteria, do you want anything? Soda, water?"

"No, thanks." I force a small smile.

She does the same before leaving the room.

Poor girl doesn't even know all these stunts are just for my attention and that her son is fine.

I take the seat Clara just left and scoot it back a bit before I sit.

I look at Johnny and roll my eyes.

"She's gone."

Johnny stirs and slowly opens his eyes. "Alex? Is that you."

"Yup."

"What's going on?"

"You know what's going on."

"What's wrong, baby?"

"Don't call me that. I'm here for your mom, not for you."

"Not here for your boyfriend after his failed suicide attempt? That's not right."

"Pretending you're depressed for attention and so I won't leave you isn't right."

"You're disgusting," he says.

I can't help but laugh. "You did all this because you cheated on me and don't want to get dumped. You can call me disgusting but, buddy, you're pathetic."

"That's not a nice thing to say to someone who just attempted suicide."

"You didn't, you faked it. For the umpteenth time."

"What's your problem?"

"You wanna know what my problem is? You're my prob-lem. Every single time something comes up and I want to break up, you do this. Then I forgive you and then you cheat on me and I tell you to leave me alone, so you do this. You don't get to put the people around you through hell just because you don't want to get dumped. Come on, Johnny. Real people really attempt suicide and a lot of them succeed. You're faking something that takes real lives. You don't see how fucked up that is? And now you're in a hospital room, you're taking up a room and the staff's time and even resources from real people who need them. I can't do this anymore, Johnny. I want out."

"Alex."

"No."

"I'll go to therapy."

"You think you have a choice after this?" I raise my eye-brows. "You attempted suicide, remember?"

"Alex, I can't lose you."

"You don't get to cheat on me and not lose me."

"Baby."

"Don't. I don't know if you realize this, but I don't care about losing our relationship, Johnny. And by the way, you're not the only one who can cheat." I get up from the chair and start heading for the door.

"What about being here for my mom?" he asks.

"Oh, now you care about the people around you? That's re-ally interesting considering you do this shit as if our feelings don't matter."

"Alex."

"Goodbye." I exit his room and go back the way I came to reach the lobby.

"How's your friend doing?" the receptionist asks.

"He's fine," I say and force a smile as I pass her desk.

I call Bryce as I walk toward the parking garage.

"Hey," he says. "How's it going?"

"I'm single. Well, not single. I have one less boyfriend. I'm not dating Johnny anymore."

He laughs. "Way to scare me."

"Sorry."

"What happened?"

"I told him I'm tired of his shit and he can't expect me to deal with the constant drama. And I may have told him I cheated too."

"Oh, wow."

"I didn't mention you."

"I wouldn't mind if you had, I just didn't think you'd bring that up."

"I was so angry, Bryce." I reach my car and press the button on the door handle to unlock it before climbing in. "I can't believe I dealt with his crap for so long."

"I can't believe you dumped him while he's in the hospital." He laughs.

"Okay, I'll admit I could've picked a better time. But on the other hand, did he deserve a better time? He intentionally put himself in the hospital without a reason again just to try to keep me from dumping him and to avoid taking responsibility for cheating. Again."

"I just didn't think you had it in you. Was that just your period making you mean?"

"Wow, thanks."

"I'm joking. When will you be back? Your mom wants to call in the pizza."

"You're still at my house?"

"Your grandma wouldn't exactly let me leave."

"Oh, why am I not surprised? I'm sorry. I'll be there in fifteen."

"Alex, it's okay. Be careful driving."

"I will." I hang up and pull out of my parking space.

I drive the countless circles to exit the parking garage and I take my two left turns to merge onto the highway and head home.

The radio stops blasting the latest pop hits and the words "Incoming Call" flash on the screen before a name pops up: Cassie.

I press the button on the steering wheel and answer.

"What the fuck is going on?" she asks before I can get a word in.

"Hello to you too." I laugh.

"Alex. Spill."

"How was your vacation?"

"No. We're not doing that. Talk."

"Johnny was being Johnny again. It was another fake attempt that he knew would get people emotional just to avoid taking responsibility for his shit."

"Okay, but responsibility for what?"

"He cheated on me. Called me up drunk a couple hours ago admitting to it."

"What the fuck is his problem?"

"Your guess is as good as mine."

"What are you gonna do?"

"I already did it. I dumped him."

"You what? Alex!"

I decide against telling her about Bryce. "It was time. Johnny was a douche."

"He was, but you dealt with him for how long?"

"Too long."

"So you're really done with him?"

"I am."

"Wow."

"Yeah."

"Wanna go to a party?"

"Time of the month, remember?" I remind her our cycles are synced up thanks to our birth control pill packs starting on the same day.

"The party's not tonight, Friday. They'll end by then."

I think for a second and agree with her judgment. "Fine. Where?"

"Some football player is throwing it. I'll pick you up so you can get hammered."

"Perfect." I laugh.

"So you're in?"

"I'm in. Listen, I just got home so I'll text you later."

"You're not at the hospital with... never mind. You dumped him, you're obviously not with him."

"Obviously not."

"Bye, bitch." She hangs up before I can say anything else so I just laugh as I turn my car off.

Typical Cassie.

I walk up the sidewalk and open the front door, already hearing Grandma's laugh.

"That's never good," I whisper to myself as I take off my shoes and head up the stairs.

"Alex, is that you?" Mom asks and I think she's in the dining room.

"Yeah." I peek around the corner cabinets in the kitchen and see Mom, Grandma, and Bryce sitting at the table with some photo albums.

"Pizza will be here soon." She smiles.

"What's everyone looking at?" I ask.

"Your baby pictures." Bryce informs me with a smile.

"Wipe that shit eating grin off your face," I say. "I can very easily get your baby pictures."

"Not so easy, there are none."

"What do you mean?"

"We don't have any. Mom didn't want any extra stuff to lug from one apartment to the next so she tossed them."

"You're kidding," Mom says.

"Nope." Bryce shakes his head.

"That's so sad." Grandma chimes in. "Lucky for you, we've got plenty of Alex embarrassing herself."

"Okay, put them away." I demand.

"Fine." Mom rolls her eyes and shuts the photo albums.

"Thank you."

"What happened at the hospital?" Mom asks.

"You told them?" I look at Bryce.

"I wasn't gonna lie to your mom."

"And it's not the first time Johnny needed you to visit him. So, what happened?"

"It was another manipulative stunt. So I dumped him."

"You what?" Grandma's jaw practically hits the floor.

"I dumped him." I walk around the table and take the seat next to Bryce.

"So now you two are dating?"

I don't say anything.

"Don't let Johnny find out. He'll throw another fit and pull another stunt." Mom warns.

"Well aware."

"How long until I can take your daughter on a real date?" Bryce asks.

"Give it a couple months."

The doorbell rings and Mom goes to see who it is.

"I told you two this would happen." Grandma smirks.

"Congratulations."

"Attitude." Bryce laughs.

"Pizza's here," Mom says as she walks up the stairs with the box of pizza and tin of garlic knots.

The smell hits my nose before she even opens the box.

"You good?" Bryce asks.

"The pizza smell fulfilled a craving."

"You didn't even eat it yet."

"But knowing that I will makes me happy."

He laughs and shakes his head.

"Bryce, how many pieces?" Mom asks.

"Two, please."

"Alex?"

"Just one."

"Mom, one?" she asks Grandma.

"You got it."

Mom walks to the table and puts a plate with one slice on it down in front of me and a plate with two slices down in front of Bryce.

I take a bite immediately and don't care that it's burning the roof of my mouth.

"What do you guys want to drink?" Mom asks as she puts plates down for her and Grandma. "We have root beer, orange soda, or water."

"Orange soda," I say.

"I'll have root beer, please." Bryce smiles.

"So polite." Mom gushes. "Can you teach Alex how to do that?"

"Very funny." I roll my eyes.

"You know, Alex, Bryce knows how to wait for everyone to sit before starting to eat."

"And he can enjoy his pizza cold while I enjoy mine hot."

Bryce wraps his arm around my waist and kisses the top of my head. "You're excused," he whispers in my ear. "It's your uterus's fault anyway."

I smile at him and take my next bite as I realize his effect on me. All it takes is him whispering in my ear for my mind to wander to a dangerous place.

His fingers gently lift the fabric of my shirt a bit and he rubs his thumb over my bare skin.

I take another bite of my pizza as Mom sets two cups of soda down for Bryce and me and sets the tin of garlic knots on the table.

"Thank you," Bryce says.

"Of course."

"So Bryce." Grandma starts. "What are your intentions with my granddaughter?"

"No. We're not having this conversation." I shake my head.

"It's an important conversation," she says.

"Nope. Not having it."

"I'm with Alex," Mom says. "They're seventeen. His intentions are in his pants."

Bryce chokes on his root beer and starts shaking his head. "That's not true. I think very highly of Alex. Do I find her attractive? Of course. I'd have to be blind not to. But I'm not in this for the physical part of a relationship."

Johnny was never this good with this conversation.

"I like Alex for her heart and her mind. Anything physical will come when it's the right time."

"Are you satisfied?" I ask Grandma.

"For now."

We finish our dinner to the lovely sound of Mom telling Grandma her mouth needs a filter.

"You guys hanging out here?" Mom asks.

"Yeah." I answer. "I need to shower though. Do you mind waiting in my room while I do that?"

"Not at all." Bryce smiles.

"We'll see you guys later," I say and lead Bryce down the hall.

We enter my room and I grab a pair of black pajama shorts.

"Can you grab me one of the tampons in the blue wrapper from that drawer?" I point to my nightstand.

"Sure." Bryce opens it and tosses me the tampon.

Johnny would've run for the hills before touching one of those.

"Thanks. I'll be back in ten."

I grab a towel from the hall closet on my way to the bathroom. I close and lock the bathroom door before grabbing the knob in the shower and starting the water. I pull the handle all the way into the red side today.

A hot shower is much needed after the day I've had.

Chapter 12

I run my hot pink straightener through my hair one last time before turning it off and setting it down on my dresser. I look in the mirror and take in my appearance. My blonde hair touches the tops of the pockets of my dark blue jeans and for the first time, I consider cutting it. My makeup is a bit heavy for my liking but goes perfectly with my black lace bodysuit that looks more like lingerie. I step into a pair of black wedges and yank the strap over my heel.

"Perfect," I whisper to myself.

I pull my phone out of my pocket and let out a sigh. Bryce is home tonight, taking care of Layla. I said I was helping my Grandma clean out her storage bins in the downstairs closet.

I should've told Bryce about this party. I text him to check in real quick.

Hey

Hey

How's it going with Layla?

What?

Oh right. She's fine.

That was weird.

Good I'm glad. I'll talk to you tomorrow?

Yeah

"You ready?" Cassie invites herself into my room.

"How did you get in my house?"

"I opened the front door and walked in."

"Why am I not surprised? Yes, I'm ready."

"No, you're not. You need jewelry."

"I don't like jewelry." I roll my eyes.

"Well, you need it. You're newly single and I'm gonna get you laid tonight."

This wouldn't be an issue if you'd tell her about Bryce.

"Put this on." She hands me a silver necklace with a simple heart charm before handing me a silver ring with my birth-stone, emerald, inside a heart. "And this."

"Am I ready now?"

"You need earrings."

"Pass."

"Nope. Put these on."

I take the simple diamond studs from her and push them through my earlobes.

"Perfect. Let's go."

I follow her out of my room and down the hallway. Her bodysuit is identical to mine, sparing the colors. We bought them together the weekend after junior prom, black for me and red for her. Her black jeans and heels go perfectly with it.

We hop in her gray sedan and she's definitely speeding.

"What's the rush?" I laugh.

"We have to make a pit stop before the party."

"To where?"

"Photoshoot for social media."

Of course.

"Where are we taking pictures?" I ask.

"You'll see."

I scroll through social media and see several other girls had the same idea. There's no shortage of skanks on the internet.

"Are we going to the waterfront?" I ask.

"Like the rest of the basic bitches? I don't think so. Just be patient."

I let out a sigh and scroll through the rest of the photos. Every girl really does use the waterfront for their pictures. One photo in particular catches my eye, a post made by Sadie Adams.

"What's up?" Cassie asks.

"Sadie posted something."

"And?"

"Nothing." I shake my head.

Johnny and I broke up, I shouldn't care who he takes pictures with let alone who he kisses at the waterfront.

"And we're here." Cassie throws the car in park and I take a look around.

"We're gonna take pictures here? There's nothing but a brick wall and some dead grass."

"Well obviously we're not using the grass. Go stand by the wall and look sexy."

"Cassie."

"Alex, just trust me. Give me your phone."

I do as she says and walk toward the red brick wall. I do a couple different poses with various facial expressions. She walks up to me and hands me my phone back. I scroll through the photos and am amazed by what she can do with a brick wall.

"I stand corrected," I say. "Your turn."

She hands me her phone and I snap some pictures for her.

"You're an angel. Ready to get shitfaced?"

"Always." I laugh.

We get back in her car and she enters and address into a maps app on her phone.

"So which football player is throwing this?" I ask as she starts driving.

"Thomas Jenkins."

"Ew."

"Ew? Every incoming freshman has a crush on him."

"Notice how you didn't say seniors?"

"Okay, so he's not the most attractive. But he's very nice. I heard he has a crush on you."

"I heard he's gonna be disappointed."

"Are you ever gonna give a new guy a chance to sweep you off your feet?"

I gave Bryce a chance.

"Not at this party."

"Alex."

"I broke up with Johnny like a minute ago."

"So? Get back out there."

I let out a sigh. "You can't tell anyone what I'm about to tell you."

"Spill."

"Promise you won't tell?"

"Promise, now give me the tea."

"You know how the house next door was up for sale for a while?"

"And it sold."

"Right. To a woman with two kids."

"Okay."

"She has a little girl, Layla, who I babysit."

"I don't see where this is going."

"She also has a son. He's our age."

"And you guys fucked."

"We did. And I'm interested in him."

"Is he interested in you?"

"Yeah."

"So go for it."

"Well, I can't advertise that I'm going for it. Johnny isn't stable enough to see me with someone new."

"Fuck him. He's fucked up too many times to earn one of your fucks to give. Is this new boy gonna be at the party?"

"No, he's watching Layla tonight."

"Bummer."

"Or it's a good thing that nobody will see us together and tell Johnny."

"I guess. You're still getting shitfaced tonight."

"Oh, for sure."

She pulls onto a road with dozens of cars parked on it and we must be at our destination.

"Jesus." She glances at all the cars and finally finds a spot to park. We climb out and walk towards the house, the music audible from all the way up the street.

"His neighbors must be thrilled." I laugh.

"Not our problem."

We walk up the walkway and through the open front door of the yellow split level house. There's a dining room to my left and a kitchen to my right and two sets of stairs ahead of me, the one on the right going up and the left going down. The left leads to a living room whose furniture has been relocated for the night so people can use it as a dancefloor.

"Hello, ladies," Thomas says. "Alcohol is in the kitchen, dancing is down the stairs, food is in the dining room. If you're gonna hook up with someone please keep it out of the bedrooms."

"You got it." I laugh. "Let's grab a drink."

Cassie and I head into the kitchen and I grab us each a beer.

"Well if it isn't Cassidy Jansen." Jessica Myers fakes a smile.

"My friends call me Cassie."

"Okay, Cassie."

"I said my friends."

I try to hold back a laugh as I pop the top off my bottle.

"Oh, hey, Alex."

"Don't talk to me." I shake my head. "I don't need your trashiness to rub off."

"Someone's still mad about their boyfriend's infidelity."

"He's not my boyfriend." I laugh. "You're gonna have to fight Sadie Adams for him, not me." I take a sip of my beer and grab Cassie's wrist, pulling her out of the kitchen with me.

"What is her problem?" Cassie asks.

"Don't know, don't care."

"Let's grab some food."

I follow Cassie to the snacks and she grabs a tiny red paper plate, tossing some chips and pigs in a blanket on it.

I steal one of the little hot dogs from her plate and pop it into my mouth.

"You took my pig." She laughs.

"Sorry, his blanket looked good."

"Idiot."

I take another sip of my beer and steal one of her chips.

"Would you like me to make you a plate?"

"No, it's more fun to steal food off of yours."

"I hope this new boy knows to have extra food available at all times."

I laugh and take a few more sips while she finishes her snack.

"We need another person for beer pong, you interested?" Thomas asks me.

"I'm good." I shake my head.

"What? You're going." Cassie demands. "She'll be right there."

"No, I won't. Find someone else."

Thomas turns and walks away, thankfully taking my side.

"You love beer pong, what gives?"

"Johnny and I had our first kiss during a game of beer pong."

"Fuck beer pong."

"Agreed." I down the rest of my beer.

"I'll go find you another drink. Go dance while you wait." Cassie disappears into the kitchen and I don't leave my spot.

I look down into the living room and see a bunch of girls wearing bralettes for shirts grinding on guys.

Definitely not gonna go join in on that.

I wish I were in more of a party mood but I feel so guilty for not telling Bryce about tonight. Even though he wouldn't have been able to come with me, this feels like I'm hiding it.

"Here you go." Cassie hands me a red plastic cup.

"What is this?" I ask.

"Fruit punch."

"With what?"

"Alcohol."

"Cassie."

"Vodka. Just drink it."

I take a sip and am caught off guard by how strong it is. "What, did you dump half the bottle in here?"

"Not me, specifically."

I shake my head with a laugh and take another sip. This one goes down a lot smoother than the first.

"Hey," a boy I don't recognize says from behind me.

I take in his football player build and have to tilt my head up to see his face. "Hi."

"You here alone?"

I hesitate for a second. "No."

"I don't see a boyfriend."

"I didn't say I was here with a boyfriend."

"So you're available."

"Nope."

"But you're not here with a guy."

"But I still have a boyfriend."

"Look, there's no need to lie. I'm not trying to date you, I'm just trying to get you upstairs."

I toss my drink in his face and take a look down at my empty cup. "And I'm just trying to get a refill."

"Next time, try being less of a dick." Cassie smiles at the now dripping boy.

We walk to the kitchen and she grabs me another fruit punch.

"Are you gonna have one too?" I ask.

She shakes her head. "I drove. I'm good with stopping after the one beer."

I take a sip of my freshly poured drink and my taste buds tell me that someone definitely poured more vodka in here.

"Wanna hang out outside? I heard a bunch of people are out there swimming."

"Sure." I shrug. "How many drunk idiots do you think will fall in?"

"At least four." She laughs.

We head downstairs and wiggle our way through the crowd of people dancing and go out the back door of the house. A couple girls seem to have lost their clothes in the yard.

"Classy." I roll my eyes and take another sip.

"Why not go in in your bra and underwear? These girls really want everyone seeing them completely naked?"

"Half the guys here already have."

Cassie laughs as Bethany Stanley catches the corner of my eye. I turn my head and see her dragging some poor guy by the wrist, clearly against his will. My eyes wander up his arm to his face.

"Bryce?" I ask.

"Alex," he says. "Hey."

"He'll have to catch up with you later." Bethany gives a tight-lipped smile and continues to yank him towards the door.

"Actually he'll have to catch up with you later." I correct her. "I'm sure you can find someone else to entertain you for the night."

"Bitch," she mutters and walks away.

"Thanks." Bryce lets out a sigh.

"How's babysitting Layla going?" I raise my eyebrows.

"How's your grandma's storage cleanout going?"

"Fair enough." I shake my head.

"And just for the record I wasn't gonna hook up with her. I don't even know her name."

"Bethany Stanley. You might want to block her on social media if you don't want her boobs sent to you every night."

"Got it."

"I'm sorry, who are you?" Cassie asks.

"This is Bryce," I say. "He's the guy I was telling you about."

"I thought we had to keep our relationship quiet," Bryce says.

"Relationship?" Cassie questions. "You said you were just interested in him."

"Shit," Bryce says. "My bad."

"Way to snitch on us." I roll my eyes.

"Fill me in," Cassie says. "You said you were interested in him."

"Well, he's also interested in me."

"Would've been nice if you had mentioned you were already a thing."

"I'm mentioning it now." I laugh.

"Well I'm gonna leave you two lovebirds alone. I don't need to see anybody making out." Cassie heads back inside.

"So how did you and Bethany meet?" I ask.

"Alex, it's not like that. I was talking to some guys and she walked up and joined the conversation."

"Great. Now get to the part where she got the idea that you're available."

"She asked if any of the guys were interested in going upstairs with her and they volunteered me. We're supposed to be keeping this quiet so instead of saying I had a girlfriend I just said I wasn't interested. She didn't like that answer."

"Yeah, because for Bethany anything other than being in a relationship is an invitation to try to get a guy to change his mind."

"I can see that."

"So you're here because?" I raise my eyebrows.

"My mom's been wanting me to meet people and somehow she heard about this party so she made me come."

"And you didn't tell me because?"

"Parties didn't seem like your thing."

"They're really not. Cassie dragged me here."

"That explains it."

I take the last sip of my drink and toss the cup into a nearby garbage pail.

Bryce pulls me into him and wraps his arms around me. "I'm sorry."

"Good."

"Let me make it up to you."

"By doing what?"

"Taking you upstairs," he whispers in my ear. "As good as that outfit looks on you, I'm sure it'll look just a bit better on the floor."

"It might. I'm not sure I want to go upstairs with you, though."

"I think you do."

"You're confident."

"I am."

"Care to explain why?"

"Because I know you're the jealous type and you need to mark your territory so the other girls here know I'm yours."

I can feel my cheeks heat up and I'm not sure if I'm blushing from the alcohol or from Bryce but right now, I don't care to figure it out.

"Babe?" I ask.

"Yes, baby?"

"Upstairs."

"Come on." He smiles and grabs my hand.

I follow his lead and we go back inside, pushing through the crowd and up the first set of stairs. I pause to take a look around to make sure nobody is watching and I see Johnny on the dancefloor, Sadie Adams grinding on him. He and I make eye contact and he freezes when he sees me, glancing at Bryce for a quick moment.

"You okay?" Bryce asks.

I tilt my head up and kiss him before pulling him up the last set of stairs with me. We turn a few doorknobs, trying to find one that's unlocked that will take us to an empty room. It takes a few tries but we finally find one. We slip in and I lock the door behind us.

Chapter 13

"I'm heading next door to babysit," I say as I peek into the living room before heading down the stairs.

"Wait a minute, my gosh." Mom shakes her head as she mutes the television.

"What?" I ask.

"What time are you babysitting until?"

"No clue." I catch my grandma using the kitchen scissors to cut something out of a flyer on the coffee table. "What are you doing?"

"Couponing." She doesn't look up from her work.

"Again?"

"Yes, Alex, again."

"You would sell your soul to save a dollar." Mom rolls her eyes.

"No, I wouldn't, I'd sell you." Grandma fires back.

I can't help but smirk at my mom. "Can I leave now?"

"Please. I don't need any witnesses to what I'm about to do."

"Oh, please." Grandma rolls her eyes. "Scissors or not, I can take you."

"Good luck." I walk down the stairs and out the front door. I walk along the edge of the cul-de-sac to Bryce's driveway. I take a deep breath as I start the walk up the driveway and the sidewalk until I reach the house. My knuckles tap on the front door a few times and Maggie lets me in almost immediately.

"Hey, Alex." She smiles.

"Hi." I walk up the stairs and stop in the kitchen where Maggie is fidgeting with some cash.

"Layla already had dinner and she's having a yogurt right now so she should be good for the night. She was up early today so she should be ready for bed a little earlier than usual. You can help yourself to anything in the kitchen, just please no alcohol until Layla is asleep. I know you and Bryce are dating so again, no sex until Layla is asleep. There's condoms in the top drawer of the vanity in the bathroom off my bedroom. It's locked but I'm sure Bryce knows where the key is. I should be home around midnight, is that too late?"

There's not a word of what she just said that didn't catch me off guard so the only part I acknowledge is the very end. "Not at all."

"Great. Here's this for tonight." She hands me some rolled up bills. "Thanks again." She grabs her keys and her purse. "Bye, Layla."

"Bye, Mommy." Layla waves from her seat at the dining room table and goes back to eating her yogurt.

Without another word, Maggie leaves the house.

Wow.

I quickly count the money and see that she gave me seventy dollars and I stick it in one of the pockets of my brown leather bag. I set my bag on the couch and join Layla at the table and see that there's an actual dining set now. A dark wooden table with matching chairs goes with the hutch placed against the wall.

"Hi, Alex." She smiles in between bites.

"Hi." I smile back. "How's your yogurt?"

"Yummy."

"What flavor is it?"

"Vanilla," she says through a mouthful of it, yogurt threatening to drip out the corners of her mouth.

"That is yummy." I take a look at her outfit, pink sweatpants with white polka dots and a matching short sleeve shirt, definitely pajamas. "You look like you're ready for bed."

"I am."

"You are?"

The front door opens and I wonder what Maggie forgot.

Probably those condoms from her bathroom.

"Bryce!" Layla runs over to her big brother who's still dirty from work.

"You're home early," I say as Bryce picks up Layla.

"It wasn't busy and since I'm still training on how to use the computers they let me out early." He throws her over his shoulder.

"They have you working on cars and using the computers?"

"They have me doing everything."

"How do you like it so far?" I ask.

"It's okay."

"Do you want to play a game with us?" Layla asks.

"I would love to play a game with two pretty girls. What are we playing?"

"Go Fish!"

"You better be careful, I'm amazing at that game." He smiles and tosses Layla onto the couch.

She gets up and scurries down the hall to her room.

"She has way too much energy for an hour before her bedtime." Bryce shakes his head and takes a seat on the couch.

I laugh and pick up Layla's empty yogurt cup and spoon. I walk into the kitchen and put her spoon in the dishwasher and toss the cup into the garbage. Tiny footsteps bounding down the hallway catch my attention and I exit the kitchen just in time to see Layla jump right into Bryce's lap.

"Oh my gosh," Bryce says with a groan.

"Why don't we sit in a chair at the dining room table and not on Bryce's legs?" I laugh.

Layla wordlessly gets up and brings the card game to the table before taking a seat. I sit across from her and Bryce sits in the chair at the end between us.

"You do it." Layla hands the cards to Bryce.

"Okay." Bryce shuffles the cards a bit and gives us each seven of them. "You go first, Lay."

"Bryce, got any sevens?" she asks.

"Dang it, I do." He hands her two cards and she puts down all four sevens.

"Alex, got any twos?" Bryce asks me.

"Go Fish!" I smile and Layla laughs, indicating that she has some twos.

He takes a card and shakes his head.

"Layla, got any fives?" I ask.

"No fair!" she whines and hands me a five.

I set down my now three fives and leave Bryce the only one without any cards down.

We play a few more rounds and Bryce wasn't lying when he said he was amazing at this game. He made a comeback and beat Layla by just one group.

"I'm impressed," I say.

"You should be." Bryce brags. "I win every time."

"He cheated!" Layla accuses.

"He cheated?" I ask.

"Liar!" Bryce shakes his head.

"No! You always cheat!"

"I'm just good at Go Fish!"

"Well, on that note, I think it's time for you to go to bed, Layla."

She nods and gets up, still pouting about her loss.

"Don't forget to brush your teeth," I say.

"I know."

"How was your day?" Bryce asks.

"Pretty good."

"Good." He leans in and kisses me. "Did you eat dinner yet?"

"Yeah." I nod.

"Good."

"So you like the job?"

"It's a job."

"Felt that."

"The guys seem cool, I'm just hoping I'll never have to deal with your piece of shit ex."

"Johnny never goes in there."

"Good."

I take a look at his red short sleeve shirt with little patches of grease scattered around the front. "You look like you got a little dirty."

"Just a bit."

"I'm gonna go check on Layla."

"I'm gonna go take a shower." He pats my leg and we get up from the table.

Bryce goes downstairs and I go down the hall to the bathroom.

"All done?" I ask as Layla sets down her toothbrush.

"Done." She hops down off her step stool and I put it away for her as she runs down the hall to her room.

I follow her and see her sitting on her bed.

"Blanket on and fan on?" I ask, remembering from last time.

"Yes."

"Okay. Lay down."

She does as I say and I lay the blanket over her.

"And your light stays on?" I double check.

"Yes."

"Okay. Goodnight, Layla."

"Goodnight, Alex."

I turn on her fan before I leave her room and walk down the hallway. Bryce's phone is on the railing buzzing like crazy. He must've left it there when Layla jumped into his arms when he came home. I pick up his phone and walk downstairs where the shower is on but he's still gathering clothes to change into.

"Hey," he says when he sees me.

"Hey. This was going off." I hold his phone out for him.

"That's where that was." He takes it and starts looking through the notifications.

"Anything important?"

"Just more nudes."

I assume he must be joking so I laugh.

"I'm serious."

"What? From who?"

"Jessica Myers and her friends."

"She must've seen us together at the party."

"My blocked list is getting to be almost a mile long."

"Why do they think you'd be okay with getting nudes from them in the first place?" I can't help but get defensive.

"Your guess is as good as mine. But it doesn't matter. I block them the second I get the pictures."

"Can you show me?"

"What? You want to see other girls naked? I don't even want to see that."

"Not the pictures." I roll my eyes. "Show me that they're blocked."

"Alex."

"Show me."

He lets out a sigh and pulls up his blocked lists on his social media accounts. I see Jessica Myers and her closest friends on all of them.

"Happy now?"

"Bryce."

"I'm not Johnny," he says. "You can trust that I'm giving you the truth when I tell you something."

I look down at the floor to avoid making eye contact with him. "I know."

"Clearly you don't or you wouldn't have needed proof."

I don't say anything as I keep staring down at the floor.

He's right. I overstepped by doubting him and demanding proof. If this were reversed, yeah, he'd be mad about it. But he'd trust that they were blocked.

"I need to shower."

"Bryce."

He ignores me and walks into the bathroom, closing the door behind him.

I hope he'll come back out and kiss me but he doesn't. I wait for another minute when I hear the hooks of the shower curtain slide on the metal curtain rod. I go into his room and sit down on his bed. His shower only takes about five minutes and after another three, he's walking into his room.

"What?" He rolls his eyes.

"Can we talk?"

"So you can accuse me of lying again?" he asks as he tosses his dirty clothes and towel into his hamper.

"Bryce."

"Come on, Alex. If you can't trust me, you shouldn't be dating me."

"Can you just try to see this from my side? Multiple girls are sending you naked pictures of themselves after you were at a party and were extremely close to hooking up with someone."

"Against my will."

"If things were switched and guys were sending me pictures, you'd be pissed."

"Yeah, Alex, I would. But I'd be pissed at them, not at you. That's what you're not getting here."

"I'm not getting why they're sending pictures to a guy they've never met just because they're friends with Jessica Myers."

He doesn't say anything.

"Bryce."

He's still silent.

"What are you not telling me?"

"We hung out."

"You hung out with who?"

"Jess and her friends. At the party."

I think I'm gonna be sick.

"It was only for half an hour, if that."

"I'm going back upstairs."

"Alex."

"I want to trust you, Bryce. But shit like this makes it really fucking hard."

"I know."

"Did you hook up with them?"

"No, you saw Bethany try."

"I don't mean at the party."

"No. The closest I came was with Jess, here, when you were babysitting."

"If you call her Jess and not Jessica one more time, I'm gonna vomit."

"It's a name, what's the big deal?"

"Her name is Jessica. Everyone calls her Jessica, her friends call her Jess. Don't call her Jess."

"I didn't think it was an issue."

"Well, it is." I cross my arms over my chest.

"I'm sorry. Can we stop having this argument now?"

I take a deep breath.

"You really want to keep fighting?"

"I don't want to keep fighting." I shake my head. "I just want other girls to stop sending my boyfriend their boobs."

"Hey," he says softly. "I didn't ask for the pictures, you know that, right?" He pulls me in for a hug.

"Yes, I know that." I roll my eyes.

"So you're not mad at me, you're mad at the situation."

I let out a sigh.

He kisses my forehead and hugs me tighter.

"I'm sorry."

"You don't have to apologize. You just got out of a relationship where you couldn't trust the guy you were with. I can be patient until you can trust me."

I smile up at him and kiss him.

Johnny was never this patient with me.

"Want to hang out down here for a bit?" he asks.

"I can't."

"You'll have more fun down here."

"You're not wrong, but I'm here to babysit. I have to get back upstairs."

"Lay is asleep, relax."

"I'll relax when I'm upstairs in case she wakes up."

"Fine." He gives me one last kiss and tucks a loose strand of my hair behind my ear. "I'll be up in a sec and we can watch a movie."

I head back upstairs and go check on Layla. When I see that she's fast asleep, I go into the living room and take a seat on the couch. Within a minute, Bryce is making his way up the stairs.

"Did you finish being a good babysitter?" he asks.

"Yes, I did."

"Good. I'm gonna make some popcorn." He tosses his phone onto the couch cushion next to me.

I hear the microwave door shut as Bryce's phone starts buzzing again.

"Your phone is going off!" I call.

"Can you check to see who it is?"

I turn his phone over and see a text message from a girl named Olivia.

Hey babe

"So who's Olivia and why is she calling you babe?" I ask.

"She's just a friend."

"Does she know that?"

"Yes, Alex, she does."

"Then why is she calling you babe?"

"That's just how our friendship is."

"No friends that I know call each other babe unless they're both girls and probably sorority sisters." I walk into the kitchen.

"Alex, you're making a big deal out of nothing."

"How do you know her?"

"She's from back home."

Hearing him talking about Maryland and another girl as home sends a dagger through my heart.

"That still doesn't explain why she's calling you babe."

"I already told you, that's just how our friendship is."

"That's a bullshit excuse."

"Alex, I'm not Johnny. Give me my phone and I'll tell her it needs to stop."

I hand him his phone and he types something and sets his phone down on the counter.

"Better?" he asks.

I nod.

"Okay."

"Thank you."

"I want you, Alex. Regardless of who else is around."

Chapter 14

My phone buzzes in the pocket of my sweatpants and I pull it out to see a text from Bryce.

You going to that pool party at Grandma Peggy's later?

That's today?

Yes lol how did you forget and I remembered

I have no idea. I'll be there tho

"Mom!" I call from my spot on the couch.

"What?" she yells back from the kitchen.

"Grandma Peggy's pool party is today?"

"Yeah."

"Thanks for the reminder."

"I didn't know you'd need one." She laughs. "Did you have other plans?"

"No, but I could've made some."

"But you didn't."

"But I could've."

"And it wouldn't have mattered. You would've made plans with either Cassie or Bryce and they're both going. You would've had to change the location and that's it."

I roll my eyes. "What time does it start?"

"Two."

"But it's already one!"

"Oh, good, you learned how to tell time."

"Mom!" I roll my eyes.

"How much time do you really need to get ready?"

"A lot, actually. I have to shower and pick out a bathing suit and an outfit and pack a change of clothes."

"But you don't have to do your hair or makeup."

"I need to get moving." I ignore her and get up from the couch.

What do I want to wear?

I walk into my room and open the drawer of my dresser that holds my shorts. Black shorts don't feel like they fit the vibe of one of Grandma Peggy's pool parties so I dig through my blue ones. I pull out a cute pair of dark blue ones that have a line of buttons instead of a zipper and hold them up next to a light blue pair with some rips on them. The light blue ones have a looser fit which is probably the better choice since I'll be wearing them over a bathing suit. I put the dark blue ones away and open my drawer of tank tops. I pull out a yellow tank top with a pretty low cut v-neck and hold it next to the shorts. Perfect. I open the drawer that holds my bathing suits and start digging through my bikinis. There's gonna be kids around so I need something with some decent coverage.

That gets rid of about three-quarters of my options.

I pull out a solid red strapless top with matching red bottoms and a turquoise and black triangle top with solid black bottoms. After spending close to three minutes comparing them and weighing the coverage options, I settle on the turquoise and black one. I gather both pieces of the suit along with my outfit and head into the bathroom so I can shower.

A towel might help.

I grab a light pink towel and start the shower so the water can warm up while I get undressed.

After taking the fastest shower of my life, my legs are shaved and my hair is washed. I quickly dry off and slip on my bikini.

Something about putting on a bathing suit right after a shower instead of underwear will always feel wrong to me.

I pull my shorts over the bottoms and slide my tank top on over my head. Once I've gathered my dirty clothes and used towels, I leave the bathroom and head back to my bedroom. I toss my clothes and towel into my hamper and plug in my blow dryer. Blow drying my hair has never been one of my favorite things so I dry it just enough to toss it up in a messy bun. I grab a pair of black leggings and a loose, white cropped t-shirt and stuff them into the light blue tote bag Mom and I always use for Grandma Peggy's pool parties before adding a bra and underwear to the bag.

"Are you almost ready?" Mom yells.

"I need a towel!"

"I grabbed you one, it's on the railing! Do you have our bag?"

"Yes!"

"Let's go!"

I slip on a pair of black flip flops and throw the straps of the bag onto my shoulder.

"Here's your towel." Mom grabs the green towel off the railing and puts it in the bag. "And some sunscreen."

"That I won't use."

"And your future skin cancer will be on you."

"Okay." I follow her down the stairs with a laugh.

We walk the quarter of a mile to Grandma Peggy's house and go around to the backyard. A couple people are already in the pool and I see Maggie, Bryce, and Layla sitting at the table on the patio with Grandma Peggy.

"You guys came!" Grandma Peggy smiles when she sees me.

"Of course." Mom hugs her.

"You didn't invite Johnny, did you?" she asks me.

"No. He won't be coming to any of these ever again."

"Thank God. Now if we could just get you to leave him."

"I did."

"What?"

"I broke up with him. He cheated on me."

"Oh, I'm so sorry. Was there another staged attempt?"

"Unfortunately."

"How soon after the cheating?"

"Well, he cheated on me while he was drunk, I dumped him immediately, and he still hadn't sobered up by the time he was moved out of the emergency room and into a standard room."

"He works fast." She shakes her head. "I'm glad you made it out."

"So am I," Bryce says as he wraps his arms around me.

"Oh, so you two are together now." Grandma Peggy smiles. "I can get behind this relationship."

"So can I." Mom agrees.

"And me." Maggie chimes in.

"So everyone's happy." Grandma Peggy smiles. "It's a good day. Well, there's volleyball, Kan Jam, badminton, the pool is open and heated, there's snacks, soda, alcohol. As long as your parents approve, there's plenty of alcohol for you guys to have some. I've got more of everything so if something runs out, let me know."

"Thanks." Mom smiles.

We grab seats at the table, Mom goes next to Maggie and I take the one next to Bryce.

"Swim first or eat first?" Mom asks.

"Definitely swim." I pull my tank top off and put it in the bag and do the same with my shorts.

"Sunscreen?" Mom offers.

"We already had this conversation." I laugh. "My future skin cancer is on me."

"As long as you know that."

Bryce and I head over to the inground pool and I see that Grandma Peggy's daughter, Penelope, and two of the kids, Emmy and Brandon, are already swimming.

"Alex!" Emmy yells.

"Hi, sweetie!" I smile. "Mind if we join?"

"Go ahead." Penelope nods. "It's so good to see you."

"It's been a while," I say as I descend the steps into the warm water of the heated pool that could double as a hot tub. "Have you met Bryce yet? His family just moved in a few weeks ago."

"No, I haven't. It's nice to meet you." She smiles.

"You too," Bryce says. "How old are your kids?"

"Emmy is five, Brandon is three, and I've got one napping inside still who's two."

"My little sister is four. She's kinda shy so she might not swim unless my mom does."

"Let's get them in."

"Good luck." Bryce laughs.

"Mom!" I yell.

"Are you drowning already?" she calls.

"You're not funny! Get in the pool and bring Maggie and Layla."

"That won't work." Bryce shakes his head.

"I give it one minute."

"So, Alex, I heard about the incident with Johnny during the get together at your place two weeks ago."

How many people are gonna bring him up today?

"Yeah, that was rough." I nod.

"Is he coming today?"

"No. I actually broke up with him."

"Wow. I didn't think that would happen."

"Well, it did," Bryce says. "She's with me now."

"Really? I'm glad."

"So am I." I smile.

"Hey, Tara." Penelope smiles.

I turn around to see Mom getting in the pool with Maggie and Layla.

"Hi." She smiles back.

"Told you," I say to Bryce.

"Yeah, yeah." He rolls his eyes.

Something lands in the water behind me, just barely missing my back based on the severity of the splash I felt. I turn around and see Cassie walking up the lawn, grinning like an idiot.

"Heads up!" She laughs.

I pick up the wet soccer ball and throw it back at her. "You're a child!"

"Yes, ma'am." She sets her bag down and pulls off her shirt and shorts before joining us in the pool.

"That's Maggie, she's Bryce's mom, and that's his sister Layla," I say. "This is my best friend, Cassie."

"It's nice to meet you," Maggie says.

"You too." Cassie smiles.

"How was your vacation?" Mom asks.

"Oh my gosh, it was amazing." She smiles. "We went to the Friends set, remind me to show you pictures."

"I'm so jealous, that's my favorite show ever."

More families start to arrive and within a half hour, the pool is a bit too crowded for my liking.

"Wanna go play volleyball?" I ask Cassie and Bryce.

"Sure. Me and you against boy toy over here," Cassie says.

"Why am I by myself?" Bryce laughs.

"You're a man. You're stronger so you have an advantage." She shrugs.

"Damn penis privilege." He shakes his head.

"I don't think that's what that means." I laugh.

We climb out of the pool and grab our towels so we can dry off a bit before heading over to the volleyball net. I pick up the ball and head to one side with Cassie while Bryce heads to the other.

"Who said you get to go first?" he asks.

"Me. Go easy on us."

"It's two against one and I have to go easy on you?"

"You want to get laid tonight or not?" Cassie laughs.

"Cassie!"

"She's probably got a point." Bryce laughs.

"I'm ending this conversation." I hit the ball over the net and it practically goes right to Bryce.

He hits it back and Cassie sets it so I run towards her to hit it over the net again. Bryce just misses it, giving us the first point of the game.

"Smart man!" Cassie yells with a laugh.

It takes us nearly forty minutes to finish our game with Cassie and I winning by just one point.

"Food is ready!" Grandma Peggy yells to everyone. "There's burgers, hot dogs, chicken, and wings!"

We head over to the patio and are the first to grab food. I take a hot dog, a few wings, some chips and salsa, and some pasta salad before grabbing a strawberry daiquiri Seagram's from one of the coolers. Once we each have our plates loaded with food, we head to one of the tables to eat. It only takes me a couple minutes to clear my plate and finish my drink.

"I'm going for seconds, anybody want anything?" I offer.

"You eat like a grown ass man." Cassie laughs.

"It's one of her more attractive qualities." Bryce nods.

"Get your own refills now." I roll my eyes.

Bryce joins me at the snack table and wraps his arms around me from behind as I throw some more chips and salsa onto my paper plate.

"Hi." I smile.

"Hello."

"So there's something I've been wanting to talk to you about."

"What's up?" I ask as I grab a can of Sprite from one of the coolers.

"Not around everyone. You done grabbing food?"

"Yeah."

"Come here."

I follow him off the deck and to the far corner of the lawn where the abandoned volleyball net hangs.

"Okay."

"What's going on?" I ask.

"So Johnny showed up at work the other day."

"He what? Why? Was he there to see his dad?"

"No. He wanted to talk to me."

"About what?"

"You."

"Why?" I roll my eyes.

"He said that you were more in love with him than you could ever be with me and he talked about all these plans you guys had made for life after high school."

"We had plans to apply to the same colleges and see if we got into any of the same schools to go together. I wouldn't call those plans, it really wasn't that deep."

"He mentioned those. He also mentioned kids."

"We never talked about having kids."

"He said otherwise. He made it sound like your college plans were loose because you were gonna have a kid by then. He said your mom even mentioned being safe to you guys the last couple times you hung out."

"Well, yeah, but that's because my mom had me when she was a teenager and she knew we were having sex. I promise, there were no plans made there."

"I know this probably isn't my business, but I feel like I need to ask now. When's the last time you guys had sex?"

"The day before you guys moved in."

"Really?"

"Really."

"So you haven't been able to bring yourself to sleep with him since you met me?" He smirks.

"Sure, put it that way." I laugh.

"Okay, just one more thing. He also made it sound like you guys were still in contact."

"We're not."

"He said something about you guys talking through Instagram."

I roll my eyes. "He's talking, I'm blocking. He's made three fake accounts to message me since I broke up with him."

"Jesus."

"You can check if you want. I'll get my phone right now and you can look through everything."

"Alex, I don't need to go through your phone. I trust you, I just wanted to ask."

"I promise you, there's nothing to worry about with him."

"Good."

Chapter 15

"Hey there." Mom smiles as Bryce and I walk into the kitchen.

"Hi," I say.

"You two doing anything tonight for the holiday?"

"Nope. The Fourth of July might as well be the fifth." I laugh.

Bryce and I thought about going to the waterfront to watch the fireworks but ultimately decided against it. The crowds wouldn't be worth it for a shitty view.

"Why don't you guys go out now then?"

"What do you mean?"

"Go do something fun."

"Like what?"

"Go out to breakfast, go walk the waterfront before it gets packed."

"Want to?" I ask Bryce.

"Sure. I actually haven't been to the waterfront yet."

"Really?"

"Really."

"Let's go." I grab my keys and lead him down the stairs. I slip on my black sandals while he puts his white sneakers on.

"Be home at three!" Mom calls.

"Why?"

"Because I said so."

"I've never had my curfew be three in the afternoon."

"Well, it is now."

"Why?"

"Because."

"Uh, okay." I open the front door and let Bryce out first. I follow him and close the door behind us.

We get in my black compact SUV and I'm still amazed Bryce can sit in it without hitting his head on the ceiling.

"What do we want for breakfast?" I ask.

"Pancakes?" he asks.

"Those are always a good idea."

"Where can we get good pancakes around a here? A diner?"

"The diners around here aren't great. There's a little cafe that's really good though."

"Sounds good, babe."

I try to ignore the butterflies in my stomach as I back out of the driveway and start driving up the street.

"Can I ask you something kind of personal?" Bryce asks.

My heart starts to race. "I guess."

"Have you given any more thought to meeting your dad?"

I let out a sigh.

Truthfully, I haven't thought about it. Not a single time. He stabbed my mother and murdered my unborn baby brother.

Why would I want to meet him? Besides, I've gone seventeen years without a father, I don't need one now.

"No."

"I think you should think about it."

"Why?"

"I just think you should see him in person."

"Why do you care so much? You want to see someone's dad? Go visit yours."

"I can't, Alex. That's why I keep bugging you about it. My dad got my mom pregnant and left. No goodbye, no nothing, he just took off. She never heard from him again. I have to wonder every single day. You have the chance to not do that."

"I don't do that."

"But you will. One day, when it's too late, you're gonna wonder. I don't want you to have to live like that."

I let out another sigh.

"Just think about it, okay?"

"Okay." I give in. "Have you ever thought about trying to track down your dad?"

"No."

"Why not?"

"My mom said he disappeared."

"So you track him down."

He's silent.

"What's his name?"

"I'm not sure."

"You don't even know his name?"

"My mom won't tell me."

"That's your dad, Bryce. She has to tell you his name. She doesn't have to introduce the two of you, but you should be able to look for him on your own if you want to."

"I've asked, she won't budge."

"Why?"

"No idea."

"Do you think you know him? Is he one of those uncles who's not really an uncle?"

"Definitely not."

I pull into the parking lot of Sun Cafe and park on the side of the building. "Put this conversation on pause?"

"Agreed."

I turn off my car and we climb out. Bryce grabs my hand and smiles at me.

"What?" I ask.

"Nothing. You just look pretty."

I look down at my black denim shorts and loose-fitted white cropped short sleeve shirt.

He genuinely thinks I'm pretty.

Bryce opens the glass door to the cafe for me and I step into the cool air conditioning.

Summer in New York is no joke.

"Hi, just two?" the perky hostess asks.

"Yeah." I smile. I use the time she takes grabbing menus and silverware as an opportunity to read her nametag and I try to figure out if Johnny has ever cheated on me with an Anna.

Not important, Alex.

"You can follow me." She leads us through the bright turquoise hall to the yellow dining room.

I take a seat in my silver metal chair and Bryce does the same.

"I'll be right back with some water for you two." Anna smiles and disappears into the back.

"How do you like living here?" I ask.

"It's a lot different than Maryland."

"I bet. Good different or bad different?"

"Both. New York doesn't have my friends but Maryland doesn't have you."

I smile as the hostess returns with our water.

"Can I start you two off with some coffee or maybe some tea?" she asks, her black apron covering the bottom of her white short sleeve shirt and the top of her blue jeans.

"I'll have tea," I say.

"Coffee for me, please." Bryce smiles.

"I'll bring those out for you right away." She smiles and leaves our table.

"What's this place called?" Bryce asks.

"Sun Cafe."

"So that's why it's so bright in here."

"Well, it's not called Moon Cafe." I laugh.

"Fair point. I'm really glad we're doing this."

"What? Breakfast?"

"A date." He reaches across the table and grabs my hand. "I'm finally getting to give you what you deserve out of a relationship."

I smile and the brown-haired hostess returns with our drinks. She sets a silver insulated pitcher down on the table. "Here's the water for your tea, and your teacup and teabags."

"Thanks." I smile.

She sets down a mug for Bryce and pours some black coffee into it. "And your coffee. Your server will be over in just a minute to take your food order."

She disappears back down the hallway and Bryce grabs his menu. I slap it out of his hands back onto the table.

"What are you doing?" he asks.

"You don't need that. I know what we're getting."

"I know I said I want pancakes but can I at least browse to see what else they have?"

"You can browse when you don't want pancakes."

He laughs and shakes his head. "You're something else."

"You love having a girlfriend who's something else."

"It does have its perks."

"So one question."

"What's up?"

"Do you like your pancakes with blueberries, chocolate chips, or plain?"

"So you don't know my order." He smirks.

"I mean, I'm pretty sure the answer is chocolate chips."

"Okay, so you do know it."

I smile and a red-haired waitress makes her way over to us.

"Good morning. How are we doing today?"

"Pretty good," I say.

"Great. Are we ready to order or do we need another minute?"

"I'm gonna have the stack of three buttermilk pancakes with sausage links and he's gonna have the stack of three chocolate chip pancakes with bacon. And could we also get the fruit salad for the table?"

"Of course. I'll get that in for you right away." She closes a black notepad and tucks it into her black apron with her pen before walking away.

"Come here often?" Bryce laughs.

"You'll be here every week once you try this too."

"This better be worth the hype."

"It absolutely will be."

"I'm gonna hold you to that."

"You can hold me to whatever you want." I smirk.

He raises his eyebrows and I laugh.

"The food's great."

"How long does it usually take to come out?"

"The fruit salad will only be a minute. The pancakes shouldn't be too far behind."

The server returns with a big silver bowl of fruit salad and a couple smaller white bowls just as I finish my sentence.

"Here you go. The pancakes will be just a few more minutes." She smiles.

"Thanks so much." I smile back.

Bryce grabs the black slotted spoon and scoops some strawberries, pineapple, honeydew, grapes, blueberries, and watermelon into his bowl. He picks up the second bowl and looks up at me. "Little bit of everything?"

"No blueberries or honeydew please."

"Just pineapple, strawberries, watermelon, and grapes?"

"Yes, please."

He scoops some fruit for me, careful to avoid the ones I don't like, and sets my bowl in front of me.

"Thanks."

He takes a bite of fruit and I do the same. The strawberries are sweet and juicy and the watermelon is the perfect refresher for July in New York.

"So what is there to do at the waterfront?"

"It's cute. There's music, little shops, lots of restaurants, cute spots to take photos. And it shouldn't be too crowded when we're there."

"That's good."

Our server returns with a plate in each hand. "And here's your pancakes." She sets the chocolate chip pancakes in front of Bryce and the buttermilk ones in front of me.

"Thank you." I smile and she walks away.

"They smell amazing," Bryce says.

"Agreed." I grab the bottle of maple syrup and pour some onto my stack before passing it to Bryce.

"You want some pancakes with all that syrup?" Bryce laughs.

"Pass."

We enjoy our pancakes in near silence, neither of us wanting to stop eating long enough to say more than a single word.

"Can I take these plates out of your way?" the waitress asks with perfect timing.

"That'd be great. Could we get the check when you get a chance?" Bryce asks.

"Of course, I'll bring that right over." She smiles as she scoops up our plates.

"So how far is the waterfront from here?" Bryce asks.

"About five minutes."

"That's it?"

"That's it. It's not far from the house, I'm surprised you haven't been."

"Might've been nice for my tour guide to tell me about it." He laughs.

"Fair enough."

The waitress returns with our check and sets it on the table for us. "You can pay with Anna up front on your way out."

"Great, thanks." I smile.

Bryce grabs the check before I can.

"What are you doing?" I ask.

"Paying for breakfast."

"I can pay."

"Good for you."

I smile and we get up from our table, leaving a few dollars for our server. I follow Bryce to the front of the cafe, letting him pay for our meal.

"You're all set. Have a great day." Anna smiles.

I thank Bryce for breakfast as we walk to my car and he stops me before I can get in.

"What?" I ask.

He cups my face in his hands and kisses me. I kiss him back and my hands rest on his back. I can't help but smile against his lips for a second before I pull away.

"What was that for?"

"I just forget how hot you are sometimes so when I remember I get the urge to do some really freaky shit to you. We're in public though so for now that's all you get."

I let out a laugh and we get in my car. I back out of my parking space and pull out of the lot, getting on the highway. I switch into the middle lane and drive about a mile. The right lane ends and a few hundred feet later I see an exit sign for the waterfront. I flick my directional on and take the exit, making a left when I come to a stop sign.

"Are we here?" Bryce asks when the river comes into view.

"Yeah." I see that the parking lot I usually use is filled so I park on the side of the road and turn my car off.

We climb out and head for the sidewalk. There's drums echoing in the valley formed by the mountains on either side of the river.

"It's really pretty here," Bryce says.

"It is."

He grabs my hand in his and I smile up at him.

"What?"

"You just make me happy."

"Good." He leans down and kisses my forehead.

I look down the sidewalk and see dozens if not hundreds of people already sitting on laid out blankets gathering snacks. "I can't believe how busy it already is."

"What's up that way?" Bryce points ahead of us.

"There's always food trucks and ice cream trucks here for the holiday. Local small businesses usually set up tables and sell some stuff too."

"Nice."

"It's usually not this crowded until later. They must be doing something special this year."

"Like what?"

"No idea."

"We can come back another day when it's not packed and we have some room to enjoy the view."

"Are you sure?" I ask.

"Positive. Besides, I can't kiss you without us catching some dirty looks when it's this busy."

"Okay." I smile.

We walk back to my car with our fingers tangled in each other. Bryce opens my door for me and I smile as I realize that Johnny never did anything like that.

I start the car and pull out into traffic.

"Do you want to come over when we get back? My mom mentioned something about taking Layla to visit our grand-parents today."

"Sure." I merge onto the highway and get in the left lane.

"You know that means we'll have the whole house to ourselves? Not even a sleeping Layla will be there."

"I already said yes." I laugh. "You don't have to try to sell me on it even more."

"I'm just building the anticipation."

"Of the freaky shit you mentioned earlier?"

"And other shit."

"Well I do love shit."

"Who doesn't?"

I stay on the highway for a few miles before finally exiting.

"I hate that road more and more each day." I shake my head.

"Route nine?"

"Yeah. There's too many damn lights."

"And idiots."

"One hundred percent."

"Speaking of lights, this one sucks." I point to the one on the corner of Summer Street and Bryant Lane.

"Why?"

"If you're coming from this direction during rush hour it stays red for thirteen minutes straight."

"Why?"

"Because traffic sucks."

"I'd imagine a long ass light makes it worse."

"It does but no matter how many people complain they don't change the timing of it."

Thankfully the light stays green long enough to let us through and today does not have to be the day Bryce gets a demonstration of the torture.

I turn into our neighborhood and see a few people testing out fireworks.

"Nothing like breaking the law on a federal holiday." Bryce laughs.

I pull onto our street and see a line of cars almost immediately. "What the hell is this?"

"You guys take the Fourth of July seriously around here."

"Not usually. I think someone's having a party." I see balloons on Bryce's mailbox and a couple of girls are walking up his driveway. "You're having a party."

Chapter 16

"What the hell?" Bryce looks at his house in shock. "How do you even know enough people here to throw a party?"

"I don't. They must have the wrong house."

"All of them?"

"This is insane."

I park in my driveway, my car narrowly fitting between two others parked on the road to make it into the driveway.

"Can I stay at your place tonight?" Bryce looks at two girls walking through the road towards his house as we get out of the car.

"Sure."

"Wait a minute. I know them."

"Who?" I ask, looking at the girls.

I don't recognize them from school.

"They're from Maryland."

"You invited a bunch of your old friends up here?"

"No."

"Then who did?"

"I don't know."

"Well, what now?"

"What do you mean?"

"You know them so are you going over and joining your party or are we hiding at my place until tomorrow morning?"

"I guess we're going over there."

"We?"

"Yeah, we. I'm not gonna go hang out with a bunch of people from home without you."

"Why not?"

"You can meet some of my old friends."

"Bryce-"

"Alex, come on."

I let out a sigh and press the lock button on my keys. "Fine."

"Thank you. You're the best." He grabs my hand and pulls me towards his house.

Everyone attending seems to be going around to the back of the house so I'm surprised when he leads me to the front door.

"What are you doing? Don't you want to go back there?"

"In a minute." He lets us into his empty house and takes us to his room. "You can leave your keys on my desk."

"Thanks," I say as I drop them down on it. "So you have no idea who's actually here?"

"None."

"This is so weird."

"Agreed."

"So about the two girls you recognized."

"Yeah?"

"Did you ever, um, hook up with them?"

"No," he says and pulls me in for a hug.

"Good."

"I guess we should go out there."

"I guess so."

He flicks off his bedroom light and I follow him up the stairs.

"Wait."

"What?"

"What if your friends don't like me?"

"They'll like you."

"But what if they don't?"

"They will."

"But-"

"Alex. They're gonna love you."

I nod as the back door slides open and Maggie enters.

"You're home early. It was supposed to be a surprise."

"You're throwing the party?" I ask.

"I thought it would be nice for Bryce to spend some time with his old friends while he's still adjusting to New York. The holiday seemed like the perfect excuse."

"So they just agreed to come up for a party?" Bryce asks.

"Pretty much. Nick and Jacob should be here any minute."

"Nick and Jacob are coming?" His face lights up.

"And Olivia. She's gonna be a little late though."

Great. She'll be here.

"How long have you been planning this?"

"Two days."

"That's it?"

"That's it."

"Your friends miss you. They agreed to drop everything and come up just for the party."

"It's a five hour drive."

"A couple of them may be spending the night."

"Who?"

"Just the close ones are staying at the house. Alex, you're more than welcome to spend the night as well. The rest are getting a hotel and probably continuing the party there."

"I can't believe this."

The front door opens and boys cheering catches my attention.

"The party has arrived!"

"Jacob!" Bryce calls and heads for the stairs.

I watch as a blond haired boy a few inches shorter than Bryce comes into my view and the two hug.

"What am I, chopped liver?" the other boy asks before hugging Bryce.

"I can't believe you guys are here."

"Five hours in the car with this one, I can't believe we're here either." He shakes his head.

"Come here. There's someone I want you to meet." Bryce brings them into the kitchen. "This is Alex."

"Hi." I smile.

"Hey. I'm Nick." He holds his hand out for me to shake. "It's nice to meet you."

"You too."

"Jacob." He waves to me.

"Hey." I smile.

"How do you guys know each other?" Jacob asks.

"She lives next door," Maggie says. "Am I gonna get a hello?"

"Miss Maggie!" Nick pulls her in for a hug. His blue short sleeve shirt hugs his biceps and Jacob's red one does the same.

Is everyone in Maryland able to bench four hundred?

"There's something else you guys should know about Alex," Bryce says once the boys let go of Maggie.

"Which is?"

"She's my girlfriend."

"You got a girlfriend? You've only been here for a few weeks and you got a girlfriend?"

"I did."

"How the hell?"

I laugh as Bryce's friends continue to tease him.

"Did you guys bring bags to stay the night?" Maggie asks.

"Yeah, we have a duffel bag in the car." Jacob nods.

"Perfect."

"Why don't you guys go out back? There's some people already hanging out playing volleyball."

"We have volleyball?" Bryce asks.

"Tara does. She let us borrow it. She also loaned us bocce."

"Who's Tara? Girlfriend number two?" Nick asks.

"Tara's my mom." I laugh.

"Mother-daughter duo, up top, man!" Jacob goes to high five Bryce.

"Idiot." He shakes his head.

"Do you need help bringing any food or anything out?" I ask Maggie.

"That'd be great. Let me grab a couple bowls and you and Bryce can each bring some chips out. Nick and Jacob, could you just put the cans of soda in the coolers with some ice? There's a few bags in the freezer in the garage."

"No problem, Miss Maggie." They head down the stairs.

"Thanks, boys!" she calls after them as she grabs some large plastic bowls from the cabinet next to the microwave.

"I can't believe you did all this." Bryce smiles.

"Are you excited to see everyone?" I ask.

"He better be." Maggie laughs as she dumps a bag of tortilla chips into the red bowl.

"I am." Bryce grabs the bag of plain potato chips for the blue bowl and barbecue ones for the green.

We dump them in as Maggie pours the sour cream and onion ones into the yellow bowl.

"Okay. You guys can bring these out. Have fun." Maggie smiles.

I pick up the green and yellow bowls and Bryce takes the blue and red ones and leads me outside. He opens the sliding glass door and I follow him onto the deck.

There's music playing and sure enough, a small group of girls in bikini tops and booty shorts are playing volleyball.

"Do they know you don't have a pool?" I ask.

"I'm sure they're just trying to tan. Don't read too much into it."

Trying to tan or show off their tits?

There's a few guys with their shirts off obviously trying to hook up with some of the girls on the lawn.

I follow Bryce over to a white folding table and set down the bowls of chips. There's blue plastic cups and red paper plates next to an unopened package of red, white, and blue napkins for the holiday.

"Bryce!" a girl yells as she bounds up the stairs to the deck.

"Hey, Alyssa." He smiles.

She goes to pull him in for a hug and he stops her. "This is my girlfriend, Alex."

"Hey," I say, grateful that Bryce stopped that hug.

"Oh my gosh, hi. How are you? You should come play volleyball with us."

I look her up and down for a quick second, her bright blue string bikini top showing off her at least C cups. Her black shorts barely cover what's in the front, definitely not hiding what's in the back.

"Okay." I agree.

"I'm gonna go help Nick and Jacob. Those idiots probably got lost trying to find the garage." Bryce heads back inside.

"You're really pretty," Alyssa says as she starts walking down the steps.

"Thanks." I follow her down to the lawn and see two other girls who are just like her. All of them have long brown hair and are at least six inches shorter than me.

"Guys, this is Alex. She's Bryce's girlfriend." Alyssa explains.

"Like, girlfriend, girlfriend? Or just sex?" one girl in a yellow bikini top asks.

"Emily! You can't ask that!" Alyssa laughs.

"It's fine," I say. "Girlfriend, girlfriend."

"I'm impressed." Emily shrugs.

"Why? He always had a type." Another chimes in.

"Okay, I don't think she wants to hear this." Alyssa shakes her head.

Am I actually gonna be friends with this girl?

"I'm sure she knows about his reputation." Emily rolls her eyes.

Well, I definitely won't be friends with that one.

"That doesn't mean you have to go into detail."

"Let's just play." A girl in a red, white, and blue bikini top tosses the ball in the air and serves it over the net.

Alyssa hits it straight up and laughs. "Alex, save it!"

I hit it over the net and am not the least bit disappointed when Emily doesn't put her hands up in time and gets hit in the head.

"I wasn't ready!"

"Bummer." Alyssa laughs.

Emily gives up on hitting the ball and tosses it over the net. I spike it and the girl in the festive bikini runs for it and barely hits it in time.

"Emily, that's you!" she yells.

Emily clearly spends too little time doing anything athletic as she tries and fails to kick the ball.

"We're getting our asses kicked!" her teammate yells.

"Claire, do you want to join our team?" Alyssa laughs.

"Please!" Claire yells back.

"Babe!" Bryce yells. "Come here real quick!"

I jog up the stairs to the deck. "What's up?"

"How's it going?"

"Alyssa seems nice. Haven't talked with Claire much. Not a fan of Emily."

"Yeah, Emily can be a bit much at times. You just gotta get to know her."

"Ugh, do I have to?"

He laughs and kisses my forehead.

"Can I ask you something?"

"Anything."

"I keep hearing how you have a type. What's that about?"

"My ex was blonde. I'd just ignore it."

"So blondes are your type."

"You're my type."

"Good answer."

"While it's still slow, do you want to go to your place and pack some clothes for tonight?"

"Only if you go with me."

"Aw, can't I stay and look at the girls in bikinis?"

"I'm so glad you think you're funny."

"I'm hysterical."

"Come on." I grab his hand and pull him into the house. "Did you find the boys?"

"I did. Why? You miss them?"

"A bunch. My heart is just aching without them here."

"They're helping my mom grab a couple more coolers." He laughs and leads me down the stairs to the front door.

"They seem nice."

"Yeah, they're cool."

I follow him through the dead end and up my front steps. My house is empty and I wonder where my mom and grandma went.

"I think I'm gonna change into a bikini." I lead Bryce to my room.

"Why?"

"I'm the only girl wearing a real shirt."

"So? Other guys don't need to be seeing you in a bikini."

"Well, Emily seems to be a tad judgmental, so." I open the top right drawer of my dresser and dig through my bikinis. "Do I want to wear red, black, or white with sunflowers?"

"White with sunflowers."

"Good choice." I pull out the top and search for a minute before I find the matching bottoms.

"That's gonna look so good on you."

I smile and pull off my tank top and strapless bra and toss them into my hamper.

"You're changing in front of me?"

"Oh, I'm sorry. I hadn't realized my boobs were something you haven't seen before."

He laughs and kisses me.

"No. We don't have time for this."

"I think we do."

"We definitely don't."

"Fine."

I step into the bottoms of my bikini. "Can you pass me the top?"

"Here." He hands it to me and I slip it on.

I grab a pair of blue denim shorts and slide them on next before sticking my phone in the back right pocket.

Alyssa and Emily and Claire look phenomenal in their bikinis. I should start going to the gym.

"Do I look okay?"

"You look great, babe."

I grab a black bag from my closet and throw in a pair of black leggings, gray pajama shorts, and a red thong.

"Oh, I'm definitely gonna like seeing you in that." Bryce smirks.

I roll my eyes with a laugh and grab a white cropped tank top to sleep in.

"I can wear these shorts tomorrow, right?" I ask as I gesture to the ones I'm currently in.

"I'd bring another pair. The boys are planning a water balloon fight for later."

"Good call."

I grab a pair of light blue denim shorts and a cropped red cami along with a tan strapless bra.

"All set?"

"Not quite." I grab my deodorant and hairbrush off my dresser and get my toothbrush and toothpaste from the bathroom. "Okay, now I'm set." I slide my feet into a pair of black flip flops that will undoubtedly come off within the next five minutes.

"Let's go." Bryce grabs my hand and leads me outside.

I follow him through the dead end and into his house. He leads me down the stairs into his room. I set my bag down next to his bed and he pulls me into him for a kiss.

"What was that for?" I ask.

"Does there have to be a reason?"

"I guess not."

"Let's go outside."

I nod and follow him out of his bedroom and into a room on the left, directly in front of the stairs.

"This room came out so nice," I comment as I see a chocolate brown couch and a flat screen TV on the wall with a scarlet area rug on the hardwood floor.

"Yeah, it did. Mom worked hard on it. The floors took her forever."

"She did this herself?"

"We don't really have the money to hire anyone. She just watched some tutorials online and borrowed some tools from my grandpa and got it done."

"Holy shit. Your mom is my idol."

"Don't get too excited. I don't need you tackling any home improvement projects next."

"Let's go outside," I say with a laugh.

Bryce leads me out the back door and we step outside, underneath the deck. There are more snack tables and coolers down here, along with a fire pit.

"This is nice," I say.

"Half of it's yours." Bryce laughs.

I hear Maggie's voice above us. "Is Bryce back yet?"

"Down here!" he yells.

"Great! Come up real quick!"

I follow Bryce up the stairs and onto the deck.

"What's up?" he asks Maggie.

"Just wait a second."

"For what?"

"Be patient and you'll see."

We stand in silence for a minute or so before the back door opens and a blonde steps out.

"Olivia," Bryce says. "Hey."

"Hey." She smiles.

"This is my girlfriend, Alex."

"Hi," I say awkwardly.

"Hi."

This tension could be cut with a knife.

"Okay, well, Emily, Claire, and Alyssa are on the lawn," Maggie says.

"Great, I'll go say hi," she says and heads down.

"That was weird," I say.

"No, it wasn't. You're reading too much into this."

"So there's something for me to read into?"

"Alex."

"Bryce, come on. That was weird. Is she that mad that she had to stop calling you babe?"

"Alex, ignore it. It's nothing."

"You did tell her, right?"

"Yes, Alex, I told her. She's my best friend, she's protective. Let her warm up to you before you expect to be best friends."

"Let her warm up to me? Shouldn't I be the one to warm up to her after that crap?"

"Alex, I didn't mean it like that. You're both guarded when it comes to each other."

"Whatever."

"Alex."

"I'm gonna get back to volleyball. Maybe I'll get lucky and Emily will hit her when she misses the ball." I turn and jog down the stairs, finding Alyssa.

"You're back." She smiles.

"Yes, I am."

"That's such a cute bikini. Where'd you get it?"

"Thanks." I smile. "I'm not sure, it was a gift."

"I love it. Let's play. You're with me again."

"Perfect."

Alyssa serves the ball and it comes back to me so I hit it hard at Olivia, proud of myself when she ducks and the ball hits the ground.

"Point for us!" Alyssa beams.

Claire rolls the ball under the net and I serve this time, letting Claire get a shot in before I slam it at Olivia again.

"Yes!" Alyssa shouts. "Another point."

"I'm sensing some issues here!" Emily calls from the side-lines.

I ignore her and hit this one a little softer, giving Olivia a chance to hit it back. Alyssa spikes it back but Claire gets under it. I hit it at Olivia and she ducks again.

She lets out a sigh. "Alex, I know I slept with your boyfriend and all, but do you have it out for me?"

Chapter 17

I charge up the steps to the deck, hating that I gave Olivia the satisfaction of getting to me but eager to find Bryce.

"Maggie, where's your son?" I ask her when I reach the top of the stairs.

"He just went inside."

"Thanks." I open the back door and head inside. "Bryce!"

I don't get a response.

"Bryce!" I yell again, louder this time.

"What?" he yells back.

"Where the fuck are you?"

"My room!"

I stomp down the stairs and throw his door open.

"What are you doing?" he asks.

"You slept with Olivia."

He lets out a sigh.

"Bryce."

"It was one time."

I can't find any words to say.

I hoped Olivia was lying, just trying to get to me.

"There wasn't even any feeling behind it. She didn't want to go into senior year a virgin and I was leaving anyway so we just did it."

"It's that easy for you to sleep with someone?"

He shrugs and my heart shatters in my chest.

"How do I know you're not sleeping with me just to sleep with someone?"

"You're different."

"How?"

"You just are."

"Oh, that makes me feel special."

"You are special, Alex. It meant nothing to either of us."

"Like Jessica Myers."

"Alex."

"What?"

"I'm sorry that I was ever the type of guy to sleep around."

"You're just saying that because you know it's what I want to hear." I roll my eyes.

"No, I'm saying it because two of my past hookups are causing problems for us. And if I knew they would, I never would've even thought about doing either of them."

I shake my head.

"I'll tell her to leave."

"You don't have to."

"Alex, you're not gonna be comfortable if she's here and I'd rather have you here than her."

"It's fine."

"It's not. She's the type to try to rub stuff like this in people's faces."

"Yeah, I already found that out."

"What exactly did she say? How did that even come up?"

"I may have been playing a little rough during volleyball and she asked if I had it out for her since you guys slept together."

"Of course that's the first thing out of her mouth." He rolls his eyes.

"Yeah, I wasn't happy about it either."

"I'm sorry."

"You swear it meant nothing?"

"On my life."

I let out a sigh. "Okay. Let's go back upstairs."

"What were you doing down here anyway?"

"Just thinking about my incredibly sexy girlfriend in that incredibly sexy jean shorts and bikini top combo."

I shake my head with a laugh. "Come on."

"Come here." He pulls me into his chest and hugs me tight, kissing my forehead before pulling away.

I grab his hand and lead him upstairs and back outside. We sit at the table on the deck with Alyssa, Nick, and Jacob.

"So, Alex," Nick says.

"So, Nick."

"What exactly are your intentions with my best friend?"

"Okay, you're done." Bryce laughs.

"How long have you guys been dating?" Alyssa asks.

"It's complicated," I say.

"I love complicated. Give me the details."

"So I had a boyfriend when Bryce moved in. He was not a good guy and there may have been some overlap between that relationship and this one." I admit.

"Which I knew about and was fine with," Bryce says. "I met her ex and he was all kinds of psychotic."

"How bad are we talking?" Jacob asks.

"He cheated on me multiple times and when he got caught, he'd fake suicide attempts."

"How does someone fake suicide attempts?"

"He would empty out pill bottles and lay on the bathroom floor so his mom would panic and call him an ambulance and then call me so I'd panic and then the second I'd show up at the hospital he'd miraculously be fine."

"What the fuck is wrong with him?" Alyssa asks. "Was he ever abusive? Sorry I know that's personal, you can ignore that."

"It's fine," I say. "He wasn't physically but verbally, mentally, and emotionally is a different story."

"What are we talking about up here?" Olivia asks as she invites herself to the table, dropping into the seat right next to Bryce.

"Just how lucky Alex and Bryce are to have found each other." Alyssa fills her in.

Oh, I am definitely going to be friends with this girl.

"Cute." Olivia fakes a smile. "You know, Alex, Bryce is my best friend."

"I wouldn't say that," Bryce says quietly.

"You better not hurt him."

"I have no plans to."

"I'd say interfering with one of his friendships is hurting him." She rolls her eyes.

"Do you mean when I asked you to stop calling me babe?" Bryce asks. "That was my choice, not hers. I didn't want her to see it and get the wrong idea."

"That doesn't mean you change the dynamic of our friendship."

"I'm sorry you feel that way." He grabs my hand.

I guess I'm not the only one upset by her telling me they slept together.

Emily comes up the steps and sits down next to Olivia. "What'd I miss?"

"Oh, not much," Olivia says. "Just the happy couple gushing over each other."

"Gross."

"Isn't it?"

"Jealousy isn't all that appealing either." Alyssa rolls her eyes.

"Didn't you used to have a crush on Bryce?" Olivia flips her hair over her shoulder with a smug smile.

"In the third grade?" Alyssa laughs. "Yeah, I think so. Don't mention that in front of Jacob. We did get married in preschool after all."

I try to hold in my laugh but can't.

"I remember that wedding." Bryce smiles. "It happened right next to the slide. Didn't Emily marry Nick that day too?"

"That's right." Nick nods.

"Double wedding of the century." Alyssa laughs.

"Who'd you marry?" I ask Bryce.

"Nobody. I was too busy saving myself for you."

"So sweet." I lay my right hand on his cheek.

"He is sweet." Olivia glares at me. "You're very lucky to have him."

"I'm aware." I nod.

"And I'm not just saying that because he's good in bed." She smirks.

"You know what, Olivia?" Bryce gets up. "I think it's time for you to head out."

"I literally just got here."

"And you're doing way too much." Alyssa shakes her head. "You can't possibly be having any fun and enjoying seeing Bryce because you're too busy trying to start problems with his girlfriend."

"I just said I know how lucky she is." She shrugs.

"And you know why that was inappropriate." Alyssa rolls her eyes just as I realize I've officially hit my breaking point with Olivia.

"I'll be inside," I say to Bryce. "Get her out."

"I'll go with Alex," Alyssa says. "I'll get arrested if I stay within hitting distance of that bitch any longer."

"Well happy Fourth of Fucking July." Olivia rolls her eyes.

Alyssa and I go inside and sit on the couch in the living room.

"The air conditioning feels so good," I say.

"It really does. You okay?"

"I'm kind of wondering if Bryce and I are really compatible now. Olivia is his best friend and she's acting like that."

"She's not usually like this. Bryce hasn't had a girlfriend in a while and I think she just got used to being the girl he's closest to. It doesn't make it right, but I think she's just feeling threatened by you."

"I just can't believe he didn't tell me they slept together." I shake my head. "That seems like something you mention given the circumstances."

"It was right before he left and I know he regretted it. I just think he didn't want to worry you over something that really meant nothing to him."

"If it meant nothing, why'd he regret it?"

"Olivia got a bit clingy after it happened. She begged him not to move and she even offered to let him move in with her. He knew the whole thing changed their friendship in a really negative way."

I let out a sigh.

"I know you're not the reason he has to choose between the two of you, but he'd choose you over her any day. He'd choose you over anyone."

I nod. "Thanks."

Maggie walks in and sees us on the couch. "What are you two doing inside?"

"Avoiding Olivia," Alyssa says.

"What'd she do?"

"She thought it was a fantastic idea to tell Alex that she slept with Bryce."

"Of course she did. She wants to try to wreck another one of his relationships. Unbelievable."

"She's done this before?" I ask.

"That girl has done more to hurt his love life than I can keep track of."

"Well, I think their friendship might be ending," Alyssa says.

"It's about time. Speaking of time, is it seven yet?"

I check the time on my phone. "Ten to."

"Do you girls mind helping me get the food ready for the grill?"

"Of course," I say.

"Great. Alyssa, can you grab the two plates of burgers and hot dogs from the fridge in the garage?"

"Sure." She heads down the stairs.

"And Alex, can you grab the plate of chicken and the package of American cheese from the fridge up here while I grab Bryce?"

"No problem." I open the fridge as Maggie goes out to the deck. My eyes scan the shelves for the plate. I finally find it on top of a container of pasta salad and pull it out, grabbing the cheese from the cold cut drawer.

Alyssa comes back upstairs and sets the plates on the counter next to the stove. I put the plate of chicken and the package of cheese next to her plates.

Maggie comes back inside with Bryce behind her.

"What else can I help with?" I ask.

"Bryce, keep her." Maggie smiles. "I plan to."

"Do you mind cutting up those tomatoes?" Maggie asks me as she points to some tomatoes in a basket next to the fridge.

"Sure."

"Thanks. There's a cutting board in the cabinet directly under them."

I open the cabinet and pull out one of the smaller cutting boards. I remember where the knives are from my time babysitting Layla so I open the drawer and pull one out.

"Where's the lighter?" Bryce asks.

"It's already on the counter." Maggie answers.

"Thanks." He turns and walks back outside.

"Alyssa, can you get the bowls of pasta salad, macaroni salad, and potato salad out of the fridge and just leave them on the counter? Oh, and then grab some serving spoons from the drawer next to the oven?"

"You got it." Alyssa answers.

I finish cutting the tomatoes so I lay the slices on a plate.

"Alex, do you mind putting some lettuce on that plate, too? And some pickles?"

"Of course." I grab the head of lettuce and the jar of pickle chips from the fridge. I put a good amount of lettuce on the plate and use a fork to pull some of the slices of pickles from the jar and lay those on the plate too.

"Can someone help me bring out the burgers, chicken, and hot dogs?" Bryce asks.

"I can," I say.

He grabs the plates of burgers and hot dogs and I grab the plate of chicken. I follow him out onto the deck and over to the far end where the grill is. He uses tongs to place the chicken and burgers on the grill.

"Are you having fun now that Olivia is gone?" he asks.

"Yeah." I nod. "I'm sorry it came down to that."

"It's not your fault. Like I said, I'd rather have you here than her."

"Was she mad?" I ask.

"Extremely. I had to block her number before she even made it up the road."

"Jesus."

"It is what it is. I probably should've cut her off sooner if I'm being honest. She's been a pretty crappy friend over the last few years."

"Your mom mentioned she's ruined another relationship of yours in the past."

"Yeah. She was always sending me texts asking to hang out and saying not to tell the girl I was seeing about it."

"Why'd you stay friends with her for so long?"

He shrugs. "It was complicated. She didn't have the easiest life or very many friends. I kinda felt bad for her."

I nod.

"She's gone now. She's not gonna start anything again."

I nod, eager to change the subject. "Do you want me to bring those plates back inside?"

"In a sec. Let me put the hot dogs on first and then you can take all three and bring me out a platter to put them on."

"Okay."

"The guys are planning that water balloon fight I mentioned for right after dinner."

"I'll make sure I don't change out of my bathing suit."

"You could put on a white t-shirt if you'd like." He smirks.

"Don't be an idiot." I laugh.

He puts the hot dogs on the grill and starts flipping the chicken. "You can take the plates in now."

"One sec." I place my left hand on the back of his head and tilt his head down for a kiss. "Okay. I'll be right back with that platter."

He smiles and finishes flipping the chicken as I gather the plates. I head back inside and load the dirty plates into the dishwasher.

"Do you have a platter for Bryce to put everything on?" I ask Maggie as she pours dressing over a bowl of salad.

"Oh, yes! It's in the cabinet above the fridge."

I open the cabinet and pull out a blue plastic serving platter.

"Could you bring out the pasta salad and put it on the table out there?"

"Sure."

"Does anything else need to go out?" Alyssa asks.

"Can you bring the macaroni salad and the potato salad?"

"No problem."

I carry out the platter and the pasta salad and set the pasta salad on the table that held the chips and cups earlier. Alyssa sets down the macaroni salad and potato salad while I bring Bryce the platter.

"Thanks, babe."

"You're welcome. Is it almost done?"

"Yeah, can you just grab me the cheese for the burgers?"

"Sure." I head back inside and get the package of cheese and bring it out to him. "Here."

"Thanks."

"I'm gonna help your mom finish bringing everything else out." I go back inside again and see Maggie gathering more paper plates and bowls and plastic utensils.

"Oh, good. Can you help me bring these out?"

"That's exactly why I came in." I pick up the plates and put the bowls and utensils on top of them.

"We should be good on cups and napkins but can you double check when you bring these out?"

"Yeah, no problem." I bring them out and set them on the table. There's plenty of cups and probably a few hundred napkins left. I return to the kitchen and report back to Maggie.

"Okay, then we're all set. Thank you for your help, girls."

Alyssa and I head back outside and go over to the grill where Bryce is pulling everything off.

"Everything looks so good," I say.

"Agreed." Alyssa smiles.

"I'm glad you two are getting along," Bryce says. "Now that Olivia's blocked, you're probably my closest girl friend."

"Oh, good. I moved up a rank." She laughs. "And don't worry, we haven't slept together."

"She couldn't pull me if she tried," Bryce says.

"I wouldn't want to."

I laugh as Bryce shuts off the grill and brings the platter to the table with the rest of the food.

"It all smells amazing," Alyssa says.

"Is this everything?" Bryce asks.

"It should be." I nod.

The sliding back door opens and Maggie steps out. "Everything looks wonderful!"

"We were just saying the same thing," Bryce says.

"Help yourselves first before I tell everyone it's ready." Maggie gives us a minute before walking over to the edge of the deck. "You guys! Dinner!"

All the hungry teenagers race up the stairs in a massive swarm and I'm thankful Maggie gave us a head start. I finish putting mustard on my hot dog and bring my bowl of salad and my plate to the table.

"Did you invite the whole senior class?" Bryce asks Maggie with a laugh.

"Pretty much." She shrugs. "I wasn't sure how to decide who to invite and who to skip."

We eat our dinner and I notice plenty of people going back for seconds. After another twenty minutes pass, Jacob and Nick quietly excuse themselves from the table.

Oh no.

It only takes a minute for them to reappear at the bottom of the stairs and start launching water balloons up at the girls.

The high-pitched screams threaten to rupture my eardrums and I go to hide behind Bryce but he's no longer there.

Oh, I know he did not just leave me here.

A water balloon hits me from behind and I turn to see that it was thrown by none other than my boyfriend.

"Traitor!" I yell.

He laughs and throws another, hitting my hip. I run down the stairs and steal a balloon from Jacob's bucket, chucking it at Bryce.

"What the fuck, Alex?" he asks when he sees that I'm the reason for the wet spot and orange balloon fragments on his chest.

"Payback's a bitch." I smile.

He charges at me and wraps me in his arms, kissing me hard.

The screams die down and the boys must've finally run out of balloons.

"That wasn't much of a fight." I laugh. "The girls had no defense."

"Oh, did I say water balloon fight? I meant water balloon attack." Bryce laughs.

"Very funny. I need to go change."

"Unfortunately, so do I."

We head inside through the door under the deck and I follow him to his room.

I grab my bag and pull out my gray pajama shorts and white tank top.

"Your door is locked, right?" I ask.

"Yeah."

"Good." I take off my bikini top and slip off my shorts and the bottoms. I pull on my fresh clothes and see Bryce in a white t-shirt and black and white basketball shorts. "And you always say I look good." I laugh.

"You do."

"Bryce! Alex!" Maggie calls.

"Yeah?" Bryce yells back.

"Fire pit is lit! We're making s'mores!"

"Let's go." Bryce leads me back outside and we sit in red Adirondack chairs by the fire.

I sit between him and Alyssa and grab one of the silver metal skewers. Bryce hands me a marshmallow and I slide it onto one of the prongs and hold it over the fire just above the flame.

"You don't burn them?" Bryce asks.

"Ew, no." I grimace. "Warm is way better than toasted."

"Weirdo."

"Yes, you are." I laugh.

When I'm sure my marshmallow is warm, I pull it away from the fire. I place a piece of chocolate on a graham cracker and put my marshmallow on top of the chocolate before covering my masterpiece with another graham cracker. I take a bite and have to try not to moan.

I finish my s'more and Bryce is smiling at me.

"What?"

"You're just cute."

"If I'm so cute can we take some cute couple photos?" I ask, hopeful he might actually say yes.

"Sure." He smiles.

"Really?" I smile. "Alyssa, can you take some pictures of us?"

"Of course. Give me your phone." She holds her hand out as she gets up from her chair.

I hand it over and Bryce leads me to a secluded spot on the lawn away from the groups of people talking or making out.

"Oh my gosh, and the sunset is behind you guys. These are gonna be so cute!" Alyssa gushes.

I wrap my arms around Bryce and he does the same.

"Wait!" Maggie calls to us. "I have sparklers!"

I gladly accept a sparkler from her and Bryce lights it for me."Hold on, pick her up." Alyssa orders.

Bryce does as he's told and I wrap my legs around his waist, careful not to hit him with my sparkler as I wrap my arms around his neck.

"Hey, Alex," he says. "I'm already falling in love with you."

A smile spreads across my face and I kiss him. "I'm already falling in love with you too."

Chapter 18

My eyes open and a pair of lips connect to my forehead. Bryce.

"Hi," I whisper.

"Hi, babe."

"What time is it?"

"Eight."

"Gross."

"Do you want to go upstairs for a bit? We're the first ones up."

"Sure." I let out a yawn and pick my head up from his shoulder.

I look around and see Alyssa, Nick, and Jacob all still sleeping in their dark blue sleeping bags.

We carefully get up, trying to be as quiet as possible so we don't wake anyone. I grab Bryce's hand and follow him up the stairs. We sit down on the couch and I curl up next to him.

"Did you have fun last night?" I ask.

"Yeah. You?"

"Yeah. Alyssa seems great."

"She is."

"I kinda wish she lived up here."

"She's definitely considering a few colleges up here."

"Really?"

"Yeah. Her cousins live somewhere around here. She's actually visiting them for a few days after this."

"That's nice."

"Yeah. I think I'm gonna make some coffee."

"That's a good idea." I follow him into the kitchen and watch him put a coffee filter in and scoop some coffee grounds into it. He adds water to the coffee maker and presses the start button.

"What are you thinking about?" he asks.

"Did you mean it when you said you were falling in love with me last night?"

"Yeah." He smiles and tucks a piece of my hair behind my ear. "I did."

"Good." I stand on my toes and kiss him.

"Now what are you really thinking about, babe?"

"That obvious?"

"Yeah." He nods with a laugh.

"I think I want to meet my dad."

"Really?" He raises his eyebrows.

"This was your idea." I laugh. "Don't make me second guess it."

"I'm not, I'm just surprised. You seemed really against it yesterday."

"I was."

"Then what changed?"

"I just realized I've been angry at him my entire life and I don't even know who I'm angry at. It's kind of exhausting."

"I bet."

"I obviously have to talk to my mom about it before I can even try to go but if she lets me, can you go with me?"

"Of course. Wherever you need me to be is where I'll be."

I hear footsteps on the stairs and turn around and see Alyssa.

"Hey," I say.

"Hey."

"The boys up yet?" Bryce asks.

"No. It's only eight, they won't be up for another four hours."

"They'll be up as soon as the coffee is ready because I'll wake them."

"Good morning." Maggie smiles as she enters the kitchen.

"Morning," we say.

"Did you guys sleep okay?"

"The boys are sleeping a little too well." Bryce rolls his eyes.

"Smart decision to make coffee before waking them."

"Agreed." Alyssa laughs. "I do not want to be the one to go down there."

"I don't blame you." Maggie shakes her head.

"Is Layla around?" Alyssa asks.

"No, she spent the night at her grandparents."

"Aw, I was hoping to see her. How is she handling the move?"

"She's coming around."

"Coffee's ready," Bryce says and grabs a bunch of mugs from the cabinet next to the fridge. "Who's having?"

"Me," Alyssa and I say together.

"And me," Maggie says. "And definitely Nick and Jacob."

"Of course." Bryce pours some coffee into four of the six mugs. "There's all different flavors of creamer in the fridge, you guys can help yourselves."

Maggie sets the bottles on the counter and I grab the dark blue mug and pour some French vanilla creamer into my coffee. Bryce goes for the hazelnut and Alyssa uses the caramel. Once our coffee is prepared, we go into the living room and sit back down on the couch.

"The house looks amazing, Maggie," Alyssa says.

"Thanks. I got a lot done but the upstairs bathroom and the kitchen still need a lot of work."

"Which we could do faster if you'd hire someone." Bryce points out. "I get doing other stuff on your own, but kitchens are no joke."

"If I hire someone, I have to cut back the budget for the cabinets and appliances. I don't want to cut corners, I want to redo the kitchen once. It's just not the right time."

"Should we wake up the boys?" Alyssa asks.

"Be my guest," Bryce says.

"Not happening."

"I'll do it." Maggie laughs and goes downstairs. "Wish me luck."

"So you're looking at colleges up here?" I ask Alyssa.

"Yeah. I've got some family that lives here so I might stay with them and save money on dorming."

"That's a good idea. You're still getting the experience of going away to school and being away from your parents without having the price tag of it."

"Exactly."

"Do you know what you're gonna major in?"

"Sort of. I'm still trying to decide between either teaching or nursing."

"Cool."

"What about you?"

"I think I'm gonna start at community college. I don't have a clue what to major in."

"I'm glad I'm not going that route." Bryce laughs.

"You're not gonna go to college?" Alyssa asks.

"Nope. School's just not my thing."

"What are you gonna do?"

"Not sure yet. Maybe trade school for a bit."

There's stomping on the stairs so I look over and see the boys making their way up.

"Good morning," Alyssa says.

"Fuck off." Jacob flips us off and Nick lets out a yawn.

"Someone's cranky." I laugh.

"They're not morning people." Bryce laughs.

"Can you blame us?" Nick groans.

"There's coffee in the kitchen," Bryce says.

They wordlessly walk to where the coffee is.

"Wow." I laugh.

"They'll be nicer after their first cup."

"What's the plan for today?" Alyssa asks.

"Breakfast would be a good start," Bryce says.

"You guys want French toast, pancakes, or both?" Maggie asks.

"Probably both." Bryce shrugs.

"Give me half an hour."

"Do you want help?" I ask. "I don't mind."

"Sure."

I follow her into the kitchen and Alyssa does the same. The boys are still fixing their coffee, clearly extremely slow to get moving in the morning.

"How'd you guys sleep?" Maggie asks them.

"Great." Jacob groans as Nick sips his coffee.

"Why don't you boys go sit with Bryce and we'll let you know when breakfast is ready." Maggie pulls the carton of eggs from the fridge along with the milk and sets them on the counter. She grabs a box of pancake mix and brings that over next. "Alex, can you take about six eggs and make some scrambled eggs?"

"Sure."

"Great. There's a pan in the cabinet next to the oven you can use and there's cooking spray in the cabinet to the right of the microwave."

I grab the pan and spray it with some of the cooking spray before cracking the eggs into it. Alyssa is putting a pan of cinnamon rolls in the oven while Maggie pours pancake batter onto the griddle in small circles. Next, Alyssa tosses some sausage links into a frying pan with some water before cutting up some fruit.

"Is it ready yet?" Jacob asks with a groan.

"Not yet," Maggie says.

"What's taking so long?"

"Leave them alone!" Bryce calls.

"I'm hungry!"

"You're being an ass!"

Jacob groans and leaves the kitchen.

Someone hasn't finished his coffee.

I scoop the eggs into a serving bowl and bring them to the table as Alyssa brings a bowl of fruit over. Maggie lays the first batch of French toast out on a platter before doing the same with the first of the pancakes on a separate platter. Alyssa pulls the cinnamon rolls from the oven and starts pouring the icing onto them while I pull the sausage links from their pan and put them into a tiny bowl. I bring them to the table before Alyssa brings the cinnamon rolls over. Maggie fills the platters with French toast and pancakes and sets those on the table before putting out plates and silverware.

"Okay," Maggie says. "Now breakfast is ready."

The boys come in and take their seats at the table.

"We've got milk and orange juice if anyone wants something other than coffee," Maggie says as she sets a glass out for each of us. "I'll be tidying up Layla's room if anyone needs anything."

"Mom, you should eat with us."

"Oh, no, you guys want to be able to gossip and fill each other in on your lives without me around."

"Mom, come on."

"You should," Alyssa says. "Besides, there's nothing we'd say without you here that we wouldn't also say in front of you."

"That's true." Bryce nods.

"Are you guys sure?"

"Yes. Sit down."

Maggie thinks for a second before grabbing herself a plate and silverware and pulling out the only empty chair and taking a seat.

"The pancakes are really good," Bryce says.

"Everything is." Alyssa nods.

"Agreed."

"So Alyssa, are you seeing anyone?" Maggie asks.

"No. I think I'm gonna wait until I leave for college next year to start dating again."

"That's smart. It wouldn't be fun to get attached to someone new right before everyone leaves."

"Exactly."

"How's your sister doing?"

"She's good. Still planning to move out by September."

"Did she hear back about the interview she had or not yet?"

"She did. She got the job so she's set to start teaching for the upcoming school year."

"What grade?" I ask.

"High school math."

"Oh, wow."

"Yeah."

"Good for her." Maggie smiles.

"Yeah, she's excited."

"What about you two?" Maggie nods at the boys. "Any girls in the picture?"

"Nick is flirting with Chloe," Jacob says.

"Bryce's Chloe?" Alyssa asks.

Bryce's Chloe?

"Yeah." Jacob nods.

"When did that start?" Bryce asks.

"A few days after you left." Nick admits.

"Oh. Okay."

"Okay?"

"Okay. She's my ex. And that's a stretch because it was a middle school relationship."

"You're not mad?" Nick asks.

"Dude, look at her and then look at Alex. I think I have the ten and you have the two."

Damn.

"Wow." Nick laughs.

"Not wrong." Jacob shrugs.

So Bryce upgraded since middle school.

"Let's maybe take it easy." Maggie laughs. "Are you seeing anyone, Jacob?"

"No. Why, you interested?" He smirks.

"Oh my gosh." She laughs. "You haven't changed a bit."

All the memories they have must be amazing.

I'll never know Bryce's friends like he does. Sure, seeing them for the party was fun, but I'll never have memories with them like he does. Never as many, never as deep.

We finish eating and help Maggie clean up. When the dishwasher is loaded and all the pans have been cleaned, everyone starts planning their day.

"What time are you guys heading out?" Alyssa asks the boys.

"As soon as we're dressed," Nick says. "I have to work the dinner shift."

"You're still at the restaurant?" Bryce asks.

"Yeah. It's not the same without you."

"I bet." He smiles and the boys go downstairs to change.

"Alex, you should give me your number," Alyssa says. "I'll definitely be back up to visit family and I might end up here for college. We could hang out."

"Definitely." I smile.

She hands me her phone and I type my number in.

Alyssa goes downstairs as the boys return and give Bryce a hug.

"It was good seeing you," Nick says. "Keep in touch."

"Will do. Thanks for coming."

Jacob whispers something to Bryce and follows Nick out the front door.

Alyssa comes back up the stairs and hugs me and then Bryce. "This was really fun. It was great meeting you, Alex."

"Same here." I smile.

"Have a safe drive home whenever that is." Maggie laughs.

"Will do." She picks up her bag and leaves the house.

"Do you need help cleaning anything else up?" I ask.

"No, everything has been taken care of."

"Are you sure?" Bryce asks.

"Yeah. Everything has already been cleaned and put away."

"Okay," Bryce says. "If you find something else, let us know."

"Will do."

Bryce and I go down to his room and flop down on his bed.

"Well, my friends love you." He smiles.

"Really?"

"Definitely. Alyssa wouldn't have asked for your number if she didn't like you. And Nick thinks you're really good for me."

"And Jacob?"

"He told me to put a ring on your finger before someone else does." He laughs.

"They really liked me?"

"They did."

"Good." I lean in and kiss him.

Chapter 19

"How was the party?" Mom asks the second she hears the front door open.

"Can I get inside first?" I laugh as I kick off my shoes and Bryce does the same.

"No. I want details."

"Okay." I start walking up the stairs. "Bryce is here too."

"Hi, Bryce!" she calls.

"Hey."

"So how was the party? Fill me in."

"Hold on." I walk down the hall and set my bag down on my bedroom floor before going back to the living room to answer her questions.

"So?" she asks. "You're still in pajamas so did you not get much sleep?"

"Eh." I sit down on the couch and Bryce sits next to me.

"Talk to me, how was it?"

"It was good," Bryce says.

"For the most part." I add.

"What does that mean?"

"There was some drama at the beginning."

"Can I have the details?"

"This one girl I used to be friends with was a little jealous." Bryce shrugs.

"She was basically trying to make me jealous so that she'd feel better."

"Did it work?"

"Unfortunately, a little bit, yeah."

"Bummer. Did she stay the night too?"

"She didn't make it to the nighttime festivities." Bryce laughs.

"She had to be asked to leave."

"Ouch. What else?"

"That was really it for the drama." I shrug. "The rest of his friends seem really nice."

"And they like you a lot."

"That's good." Mom smiles. "I can't believe everyone was willing to come up just for a party."

"I can't believe you didn't tell me about the party. You loaned Maggie some stuff so I know you knew."

"It was supposed to be a surprise and you would've told Bryce."

"Maybe." I admit.

"There's no maybe about it." She laughs. "Do you guys have plans for today?"

"No, we're just gonna hang out. Maybe watch a movie."

"You guys should do something."

"There's actually something I was hoping to talk to you about."

"What's up?"

"Please hear me out before you give me an answer."

"Okay."

"I want to meet my father. I've been angry at him my entire life and I don't even remember him and I haven't even seen pictures of him and I just need to know who I'm angry at. I don't want a relationship with him, I just want to meet him. I need to know if he's sorry because even though I could never forgive him, if he's sorry then maybe I can stop being so mad. I've just been carrying this around my whole life and it's not mine to carry. I need to at least have a face to put to the shitty actions."

"Okay."

"Okay?"

"You've clearly thought about it so if you want to meet him, I'll support that decision."

"Oh."

"Did you not want me to say yes?"

"I did, I just wasn't expecting you to."

"Alex, I've always told you that nothing would ever be off limits as long as you had a good reason for wanting to do it. You have a good reason for wanting to meet him. I agree that this burden is not yours to carry and I hate that he left you with it. So, if you think meeting him will take some of the weight off your shoulders, I'm all for it."

"Thank you."

"Don't thank me yet. I'll let you see him, but I am driving you there. And I do not want you going in there alone so maybe ask Cassie if she can go with you."

"Actually, Bryce offered to go with me."

"Really?"

"This was actually his idea."

"Oh. Great. No matter what your father asks, you are not to tell him anything about where we live. Not what town, not what color our house is, not who we live with. Don't mention anything about neighbors. And do not talk about me. If you want to fill him in on your life, do not mention where you go to school. Don't mention anyone's last names either."

"Wow. That's a lot."

"He'll seem nice, Alex. He's manipulative like that. Do not let him fool you. Remember why you're going and remember what he did to land himself in there. You just want to see if he's sorry so you can stop carrying the weight of what he did. You do not want to be his friend."

"I know."

"Don't let him make you forget that." She turns to Bryce. "Do not let her forget that."

"I won't." He promises.

"Good. I'll get everything set up and let you know when the visit is."

"Set up?" I ask.

"You need an appointment in order to visit and in order to get an appointment you have to be on his visitation list. Visiting someone in prison is a process."

"Oh."

"So I'll get everything in order for you and let you know the details."

"Thanks."

"Of course."

I get up from the couch and lead Bryce to my bedroom.

"That was weird, right?" I ask.

"That she agreed so easily? Very." He closes my bedroom door behind us.

"Okay, good. I thought it was just me." I plop down on my bed and grab the remote and turn on the TV. "What do we want to watch?"

"Does it really matter what we put on? I don't think we're gonna do much watching anyway." He sits down next to me and wraps his right arm around my waist.

"My mom is home." I turn my head and kiss him. "Do you think you'll ask your mom again about meeting your dad? Or at least knowing who he is?"

"I don't know." He sighs. "I don't think I'll get anywhere."

"I didn't think I'd get anywhere with my mom and look how easy it was."

"Yeah, but you hadn't tried before today."

"That's true. I still think it's worth a shot."

"Nothing's changed though."

"That's not true. You live in a whole different state. Maybe your dad is still in Maryland and she'll be willing to tell you who he is now that you're nowhere near him. Maybe he's not a good guy and she just wanted to get you away from him before telling you about him."

"I don't know. If I can't meet him, is there really a point to knowing?"

"Maybe you've already met him."

"I doubt it."

"Well, maybe it's the other way around. Maybe he lives up here and she moved you guys up here so she could tell you about him."

"Then why hide it for so many years? Why give me zero information for seventeen years of my life just to give it all up eventually?"

"Maybe she was planning to tell you all along and just didn't want to do it until you could meet him. You said he took off, right? She probably knew you'd have questions and just wanted you to be able to get your answers."

"I don't know."

"I think it's worth a shot."

"And what if she still doesn't tell me?"

"Then at least you tried. At least you don't know because of her choices and not yours."

He shakes his head.

"Babe, I really think you should try."

He thinks for a moment before he finally caves. "I'll call her."

Yes!

I mute the TV and he puts his phone on speaker. It rings a few times and Maggie finally answers.

"What's up, kid?" she asks.

"Who's my dad?"

Right to the point.

"What?"

"Who's my dad?"

"Bryce." She lets out a sigh.

"Answer me."

"I'll tell you anything you want to know if we can just do this in person."

"Really?"

"Really."

"I'm coming home now then and I'm bringing Alex. Dig out my birth certificate because I want proof."

"His name isn't on it."

"Then whose is?"

"Nobody's."

"Mom."

"I didn't know what to do, Bryce. I just put unknown. I was scared and sad and lonely."

He shakes his head. "I'll be home in two." He ends the phone call and sighs.

"Ready to get your answers?" I ask.

"I don't even fucking know."

"It's gonna be okay. And I'll be right there the whole time."

"What if I can meet him?"

"Then I'll be there for that too. But we'll cross that bridge when we get to it."

"Okay." He nods. "Thank you for pushing me."

I force a small smile and turn off the TV. He grabs my hand and I lead him out of my room.

"Where are you two going?" Mom asks.

"His house for a bit."

"Were the last almost twenty-four hours not enough?" She laughs.

"Nope." I slip my shoes back on and open the door.

Bryce doesn't move so I step out first and hold my hand out for him. He accepts it and follows me out the door. I let him set the pace of our short walk to his house. His feet slowly lead the way and I'm pretty sure we're about to be passed by a snail.

"Are you nervous?" I ask.

"Not nervous. Just starting to question if this is really a good idea."

"I think it is. You'll feel better once you know."

"I really hope you're right."

"I'm always right, it's why you're dating me." I smirk.

He opens the front door and nudges me in first.

We walk up the stairs and see Maggie sitting at the dining room table with a dark blue folder in front of her.

"Can we sit on the couch?" Bryce asks.

"I think we should do this at the table," she says.

He lets out a sigh and pulls out both of the wooden chairs across from Maggie. He takes a seat in the one on the right and I sit down next to him in the one on the left. He instantly grabs my right hand in his left and gives it a squeeze.

"I never meant to keep your father from you," Maggie says. "Things just got a little out of hand."

"You think?"

"Hear her out." I remind him.

He sighs. "Sorry."

"Your father was on vacation in Maryland visiting family when we met. I was young and stupid and I spent time with him even though I knew he had a girlfriend back home. We exchanged numbers, we hooked up, and then he went home. I thought that would be the end of it but a little over a month later, I found out I was pregnant and I called him to tell him the news. He told me that I knew he had a girlfriend and that the baby, you, wouldn't change anything. He tried telling me to get an abortion and when I told him that wasn't an option he said he would offer me no help. No money, no clothes, no diapers, no co-parenting. Nothing. And then he blocked my number. I was completely on my own to raise you."

"Great. Now who is he?"

"Bryce," I say. "Be patient."

"I've been patient for seventeen years."

"So you can wait five more minutes."

He lets out a sigh and glances up at Maggie.

"About five years ago, he reached out."

"He reached out?" Bryce raises his eyebrows. "You didn't think to tell me?"

"He reached out once in all those years. I didn't want to get your hopes up if it was gonna turn out to be nothing. He just said he was sorry and that he wanted to help me out. I said I didn't need his help anymore but I wouldn't refuse anything he wanted to offer you."

"Did he offer me something?"

"He did."

"What was it?"

"Well, let's get into this first." She peels open her folder and lays Bryce's birth certificate on the table.

"Okay," he says after looking down at it. "Father is unknown. You told me that already."

"I know. I just wanted you to see it for yourself. Hopefully have you less mad at me for the next part of this."

"Which is?"

"He and I met up."

"And you didn't bring me?"

"It's complicated. Please try to hear me out."

"What?"

"You and Layla aren't half siblings."

"You're joking."

"I'm not."

"You hooked up with him twice? Almost thirteen years apart? And not once tried to form a relationship with him?"

"We went out to dinner and he gave me a check for your college fund. Things just kind of picked up where they left off all those years ago."

"Mom."

"He said he was ready to be a man and be there for his kids. But then I found out he already has kids with a wife and a mistress."

"Oh my God."

"How many kids does he have?" I ask.

"Bryce, Layla, and two others."

"Holy shit." Bryce shakes his head. "I have more siblings."

"You do."

"Have I met them?"

"Bryce."

"Can I?"

"Bryce."

"Have I met him?"

"Yes. You just didn't know he was your father."

"Who is he?"

"Jimmy Tate."

"Jimmy Tate?"

"Well, you know him as James Tate."

"The James Tate I work for?"

"Yeah."

"Wait a minute. James Tate? That's Johnny's dad."

"Johnny, like, your ex, Johnny?"

"Yeah."

"Your ex boyfriend is my half brother?"

Chapter 20

I bite the nail of my pointer finger and check my phone. No new notifications.

Bryce and Maggie went to meet up with James Tate, leaving me to watch Layla for the afternoon. I told Bryce to keep me updated but I haven't heard from him once.

My mind is racing with all the possibilities of how their conversation could be going.

"I'm done," Layla says as she gets up from her chair.

"Did you finish your salad?"

"No."

"Park it, missy."

She lets out a groan and gets back in her chair.

I take the paper plate that held her pizza and toss it into the garbage can.

My phone buzzes in the pocket of my dark gray hoodie and I pull it out immediately. Instead of seeing Bryce's name on the notification for the text message, I see a random number.

I take a deep breath and unlock my phone, pulling up the message.

Nice to know you were at least keeping it in the family Johnny.

I roll my eyes and type a quick response.

Bite me.

He immediately starts typing again and I glance up at Layla to make sure she's eating her salad. When her fork with some lettuce and a piece of a black olive enters her mouth, I turn to walk down the hall.

"I'll be right back," I say. "Don't move until you finish your salad."

When I'm far enough away, I press the call button under Johnny's number.

I press my phone to my ear and my heart is thumping against the wall of my chest with every ring.

"Crawling back already?" he asks and I can hear the smirk in his voice. "Did my brother really disappoint you this fast?"

"Never that. You need to back off."

"Yeah? Or what? You gonna send my brother after me?"

"Johnny."

"So just out of curiosity, is he an asshole who treats you like shit or is he awful in bed?"

"That's you, for both of those."

"Hey, you never exactly complained about anything we did in bed."

"Notice how there's no denial that you treated me like shit." I roll my eyes.

"Hey, if that's what you were worth, that's not my fault."

"Don't contact me again."

"Yeah, or what?"

"Johnny, I'm warning you."

"Oh, well thanks so much for the warning."

"This is harassment."

"And what's sleeping with my brother called?"

"For your sake, I really hope you realize you need to leave me alone." I hang up my phone and block his new number before sticking my phone back into my pocket.

It buzzes immediately and I don't bother pulling it out to check who it is.

I return to the table and see Layla taking her last bite of her salad.

"All done?" I ask.

She nods as she chews and gets up from the table. I pick up her empty paper bowl and toss it into the garbage pail and put her fork in the dishwasher.

"Why don't we watch a movie? You can pick." I smile.

Layla grabs the remote control for the TV and starts scrolling through the free movies.

"I'm gonna go make some popcorn, I'll be right back." I pull a bag of microwave popcorn out of the pantry and unwrap the plastic before sticking the bag in the microwave. I grab a big blue bowl from the cabinet above the fridge and get the salt off the dining room table. The microwave beeps so I pull the bag out and tear it open, pouring the contents into the bowl before sprinkling some salt onto it. I join Layla on the couch and see that she selected the latest cartoon I'm sure all the kids her age are watching.

We make it twenty minutes into the movie and to the bottom of the bowl of popcorn when the front door finally opens.

"Layla, go get some shoes on," Bryce says and slams the front door. "Mom's taking you to Grandma's. You guys are having a sleepover there tonight."

"Yay!" she cheers and runs down the hall to her room.

"Why are they sleeping at your grandma's?"

"Because I can't be in the same house as my mother right now and she knows that if I leave, I'm not coming back."

"Today didn't go well?"

"Picture World War Two if Hitler's side was on steroids."

"I'm sorry."

"Once Layla leaves, I'll fill you in."

"Okay."

"Layla, let's go!" Bryce calls.

"Does your mom have pajamas and clothes for tomorrow for the two of them?"

"That's not my problem."

"Bryce, Layla didn't do anything to you. Go get clothes for her and I'll get some together for your mom and we'll pack a bag for them." I go down the hall and make sure Bryce goes into Layla's room before I go into Maggie's. I drag open a few drawers before finding pajamas. I pull out a pair of gray sweatpants and a red t-shirt and Bryce walks in with some clothes for Layla and a black bag.

"You can put them in here," he says and drops the bag on the bed. "I'll be in my room."

I grab a pair of black jeans and a purple long sleeve shirt and add them to the bag with a bra and a pair of underwear before going to Layla's room.

"All set?" I ask.

"Is Bryce coming?"

"No, just you and Mommy get a sleepover tonight."

"Okay." She frowns.

"Let's go meet her in the car." I lead her down the hallway and down the stairs.

"Bye, Bryce!" Layla calls.

"Bye! Have fun! Love you!"

"Love you!"

I walk Layla out to Maggie's car and open the door to the backseat.

"Hi, Alex," she says softly.

"Hi. How did it go?" I set the bag on the floor and help Layla into her car seat.

"Awful. Jimmy was an ass. Is Bryce okay?"

"He's moody. He said he'll fill me in once you guys leave."

"Can you stay with him tonight? I think it's best he's not alone."

"Of course."

"Thanks."

"We packed you guys some clothes, they're in this black bag back here."

"Thanks so much."

"Of course. Have fun, Layla."

"Bye, Alex."

"Bye, sweetie." I close the car door and wait for them to back out before going inside.

"They gone?" Bryce calls.

"Yeah." I head downstairs and into his room. I take a seat on his bed next to him. "What the hell happened?"

"Well, I don't have a job anymore."

"He fired you?"

"No. I quit."

"You quit? Why?"

"I can't work for someone who knew my mom was pregnant with me and left. Especially when they did it a second time with my sister."

"Was he at least apologetic about it? Did he offer a big, fat check for all that missed child support?"

"Nope. Aside from the college fund one he gave my mom, that is."

"All those years ago."

"Yeah. So nothing new in that department."

"So what happened? I need some more details here."

My phone starts to vibrate and I pull it out of my pocket to see another random number.

"Do you need to get that?"

I shake my head. "It's probably just Johnny again. I'm not answering."

"Speaking of Johnny, he's the only kid this guy had with the one woman he actually bothered to marry."

"Good to know the only one with a stable home life and both parents in the picture for at least a few years turned out so great." I roll my eyes.

"Obviously you know they're divorced now but apparently his mistress has tried to snag him a couple times."

"The one with kid number four?"

He nods. "Although, it's technically kid number three, Layla is the youngest. But, yeah, she tried to get him to marry her."

"How'd that go?"

"I don't think they got married but I know they don't talk anymore."

"I can't believe Johnny never mentioned any of this."

"I don't think he knew until today."

"Seriously?"

"Seriously. He showed up right in the middle of it. He was very pissed off and screaming about the betrayal and 'how could you do this to Mom' crap."

"Jesus."

"I know."

"Guess we at least know the cheating gene was passed down."

"Don't worry, this son didn't get it."

"Keep it that way. What else happened?"

"Well, kid number three of his is another daughter."

"Oh, I swear, if it's me I'm gonna lose my shit."

"I think we'd know that by now." He laughs.

"Thankfully. But could you imagine the soap opera?"

"I think I could."

"So how old is this mystery daughter?"

"Nine."

"Cute age."

He glares at me.

"I hate her."

"Thank you."

"What else?"

"He said I don't need a dad anymore so he doesn't see the point in being in my life as anything more than my boss."

"Fucking asshole."

"No argument here."

"So is that when you quit?"

"Yeah. I said Layla's four and he needs to step up and be there for her while he still can. I said he doesn't deserve to have her as a daughter but she deserves a dad. I don't want her to grow up like I did. I don't want her to wonder who her dad is and why he didn't want her."

"What'd he say to that?"

"He didn't care. It didn't affect him in the slightest."

"Scumbag."

"Yup. He doesn't know the nine year old, either."

"Do you know her name?"

He shakes his head. "All I got is her age. I know nothing else about her."

"Not even where she lives?"

"Nothing."

"Damn. So what's going on with you and your mom?"

"Well, my sperm donor ended up walking out and then Mom and I got in a fight over her awful taste in men."

"That's not good."

"Nope."

My phone buzzes again and I peek at it.

"Johnny again?"

"I think so."

"What does it say."

"Let's see." I open the conversation and look down at the messages. The words 'bitch' and 'whore' are mentioned a few times along with some other degrading curse words so I stop reading and turn my phone for Bryce to see. "I don't want to read them all."

He scrolls through the messages. "Can I block this number?"

I nod.

"Alex, I swear, I'm gonna hit him."

"I wouldn't blame you. So you guys aren't talking at all now? You and your mom?"

"Nope."

"She asked if I could spend the night here so you're not alone."

"She thinks I need a babysitter now?"

"Well, I was already getting paid to watch Layla tonight, I might as well get paid to watch you too." I laugh.

"I don't think it's legal to get paid for what we're gonna do tonight."

"Oh, yeah?"

"Yeah."

"You seem confident."

"Not so much confident as knowing my girlfriend won't turn me down after I've had a long day."

"Oh, she won't? What girlfriend is that?"

"Her name's Vanessa. She's a short blonde, kinda feisty, just the way I like my women."

"Oh, so you do know your little sister's name."

"Oh, really? You had to ruin my fake second girlfriend for me?"

"I did. Your fantasy was getting a little too real."

"So sorry."

"Blonde is your type, is it not?"

"Fair enough. Sorry."

"You had a rough day so I guess you're excused."

"I appreciate that."

"I bet." I lean in and kiss him.

"Today kinda got me thinking. Are you still on your birth control pill?"

"Yeah."

"And you're still taking it every day?"

"Not quite at the same time every day but yeah. I would tell you if I stopped."

"I'm just making sure. Some girls are crazy and will try to trap a guy with a kid."

"I'm flattered you think I could be one of them." I laugh.

"It's a high level of psycho. You should be honored to be mistaken for it."

"I truly am."

"Good. Get over here."

Chapter 21

"How are you doing, sweetie?" Mom asks.

"I'd be doing better if Johnny would leave me alone."

"He's still going?"

"I blocked his number, so he moved to Instagram. I blocked him there, so he moved to Snapchat. Blocked him there too, so he moved to Twitter. Blocked him on Twitter, so he went back to Instagram with a fake account."

"And you blocked that too?"

"Of course, I did. But because he's Johnny, he made another fake account."

"Please tell me you have some sort of proof of all this."

"I took lots of screenshots."

"Good. Has he been by the house at all?"

"He drives down the dead end and he's sat outside a couple times but he hasn't come to the door at all."

"He's sat outside?"

I nod. "He just sits in his car. Like he's waiting to see if I'll come out or if someone will come over."

"What exactly does he say to you when he messages you from his fake accounts?"

"He's cursed at me, called me a whore, told me everyone around me would be better off without me and that I should kill myself and then for some reason he always ends the messages with an attempt at getting back together."

"Are you serious?"

"Unfortunately. He'll ask why I won't just get back with him and I tell him how he treated me like dirt and then he'll throw a tantrum and say I'm wrong and I don't know what I'm talking about and I'm too stupid to know what's best for me. That's where I block him and then get another fake account requesting to message me."

"How long has he been doing this?"

"Since Bryce met up with his dad. Their dad."

"Almost two weeks? This is harassment now, Alex. You'd be well within your rights to go to the police."

"I know. I just don't want to take it to that level."

"He's the one taking it to that level."

"I know."

"I just want to make it extra clear that I never liked him."

"I know."

"Your grandmother didn't like him, either."

"I know."

"What does Bryce think of all this?"

"He's not a fan."

"Why don't you let him take care of it? I have faith in his ability to hide a body."

"Good to know."

"I'll help him if he needs an assistant. I bet Cassie will join too."

"She absolutely would."

"Grandma's got some experience in that department."

"She what?" My eyes widen and my jaw drops to the floor.

"Oh, relax. I was seeing if you were paying attention."

"Can you test me later?" I laugh. "I need to do a some shopping at the mall and I'd like to get it over with."

"You're going in that?" She looks down at my pajamas.

"I wasn't gonna change with my mother in my room."

"Fair enough." She walks out and closes my door behind her. "Can you grab some milk while you're out?"

"Sure!" I yell as I yank open the top left drawer of my dresser. I pull out a pair of dark blue denim shorts before closing the drawer and opening the one next to it. It takes some digging before I find the tank top I'm looking for: a yellow crop top with white flowers on the chest. I grab a pair of black panties and a tan strapless bra before taking a light green towel and going into the bathroom.

"You're showering first?" Mom asks through the door when she hears the water turn on.

"Well, I'm not going out in public smelling like sleep."

"Sleep has a smell now?"

I ignore her and pull off my pajamas.

I take a quick shower and dry myself off with my towel before wrapping my hair in it to dry a bit while I get dressed.

Once my shorts and shirt are on, I walk to my room and take a look in the mirror. My butt looks great in the shorts and the cropped tank shows off my abs perfectly. I brush my hair and throw on some light makeup before slipping on a pair of black and tan sandals. I toss my wallet, keys, and phone into my black purse and head out.

"Have fun," Mom says. "Don't forget the milk."

"I won't. Bye, Grandma."

"If a road is closed and you have to take a detour through a certain someone's neighborhood and you accidentally hit that certain someone with your car, don't worry about it. I'll pay to fix the damage," Grandma says.

"Oh, good to know." I walk out the door and get in my car.

It's not a bad idea.

I back out of the driveway and head to the mall. I park in the lot between the mall and the grocery store, knowing I'll forget the milk if I don't have a visual reminder. As I get out of my car, a red BMW parked a row over catches my eye.

"You're just paranoid," I whisper to myself. "It's not Johnny."

I decide to get a little closer to peek at the license plate to prove it to myself.

"Well we might be paranoid, but that's his."

I look around and don't see him anywhere so I hurry into the mall. Every ten seconds, I take a look around me to make sure I don't see him following me.

I go upstairs and quickly walk to Forever 21. I browse the racks of clothing and pick up a pink cropped tank top. Once I'm sure I've hit all the racks, I head to the fitting room.

A brunette about four inches shorter than me wearing ripped black leggings and a mint green cropped tee with a lanyard holding some keys around her neck looks up at me. "Just one item?"

"Yeah." I nod.

"You can follow me." She leads me down a short hallway and knocks on a green door before unlocking it for me. "Here you go."

"Thanks." I close the door behind me and pull off my top. I slip into the pink cropped tank and take a look in the mirror. The shirt is fitted but not too tight and stops just above my belly button. I take a picture of my reflection and send it to Bryce.

What do we think?

He sees it right away and texts me back.

GET IT

I smile at my phone and change back into my tank top. I bring the shirt over to the empty register and pay for the top.

The jeans I like are on sale at Hollister so I go there next.

"Hi, how are you?" a girl in light blue ripped jeans hanging up some dresses asks.

"Good, thanks." I smile.

"Just to let you know, our jeans are currently on sale. Let me know if I can help you find a pair or get you a fitting room."

"Thanks so much."

I walk to the shelves of the jeans I like and look through the different ones. I grab a pair of ripped black ones and a pair of light blue both in a size three before going to the register.

"All set?" the girl from before asks.

"Yeah," I say.

"And were you able to find everything okay today?"

"Yup."

She rings up the jeans and I swipe my card. I take my bag and walk back out into the mall after looking both ways to check for Johnny.

I make it about twenty feet before trouble finds me.

"Having fun swiping my brother's credit card?" Johnny asks from behind me.

I don't turn around but I do speed up. "Get a life."

"Oh, I have a life, sweetheart. You're the one who can't get your own guy so you have to go after my family members."

I shake my head. "I can't get my own guy? You make no sense. Seriously, Johnny, I got you. And I got Bryce. Long before I had any idea of you two being related, might I add. And you know what, Johnny? Does the situation with your dad suck? Yeah, it does. But you're the only one throwing a tantrum over it like a fucking toddler. Leave me alone. Stop with the fake accounts and the sitting outside my house and the harassment. You're seventeen years old. Grow up."

He grabs my arm and I try to yank it away but I can't.

"Let go of me."

"Don't you fucking dare talk to me like that."

"Let go."

"No. We're not done here."

"I'll scream."

"You won't."

"Somebody help me!" I yell. "Help!"

A man wearing black slacks and a white button down with a bright yellow vest on the other side of the walkway hears me and runs over. "Let go of her!" he yells and grabs Johnny's arm. "Let her go!"

Johnny grits his teeth and walks away with no more than a muttered curse word under his breath.

"Are you okay?" the security guard asks.

I wipe a tear off my cheek. "Can you walk me to my car? I know he's walking the other direction but he's parked near me and I don't want him to have another opportunity to cause a scene."

"Of course. You know him?"

"He's my ex."

"I take it he's not over you."

"He's not. It didn't end well. Things got really messy and now he's harassing me."

"That was a little more than harassment. You've got marks on your arm."

I look down at my forearm and sure enough, there are multiple bright red marks from his fingers.

"You have your phone on you?" he asks.

I nod.

"Give it to me really quick."

I do as he says and he takes pictures of the marks on my arm with my phone before doing the same with his.

"I strongly advise you file a report. It can be with us or through town police, whatever you're comfortable with."

"Do I have a time limit? I'd like to think about it for a bit."

"How about this? I'll give you my card and if you decide you want to file a report through us, you'll have my info. If you decide to go through town police, call me and I'll go with you. I have some buddies in the department and I can make sure you're taken care of."

I accept his card and stick it in my purse. "Thank you."

"Was he a decent boyfriend before things got messy from the breakup?"

"Not really." I admit. "He cheated on me."

"And he's got the audacity to cause a scene?"

"He does."

"Has he done anything else like this?"

"This is the first time he's put his hands on me but he's been making fake accounts to talk to me through social media for almost two weeks now. He's driven past my house a lot and decided to sit outside a couple times."

"And you haven't gone to the police yet?"

"You sound like my mother." I laugh.

"Maybe you should listen to her, then."

"I'll think about it."

I read the security guard's nametag as we reach my car. "Thanks for walking me, Ray."

"Of course. Don't forget what I said about going through town police."

"Call you first, got it."

"Good. Get home safe."

"Thanks." I get in my car and drive over to the grocery store. I take one of the spots toward the back to try to avoid door dings, knowing I'll probably still end up with one.

I walk into the store and go to the back right. It takes a second for me to find the two percent milk and about a minute to find one dated anything other than tomorrow. I grab a gallon dated a week out and head to the self checkout. I pay for the milk and don't bother bagging it. Bryce stands at the desk by the last register and I walk over to him.

"Hey, there," I say. "I heard they just hired a cute self checkout boy. Any idea where I can find him?"

"Funny."

"I thought so. You look good in red."

"This polo is itchy."

"You'll live."

"This job sucks."

"So find a new one."

"I applied to a bunch of restaurants but nobody's hiring. Not hiring me, at least."

"You'll find something."

"I made more working for Father of the Year."

"You did the right thing by leaving."

"I'll believe that when I can afford my car payment."

"I know it sucks right now, but it's gonna be okay."

"I know."

"I'll see you tonight?"

"Yeah. Thanks for saying hi."

"Of course. Love you."

"Love you."

Chapter 22

"Alex?" Mom knocks lightly on my door.

"Yeah?"

"Can I come in?"

"Yeah."

My door slowly opens and Mom awkwardly runs her fingers through her hair.

"What's up?"

"You asked about meeting your father."

"I remember."

"I got you an appointment for about two weeks from now."

"Okay."

"I just got a phone call from the prison. He was supposed to have a visitor for today in about three hours but they cancelled. So they want to know if you want to go today."

"Oh," I say. "That's not much notice."

"You don't have to take it if you don't want to. We can keep the appointment you already have."

"I'll take this one," I say. "Bryce is off from work today anyway so it works out."

"Are you sure?"

I nod.

"Okay. I'll call them back and let them know. We'll leave at one."

"Okay."

She gives me a small, clearly forced smile before leaving and closing my door behind her.

I pull my phone out and call Bryce.

"Hey, babe."

"Hi," I say awkwardly. "Can we talk?"

"Is everything okay?"

"Sort of."

"Is it Johnny? Did he do something?"

"Just the usual but that's not what I'm calling about."

"Okay. What's going on?"

"So you know how my mom was gonna make an appointment for me to talk to my dad?"

"Yeah, did she get you set up?"

"Yeah. I was supposed to go two weeks from now."

"Supposed to? Did it get cancelled?"

"No. They had an earlier opening. Apparently someone was supposed to visit him today and can't make it so I can move mine up."

"Oh, wow. Are you gonna?"

"Yeah. Can you come with me?"

"Of course. What time?"

"We're leaving at one."

"Oh, wow."

"Yeah."

"Are you ready to see him?"

"I don't know."

"Anxious?"

"Very."

"Nervous?"

"Probably."

"It'll be okay."

"I hope so."

"It will."

"I need to go take a shower."

"Okay, babe. I'll see you at one."

"See you at one." I end the call and toss my phone onto my bed. I let out a sigh and glance out my window.

The bright green leaves cover every tree branch in sight and the cloudless sky is a bright blue. If I took a picture of it, it'd look like a backdrop for a Disney movie.

Ironic how such a nice day can bring so much stress.

I get up from my bed and open my top left dresser drawer.

Do prisons have a dress code? Obviously they have one for the inmates, but what about for visitors?

I grab my phone off my comforter and call Cassie.

"Nice of you to remember I exist." She laughs.

"Oh, shut up. My life has been stressful."

"Wouldn't ranting to your best friend be a nice way to get some of that stress off your shoulders?"

"That's what I'm trying to do right now, brat."

"Then spill the beans, bitch."

I let out a laugh. "I have a lot to fill you in on. For starters, wait, are you drinking something right now?"

"Like alcohol?"

"No, just anything in general."

"Oh, yeah, I have water."

"Don't drink for a minute because if you do and you have it in your mouth it will end up all over whatever is in front of you."

"Oh my, okay. What's up?"

"Johnny and Bryce are half siblings."

"They're what?" she yells.

"I know. Apparently Johnny's dad wasn't so loyal to Johnny's mom. He's got Johnny, Bryce, Bryce's sister who's four, and a random nine year old we know nothing about."

"Holy shit."

"I know. And ever since Johnny found that out, he's been harassing me."

"Wait, how did Johnny find all this out?"

"I'm not sure if Johnny's mom knows and told him or if his dad told him himself or if he snooped and found out somehow but he showed up when Bryce was talking to James."

"Holy shit."

"I know. And now Johnny is obsessed with the whole situation."

"To be fair, I'm sure it kinda turned his world upside down."

"I know. But he's been harassing me over it."

"He's misdirecting his anger."

"For sure."

"So what are you gonna do?"

"About what?"

"Well, are you gonna keep dating Bryce?"

"Why wouldn't I?"

"Isn't it kind of weird to be dating your ex's brother?"

"Half. And a bit, I guess. But I didn't know that when I started dating him."

"You know now."

"Yeah."

"Look, you don't have to stop seeing him. Just know that this is gonna get out eventually and it's probably a good idea to know how you're gonna handle it."

"That's true. This actually isn't the main reason why I called."

"Okay. What else is up?"

"I'm visiting my dad today."

"Alex, what?"

"I know."

"Today?"

"Today. I'm leaving at one."

"Oh my God. Why didn't you start with that?"

"I figured the rest of the gossip was juicier."

"It was, but this is bigger."

"I know."

"Do you know what you're gonna say to him?"

"Not a damn clue."

"Are you sure you want to do this?"

"I'm sure. That's all I really know at this point. I don't even know what I'm gonna wear."

"So you called me for outfit advice?" She laughs.

"I did. Please help me."

"Wear something simple. They gotta search you, right?"

"I'm assuming."

"Okay. Wear jeans. No rips. You want to look nice and show him what an amazing daughter he missed out on raising."

I force a smile. "Thanks. What shirt?"

"Something plain. No designs, nothing cropped, nothing that shows too much cleavage."

"Okay. Good idea."

"And no jewelry. They'll probably just make you take it off. And I'd skip a belt and purse, too. And don't even bring your phone in. Just leave it in the car or at the house."

"How do you know all of this?"

"Doesn't everyone?"

"Not really, no."

"Well, be happy I do."

"I am. Thanks for the tips."

"Of course. You better call me tonight with an update."

"About that."

"Oh, come on. You want my help but you won't fill me in?"

"I will fill you in. I just wanted to know if we could meet up instead of talking over the phone."

"Oh, sure. Smoothies tomorrow?"

"Sure. What time?"

"What works for you?"

"Noon good?"

"Perfect. Good luck and call me if you need anything."

"Thanks."

"Of course."

I end the call and set my phone down on my dresser before grabbing a pair of blue jeans and a light pink t-shirt.

"Plain is good." I remind myself.

I take a quick shower and change into my outfit before texting Bryce some of Cassie's tips.

Got it. Don't worry. Everything is gonna be fine.

I take a deep breath and set my phone down on my bed. I blow dry my hair and run my straightener through it until I'm satisfied.

Why am I doing my hair for this guy?

I shake my head but decide to put some makeup on anyway. I go with some foundation and light pink eyeshadow but skip the mascara.

It's prison, not a fashion show.

"Can I open?" Mom asks.

I nod and remember she can't see me. "Yeah."

"Almost ready?"

I nod.

"Anxious?"

"Very."

"You don't have to go if you don't want to."

"I want to."

"Okay. And Bryce is coming?"

I nod.

"Good. I'm glad you'll have someone with you."

"You're sure you can't come in with me?"

"Alex." She takes a seat on my bed. "It's not a good idea. If I go in there, you'll have two parents behind bars and that's the best case scenario."

"Okay."

"Let me know when you're ready to head out."

"Okay."

She gets up from my bed and kisses the top of my head before leaving my room.

I slip on a pair of black sneakers and text Bryce.

Ready?

Ready.

I leave my room and find Mom on the couch.

"All set?"

I nod.

"Is Bryce?"

I nod again.

"Okay. Let's go."

I follow her outside and Bryce is standing in our driveway.

"Hi, Bryce." Mom smiles as if it's just another day.

"Hi, Tara. Hey, Alex."

"Hi."

We get in the car and I sit in the backseat with Bryce.

"Do you want to talk about anything?" Bryce asks.

"I'd rather just sit silence until we get there."

"Okay."

We spend the better part of the ride with nothing but the radio making noise before a red light ruins our good luck.

"Okay, only five minutes left," Mom says. "Some ground rules. Do not talk about me. If he brings me up, you change the subject. Do not tell him where you go to school, who your friends are, nothing. You're there to get your questions answered, not to answer his."

"I know."

"I'm just making sure. Do not expect anything from him. Just let him be who he is and understand that he is not a reflection of you just like you are not a reflection of him."

"Okay."

"Do not tell him where we live, who we live with. He'll ask about someone he knows you know, I'm sure. Do not answer him."

"I got it."

"You are there to see if he's sorry for what he did. Do not lose sight of that." She pulls up to a gate and a man in a blue shirt with GREENWOOD CORRECTIONAL FACILITY written on it steps out of the booth.

"Afternoon," he says.

"Afternoon." Mom nods. "I'm bringing my daughter and her boyfriend to visit her father. Alexandra Brant and Bryce Wilkins, here to visit Brandon Axelrod." Mom shows him some papers and he nods.

"Go ahead. Go left at the stop sign, the visitor lot is on the right. There's a door with a sign for a visitor's entrance, you can't miss it."

"Thank you." She rolls up her window as he presses a button that opens the gate and lets us through. She follows his directions and pulls into a parking space in lot four.

"I'm so nervous." I admit.

"You're good." Bryce squeezes my hand.

"I think you're doing the right thing," Mom says.

I set my phone on the center console and Bryce does the same before I open the car door and hop out, Bryce close behind. A red sign with white writing shows us where visitors are supposed to enter so Bryce leads the way. He opens the door for me and I step in.

"Hello." A woman behind a desk smiles. "Visiting?"

I nod, not quite able get words over the lump in my throat yet.

"Perfect, just sign in right here." She points to a clipboard with a pen chained to it and Bryce grabs it. "Names?"

"Bryce Wilkins and Alexandra Brant," Bryce says. "Here for Brandon Axelrod."

She writes out nametags for us and hands us each a visitor card to clip onto our shirts. "Go straight through these doors and security will check you in while Brandon is brought down."

"Thanks," Bryce says as the door buzzes and he holds it open for me.

I walk into a room with metal detectors like the ones in airports and a man in a blue shirt like the one the man at the gate had on waves me over to the counter.

"Either of you have anything in your pockets?" he asks.

I shake my head as Bryce answers for me again. "No, sir."

"Step through."

I step through the metal detector and am relieved when I don't make it beep, knowing there was no reason for me to set it off anyway. Bryce steps through and doesn't beep, either.

Thank God.

"Spread your legs," the guard says and I do as I'm told. He uses a handheld metal detector and checks my legs. "Arms up."

I lift my arms out to the sides and he checks my abdomen and arms.

"Clear. You're up." He nods to Bryce.

Bryce does the same and doesn't set that one off.

"Clear. Here for Brandon Axelrod?"

I nod.

"He'll be down in a minute. Ever been here before?"

I shake my head.

"Do you talk?" He laughs and I wasn't expecting a joke from a prison guard so all I can do is force a small chuckle.

"She's nervous," Bryce says. "Brandon is her dad."

"Wow. I didn't know he had a kid. A living one, I mean."

Well that could've been worded better. At least everyone here knows what he's capable of.

"Some ground rules. When you get in there, you're gonna see a bunch of tables. Brandon will be at one of them. Do you know what he looks like?"

"No," I say and it comes out raspy. I clear my throat and try again. "No."

"Don't worry, we'll walk you over to him. He's one of our more, uh, there's no easy way to say this." He stops and scratches his head. "He's one of our more dangerous inmates. He had his visitation privileges revoked for a while. He'll be handcuffed to the table."

"Oh."

"It's for your safety and his."

"Great."

"Your hands need to be where guards can see them. Keep them flat on the tabletop, palms down, at all times."

"Okay."

"There's no yelling, no touching, and no speaking to other inmates or visitors permitted."

I nod.

"Brandon Axelrod is all set at table five," a voice on the radio says.

"If you're ready, I'll have Rebecca bring you in."

I nod.

"Rebecca, can you escort two visitors to Brandon Axelrod, please?" he says into his radio. "Table five."

I hear another buzz and the door to my left opens, a woman in blue stepping through.

"Follow me."

I do as I'm told and we enter a large room with about two dozen tables in it. Only three are occupied and only one holds a single person.

"I guess that's him," I whisper to myself.

Rebecca leads us to the table. "Here we are. You've got one hour."

"Thank you." I sit across from Brandon and don't say anything as I set my hands on the table like I was told to do.

Bryce sits down next to me and I take in Brandon's appearance.

His hair is brown and extremely short and his face has a few fading scars on the cheeks. I don't want to find a single feature that even slightly resembles one of mine.

"Hello," he says.

His voice is deeper than I anticipated and it throws me off.

"Do I know you?" he asks.

"They didn't tell you who I was?"

"They don't tell me anything around here."

"Oh," I say awkwardly. "I'm your daughter."

His eyes widen for a quick second before he composes himself. "Alexandra."

"I go by Alex."

"Alex. You're a very beautiful young lady."

"I know."

"Good. How's your mom?"

That didn't take long.

"I'm not here to talk about my mom."

"Okay. Then how are you?"

"I'm fine."

"Oh, that's a red flag. A woman who says she's fine is never fine."

"You're saying I have a red flag? You killed my brother."

"Oh, good. They filled you in."

"Yeah, they did. And I want to know why you did it."

"I had a lot of issues back then."

"That's an understatement."

"I was going through a very dark time."

"So you put my mother through one? You stab her multiple times and murder my unborn brother?"

"There's a lot you don't know about that day."

"So enlighten me."

"We had a disagreement that morning."

"Oh, well that justifies it." I tuck my hair behind my ear and drop my hand into my lap.

"Hands on the table!" Rebecca calls.

I jump and put my hand back up.

"You scare easily." Brandon smirks. "That's good to know."

I roll my eyes.

"How's your friend, what is it, Cassie?"

"How do you know about her?"

"I have my ways."

"Well, I'm not here to discuss Cassie."

"That's fair. Can we discuss your boyfriend?"

I glance over at Bryce and he shrugs.

"What do you want to know about me?" he asks.

"Not you, her boyfriend."

"I am her boyfriend."

"No, you aren't. I know her boyfriend. He visits me all the time."

"What are you talking about?"

"That boy you've been seeing for a few years. Johnny."

"Excuse me?"

"Johnny Tate, I believe."

"Johnny's been here?"

"He has."

"When did he start seeing you?"

"Oh, you didn't know that bit of information?"

"When did he start seeing you?" I repeat.

"Not long ago. Not exactly recently, either."

"Brandon."

"I'm your father, you will not call me by my first name."

"You're my sperm donor, I'll call you whatever the hell I want."

"Then this visit is over with."

"Fantastic. Rot in hell, you piece of shit." I get up from the table and Bryce does the same.

"I don't know if you're ever getting out of here," Bryce says, "but if you do, stay the hell away from her."

"And what if I don't?"

"You're gonna wish you did."

Rebecca leads us out of the room and into the room with the metal detectors.

"That was quick," the guard who checked us in comments.

"Thankfully," I say.

"I'm guessing you won't be back to see him again."

"Never. Do you know how much longer he's in here for?"

"Not off the top of my head but I can check if you'd like."

"That's okay. Can we go?"

"Just sign out at the front desk."

"Thanks."

Bryce leads the way and signs us out on the clipboard.

"Have a great afternoon." The woman smiles and I ignore her as I open the door.

"Do not tell my mother about any of this."

"Okay."

I open the car door and climb in.

"That was quick," Mom says. "How did it go?"

"I don't want to talk about it."

Chapter 23

I pull into the parking lot of Smoothie Central and look at the time.

12:07

Only slightly late.

I walk into the smoothie store and see Cassie sitting at one of the tan round tables with a smoothie for each of us, a white one for her and a pink for me.

"Strawberry banana?" I ask.

"Duh."

"You're an angel."

"I am. Nice of you to show up, by the way." She rolls her eyes.

"Oh, shut up. I told you there was traffic." I take a seat in the chair across from her.

"I'm sure there was. Now fill me in and tell me everything. What happened with your dad?"

"I really don't want to use that word to describe him any-more." I grimace.

"It was that bad?"

"It was about a hundred times worse than you can imagine."

"What happened?"

"He had absolutely no remorse for stabbing my mother and killing my brother. He said he was going through a 'dark time' and that he and my mom had a 'disagreement' that day."

"He did not."

"He did."

"Scumbag."

"I know. But it gets better."

"Does better mean worse?"

"It absolutely does. He mentioned you."

"Me?" Her eyes practically pop out of her head. "How the hell does he know who I am?"

"Take a guess."

"I don't think I want to."

"Trust me, you do."

"Don't even tell me one of his little prison buddies got out of jail and has been stalking you for him."

"No, but that's a good guess. It's a very entertaining thought."

She rolls her eyes. "So then what's been going on?"

"Johnny has been visiting him."

"No way!"

"Yes way."

"Why?"

"I don't know."

"What do they talk about?"

"Me, I guess."

"How long has that been going on for?"

"I don't know."

"What the fuck is that guy's problem?"

"Which one of them?" I laugh.

"Both." She laughs. "But I meant Johnny."

"We should start calling them Shithead One and Shithead Two."

"I like those names."

"So do I." I laugh.

"So what did Johnny tell him? Any idea about the specifics?"

"Not a clue."

"That's fucked. What was going through Johnny's head when he started making those visits?"

"I'd really love to know."

"So would I."

"So now I need some advice."

"About?"

"Do you think I should press charges?"

"Against?"

"Johnny."

"Alex!"

"I know he's just trying to get a rise out of me, but he's been driving by in the middle of the night again. And he kind of assaulted me at the mall too. A security guard had to intervene."

"What? You didn't tell me all that."

"He threw a tantrum and he grabbed my arm and wouldn't let go. I had red marks from his fingers all over my forearm."

"Do you have proof?"

"I have pictures."

"Can you show me?"

I pull up the photos and hand her my phone.

"Holy shit, Alex."

"I know. The security guard took those actually."

"What else happened?"

"Well don't even get me started on all the fake accounts he's been making to try to talk to me. And now after hearing he's been visiting Brandon and discussing me, I don't know. He's been posting some stuff on social media now too."

"Posting stuff like what?"

"Threats."

"Threats?"

"Threats."

"What kind of threats, Alex?"

"Apparently he has a video of us having sex and he's threatening to post it. He's also threatening to go fight Bryce. I don't even know how to handle this anymore."

"Well is there actually a video of you two going at it?"

"I don't know." I shrug. "I didn't think so, but it's Johnny. Who really knows for sure when it comes to him?"

"That's true."

"I'm just scared at this point. And I don't know if I'm just being paranoid or if it's warranted."

"And are you sure this isn't just the period talking?"

"What are you talking about?" I shake my head.

"You have your period right now."

"No, I don't."

"You do."

"I think I'd know if I had my period."

"Alex, we get them at the same time. I have mine right now, which means you have yours."

"I don't have my period." I shake my head and then it hits me. "Oh my God. I don't have my period. I have to go. I'll talk to you later."

I don't hear if she answers me and I don't bother to grab my smoothie before getting up and running to my car. My keys slip out of my sweaty palms and I rush to grab them off the pavement. I have to fight to get my car door to unlock and open but once I succeed, I climb in and barely buckle my seatbelt before speeding out of the parking lot.

I narrowly run a few red lights and almost flip my car turning into the parking lot of the drugstore. My hands fumble through my wallet to dig for cash and how much does a pregnancy test even cost? Twenty bucks? More? I grab my debit card instead just in case twenty won't be enough and head in. I have absolutely no idea where the pregnancy tests even are and there's no way I'm asking someone for help and admitting I need one of these so I jog up and down every aisle, hoping they'll stand out and catch my eye. I go through every aisle and don't see them so I start making a second trip through each and finally, I find them on a shelf in aisle eight.

Which one do I grab? Does it even matter? Pee is pee, regardless of the stick, right?

I grab two boxes by different brands, one that'll show me words and one that'll show me lines, and head to the checkout.

One of these will be accurate, right?

My hands shake as I drop the boxes on the counter. The man behind the register rings them up and the sound of my heart pounding drowns out his voice when he tries to tell me the price. I shove my debit card in the machine after missing on the first few tries. I punch in my pin and the machine beeps loudly, telling me my transaction is complete. I don't wait for the receipt before grabbing my bag off the counter and sprinting out of the store.

My empty car waits for me in the lot and I hesitate for a moment. When I get in there, I have to drive home. When I get home, I have to take the test.

A tear rolls down my cheek and I let out a sob.

I need to talk to someone who can calm me down so I call Bryce.

"Hey, babe, what's up?"

"Bryce, I'm really scared. I don't know what to do. I need your help."

"Okay, slow down. What's going on?"

"I can't tell you yet."

"You can tell me anything."

"I know, but I shouldn't tell you until I know there's a problem. And it might not even be your problem."

"Alex, what? What are you talking about, what problem? Did Johnny do something? Is it Brandon?"

"No. Bryce, I'm scared. Please just tell me everything is gonna be okay."

"Alex, everything is gonna be fine. No matter what's going on, we're gonna get through it together."

"Promise me."

"Alex, I promise."

"What if I am and what if it isn't yours?"

"What if you're what? Alex, what are you talking about?"

"I can't tell you yet."

"Are you home?"

"No."

"Alex, go home and we can talk in person."

I don't know what to say to him.

"Alex?"

"What?"

"Everything is gonna be okay."

I nod. "Okay."

"Where are you? Are you okay to drive home? I can come get you. I don't care how far it is."

"I'm at the drugstore and I don't know." I admit and then remember I shouldn't worry him. "I'll be fine."

"Alex."

"I'm good. I promise." I wipe my tears and hang up.

I turn off my phone so he can't call me back. My mind is running a thousand miles a minute.

What the hell did I get myself into?

I pull out of my parking space and try to take my time getting home. When I finally reach the house, Bryce is sitting on my front steps.

I climb out of my car and hold my bag behind my back so he won't see its contents as I walk up the steps to him.

"Are you okay?" he asks.

I nod.

"Alex, you never call me up crying like that."

"I'm okay."

"Are you lying to me right now?"

"No."

"Then what's in the bag you're trying to hide from me?"

"What bag?"

"Alex."

"It's nothing."

"Then show me."

"No."

"Yes." He reaches behind me and snatches the bag from my hand.

"Bryce!"

He reaches into it and freezes when he pulls out one of the boxes. "Alex. Alex, are you pregnant?"

"I don't know."

"If you are, is it mine?"

"I don't know."

He lets out a sigh and sits down on the front steps. I sit next to him and lay my head on his shoulder.

"Are you mad?"

"I'm upset that you didn't tell me this is a possibility."

"I'm sorry."

"No. Do not apologize right now."

"It might not even be your problem."

"But it will be. Regardless of if it's mine or Johnny's."

"Bryce, I'm scared."

"It's okay."

"It's not okay."

"But it will be."

"What if it's Johnny's?"

"I don't know." He shakes his head. "I'm not going any-where either way, but I don't know how Johnny would feel about me being around if it's his."

"So even if it's Johnny's, you'll still want to be with me?"

"Why wouldn't I?"

"What if it's yours?"

"Can we maybe find out for sure that there's a baby before we finish this conversation?"

"Oh," I say. "Okay."

"Alex, I didn't mean it like that. It's just, my head is spinning and there might not even be a reason for it to be."

"I get it." I nod. "I'm gonna go take these then."

He nods. I grab the tests and head inside. A quick search on the internet tells me I should grab a cup to pee in and dip the tests into the cup so I grab a blue plastic cup from the kitchen. I know Mom is at work but Grandma is home so I look around to make sure she won't see me head into the bathroom. Once I'm sure it's clear, I walk to the bathroom.

I double and triple check that the door is locked before setting the tests and the cup on the counter. My hands shake as I unbutton my shorts and slide them down a bit and do the same with my panties. I grab the cup and take a few deep breaths.

Okay, Alex. Just don't miss the cup.

Once the cup is about halfway filled, I set it on the counter before wiping and pulling up my pants. I grab the boxes of tests and open one. I pull one out and my hands shake as I pull the piece of plastic off and dip the test in the cup. My breaths are loud and I will myself to calm down as I cover the test with the plastic again. I do the same with a test from the other box and set it down on the counter with the first.

"And now we wait," I whisper.

I set a timer and sit on the bathroom floor. My eyes close and I catch myself saying a prayer when the timer goes off and interrupts me. I take a few quick breaths before using the counter to pull myself to my feet. My hands each grab a test. I look down at them and they both give me the same result, one in words, the other with lines. I take a deep breath and open the second test from each box. I dip them into the cup and cover them with the plastic caps and set a timer again.

"Okay, round two."

I try to ignore the knot in my stomach as I watch the numbers on the timer change. I take a few deep breaths and it finally beeps.

I look down at the next two tests and they show me the same result as the first two.

Four tests, all telling me I'm pregnant.

I leave my supplies on the counter and exit the bathroom.

"Grandma!" I yell. "Where are you?"

"Downstairs, sweetheart!"

I run downstairs into her room. "Can we talk?"

"Of course. Come sit." She pats the spot on the couch next to her and I sit down.

I take a deep breath.

"What's going on?" she asks.

"Grandma, I need to talk to you."

"Okay, well, I'm here. Is everything okay?"

I run the tip of my tongue over the back of my teeth and try to find the words.

"Alex?"

"I didn't know who else to go to." A tear wiggles out of my eye.

"Alex, what's going on?"

"I have no idea how to tell you this."

"Spit it out. Did you and Bryce break up?"

"No, we didn't."

"Alright, then what's up? Alex, you're acting like the world is ending."

"I'm pregnant."

Chapter 24

9 Months Later

"Just one more push, sweetie. You're doing great." The nurse in baby pink scrubs urges me.

Thanks to my epidural, the pain isn't too bad, but the pressure is a bitch.

"I can't do it!" I cry as another tear rolls down my cheek.

"You can, you're already doing it. Just one more push."

"Keep squeezing my hand." Bryce kisses my forehead and I do as he says.

I force myself to give one last big push and I wouldn't be surprised if Bryce has be taken down for an X-ray to see how many fingers are broken.

When I really start to feel like I can't push anymore, I finally hear the first cry.

My tears of frustration and stress from the last thirty-six hours of laying in this hospital bed instantly turn into those of joy.

"Congratulations." The doctor smiles. "It's a boy."

"It's a boy?" I ask.

"It's a boy." He holds my son up for me to see before the nurses take him to get cleaned up.

"I want to hold him," I say.

"Just one minute, we'll be very quick."

"You did so good." Bryce smiles.

I pull him in and kiss him.

"Thank you for being here."

"I wouldn't want to be anywhere else."

"You wanted to get a paternity test, correct?" Dr. Watson asks.

I nod.

"Okay, I'll need to get a DNA sample by swabbing the inside of your cheek," he says to Bryce.

"Okay."

"Can I hold him now?" I ask as Bryce's cheek is swabbed.

"They're just swabbing his cheek and then you can."

I can't see anything through the nurses' backs and I'm just itching to be able to see his face again.

"Do you know who the father could be if it's not Bryce?" Dr. Watson asks.

I nod. "Unfortunately it would be my ex boyfriend."

"Is he here?"

I shake my head. "I told him about the pregnancy but he wasn't interested in being a dad. He said he didn't care about getting updates or being here for the birth or anything. I still told him I was in labor but he never cared to acknowledge it."

The apple really doesn't fall far from the tree.

"So it's either Bryce or your ex?"

I nod.

"Okay. So either way we'll have our answer."

I hadn't thought of it that way.

I think back to nine months ago. Johnny was harassing me with fake accounts, he was driving by my house nonstop, sitting out front in the middle of the night, assaulting me at the mall, visiting my father in prison.

It took a police report and a couple court dates, but I was finally granted a restraining order.

He had to stop driving by, he had to stop messaging me from fake accounts, and he had to discontinue his visits with Brandon.

Given the fact that I was pregnant with a child that could be his, not all communication could be broken. I was ordered to give him updates such as finding out the sex, which I opted not to do until the birth in case he's not the father. He chose not to come in to provide a DNA sample. If I want him to, it'll take a court order. None of my updates received a response.

"Here he is." The nurse smiles and lays my baby on my chest.

I look down at his bright blue eyes and tiny pink lips and chubby little cheeks. His screaming doesn't bother me and after a few seconds, he settles himself down.

"He's adorable." Bryce smiles.

"He's perfect." I kiss his forehead.

"Do you have any name ideas?"

I shake my head. "Not yet. I thought I'd know it when I see him."

"We've got time." Bryce wraps his arm around me.

"Would you like us to grab your visitors?" Dr. Watson offers.

"Just our moms for now," I say before turning to Bryce. "Are you okay with letting Layla wait with Cassie?"

"Yeah."

"Okay."

"Aaliyah, could you go grab the grandma and potential grandma?" Dr. Watson asks a nurse.

"Of course." Aaliyah walks out.

"What do you think of the name Eli?" I ask Bryce.

"Eli. I like it."

"So do I."

"Middle name?"

"Still stuck on that part."

"Well, at least it's a start. Eli."

"Eli." I look down at him in my arms.

He's definitely an Eli.

"Here we are." Aaliyah enters the room with our moms.

"Oh my gosh." My mom smiles. "Boy or girl?"

"Boy." I smile down at him. "Eli."

"Oh, Eli." She wipes a tear off her cheek. "Can I hold him?"

I pass Eli to my mom and Maggie peeks over her shoulder to see him.

"Oh, he's adorable." She beams. "Those cheeks."

"I know." I smile.

"Long labor." She smirks.

"Brutal labor."

"I'm surprised you did it without me in here," Mom says. "I thought you'd crack and want to break my hand."

"She broke mine instead." Bryce laughs.

"He's really a beautiful baby." Maggie smiles. "Everything's normal? He's healthy?"

"He's perfect," I say.

"Good."

"And the paternity test?" Mom asks.

"On its way to the lab," Dr. Watson says. "I put a rush on it so we'll have the results by the end of the day."

"Perfect."

"I still don't know why you bothered." Maggie shrugs. "Bryce isn't going anywhere regardless of what it says."

"I don't want my son to wonder who his dad is. I don't want him to feel like I lied to him. If it's Bryce, perfect. If it's Johnny, then Eli will know what an amazing guy Bryce is for stepping up and being there for us despite all this."

"Whose last name will he have?" Mom asks.

"I don't know."

"Obviously it's up to you," Bryce says, "but if he's mine and you want to give him my last name, I wouldn't be opposed to it."

"Okay."

I wish everyone would shut up about the paternity test and the last name debate. Being the pregnant girl at seventeen and giving birth at eighteen would've been hard enough on its own but on top of it, I have to question who the father is and what last name I should give my baby. My guidance counselor may have offered to help with whatever I need when I switched to online classes to graduate early, but I don't think offering help in this particular area was what she meant.

"Are you planning to breastfeed?" Maggie asks.

"My milk actually hasn't come in," I say. "I know there's tricks I can try but I'd rather not have one more thing to stress over."

"That's valid. Formula is just as good. As long as he's being fed, you're doing the right thing."

"Have you had breakfast?" Mom asks. "It's only ten, I'm sure lots of places are still serving something good."

"I haven't actually," I say. "I'm starving. Can you find me pancakes?"

"Plain?"

"Chocolate chip if you can get them."

"Got it."

"If there's no shot at chocolate chip, plain is fine."

"I'll do my best and hit a McDonald's if I have to. Bryce, what can I get you?"

"I'm good with pancakes."

"Maggie, do you want anything?"

"I'm okay, thanks."

"I'll be back soon. Who's next to hold him?"

"My turn?" Maggie asks.

"Of course." I smile.

Mom passes Eli to Maggie and comes over to me. "I'm so proud of you." She kisses the top of my head. "I'll be back soon."

"He's beautiful," Maggie says.

"I just want to thank you for how amazing you've been the last nine months," I say to Maggie. "You could've gotten mad and said Bryce is better off without me or judged me or told Bryce he's not allowed to see me anymore but you didn't."

"I've been where you've been, Alex. Finding out you're pregnant as a teenager is far from easy. I would never try to make this, or anything else for that matter, harder for you."

"Can it be my turn to hold him now?" Bryce asks.

"I guess." Maggie laughs and passes Eli to Bryce.

I look over at Bryce holding Eli in his arms. He looks like a giant teddy bear holding such a tiny person. I can't help but smile and hope even more that the paternity test will tell me Bryce is the father.

"What?" Bryce asks when he catches me staring.

"You look good holding a baby."

"Nope." Maggie laughs. "No more babies until this one is walking. And trust me, that's for the sake of your sanity."

Bryce laughs and rolls his eyes.

"Your friend Cassie seems really nice."

"She is." I nod. "She's been a lot of help."

"Can I go grab her and Layla now?"

"Sure. Can you just give us a minute with Cassie at first?"

"Absolutely. I'll be right back." Maggie leaves the room.

"What about Blaine?" Bryce asks.

"Blaine?"

"For his middle name."

"Eli Blaine." I smile. "Eli Blaine."

"Does the fact that you're repeating it mean you like it?"

"I think so."

He leans in and kisses me. "I love you so much."

"Will that change if the paternity test says you're not the dad?"

"No. I'll be bummed but I'm not going anywhere."

"You'll be bummed? You'll be bummed to not be a teen dad?"

"You know what I mean."

"I do but I want to hear you say it."

"Johnny doesn't deserve you and he doesn't deserve Eli and he definitely doesn't deserve moments like these. And he wouldn't even want them anyway. Think about it, Alex. There's a chance this is his kid and he knew you were in labor and he didn't show. You're both better off with me than you are with him."

"I know."

"And speaking of being better off with me, there's something I wanted to talk to you about."

"What's up?"

"I think we both know I'm not going anywhere. And I think we should-" the door opens and cuts him off.

"Boy or girl?" Cassie asks with a smile.

"Boy," I say.

"Congratulations!" She gives me a tight hug and quickly pulls away. "Ew, you're sweaty."

"You go give birth and then we'll talk."

"I'm good, I'll pass on that. But I'll gladly hold him if I can."

"If Bryce is willing to give him up."

"Please?" She smiles at Bryce.

"Fine." He passes Eli to Cassie.

"What's his name?"

"Eli," I say. "Eli Blaine."

"That's such a cute name. And he's such a cute baby."

"I'm glad you think so." I smile. "Because there's something I wanted to talk to you about."

"Okay."

"It's about Eli."

"I'm listening."

"You've been such a good friend to me for so many years and especially during my pregnancy. You've been there for me through it all and I'm so thankful that Eli will have you in his life so you can be there for him too. But I was wondering if maybe you'd like to be his godmother."

"Me?" She smiles.

"You."

"Really?"

"Really. You don't have to if you don't want to. I know it's a huge responsibility. You can take some time to think about it if you want."

"I'll do it."

"You will?"

"Of course. I will gladly steal this little cutie if something happens to you guys."

"Let's not get too excited over my potential untimely death." I laugh.

"Oh, shut up. Don't take this away from me."

"Can you let your mom know she can bring Layla in?" I ask Bryce.

"Sure." He gets up and leaves the room.

"How bad was labor?" Cassie asks.

"I don't want to talk about it." I shake my head. "It hurts just thinking about it."

She lets out a laugh. "Do you want more babies in the future anyway?"

"Absolutely."

"Well, you do make cute ones. Any word on the paternity test?"

"Not yet. We'll know by the end of the day."

"Whose do you think it is?"

"I don't know." I admit. "I've tried counting back the weeks but their estimate is just an estimate, it's not exact. And with how much overlap there was with Bryce and Johnny, it's really hard to try to figure this out."

"Whose do you want it to be?"

"What do you think?"

"You don't want court ordered supervised visitation with your baby daddy?"

"Surprisingly, no."

She laughs at herself and the door opens, Bryce leading Maggie and Layla into the room.

"Baby!" Layla yells when she sees Eli in Cassie's arms.

"I told you the baby was here." Maggie smiles.

"Do you want to hold him?" I ask Layla.

She doesn't say anything and instead looks down at the floor.

"She's a little nervous," Maggie says.

"Come sit up here with me." I force my legs to cross and pat the area of the bed in front of me. Layla hops up with some help from Maggie and I adjust her in front of me so her back is facing me. "Can I have that pillow?"

Bryce hands me the pillow from the cot and I put it in Layla's lap.

"Okay. Cassie, can we borrow him?"

"I guess."

I position Layla's arms before taking Eli from Cassie and setting him in her arms, being sure to keep my hands under him to support his weight.

"What do you think?" Maggie asks. "He's cute, isn't he?"

Layla nods and I take a peek over at her face and see her smiling.

"Why are you being shy?" Bryce laughs. "This is all you've talked about the last few months."

"He's tiny," Layla says.

"He is tiny." I agree.

"What's his name?" she asks.

"Eli."

"Eli."

"This is too much cuteness," Cassie says.

"Can we keep him?" Layla asks.

"Oh my gosh, it just got cuter."

"Are you gonna cry?" I ask Cassie.

"How could anyone not?"

The door to my room opens and Mom enters with two plastic bags.

"Pancakes?" I ask.

"Lots of pancakes."

"Did they have chocolate chip?"

"They did when I said my daughter just finished pushing a human out of her cooter."

"Good." I laugh.

Mom digs through one of the bags and pulls out a plastic container. "Here's yours."

Bryce takes Eli from Layla and she hops off the bed to sit by Maggie. I quickly accept the container of pancakes from my mom and pull the lid off. "Am I supposed to eat with my hands?"

"Here." She passes me a set of black plastic utensils wrapped in clear plastic.

"Thanks." I grab my fork and dig into my pancakes.

The first bite hits my tongue and this is exactly what I needed right now.

"How are they?" Mom asks.

"Perfect," I say through a mouthful of food. I look over at Bryce balancing his plastic container of pancakes on his right knee while he holds Eli with his left arm. "You've got this parenting thing down better than I do." I laugh.

"I do."

"You can thank Layla for that," Maggie says. "He was always helping out with her when she was a baby. I trained him to change diapers too."

"Good to know." I smirk.

We eat our pancakes as everyone passes Eli around, fighting over who gets to hold him next.

"Knock, knock," Dr. Watson says as he enters my room.

"Checking in?" Maggie asks.

"Actually, no. Can I have a minute with these three?"

"Oh, okay."

"Is everything okay?" Mom asks.

"Everything is fine, I just need a moment."

"Okay."

"We'll be right outside if you need us," Cassie says and squeezes my hand after passing Eli back to me.

I nod and watch them leave the room, squeezing Eli a bit tighter as they do.

"Is everything actually okay?" Bryce asks.

"Everything is perfect. The results of the paternity test are in."

"Oh," I say. "That was quick."

"A couple people owed me some favors so you guys got pushed to the top of the list."

"What are the results?" Bryce asks. "Am I the father?"

"Congratulations, Bryce." Dr. Watson smiles. "It's a boy."

"Eli is really Bryce's?" I ask.

"He is. Congratulations."

I look over at Bryce and he's already smiling at me.

"He's mine." Bryce smiles. "Ours. He's ours."

"I know." I smile.

"I love you so much."

"I love you." I lean in and kiss him. "I'm gonna let Johnny know."

"Okay."

"Hand me my phone?"

"Here."

I unlock my phone and dial Johnny's number. As usual, I'm sent to voicemail. "Hi, it's me again. I just wanted to let you know the results of the paternity test came in and it's not your baby. It's Bryce's. You're off the hook. You don't need to worry about anything and you'll never hear from me again. You don't have to call me back, I just wanted to make sure you knew." I hang up my phone and set it on the bed beside me.

"You okay?" he asks.

I nod. "I just can't believe there was a chance that this baby was his and he wanted no part of any of it."

"Well, Eli isn't his. He's mine. And I want all of this."

I smile and my phone buzzes. I look down and see a text from Johnny.

Good. I hope my brother enjoys his whore.

I show the text to Bryce and he takes my phone from me.

"We don't need this anymore." He sets it on the tray table.

"Yeah."

"Should we talk about the last name?"

"I guess."

"I don't think it's a secret that I'm not going anywhere. Regardless of what happens, I'm gonna be here for both of you. Always."

"And what if you and I don't last? Are you still gonna be here for him?"

"Of course. But I want us to last, Alex. I want us to make it work."

"So do I."

"Good. Because I would love for him to have my last name." Eli Blaine Wilkins.

It does have a nice ring to it.

"I want him to have your last name too."

"Really?"

"Really."

"Good. That's not all I have to say about this, though."

"Okay. What else is there?"

"I want us to be a family, a real family. I want all three of us to have the same last name." He pulls a tiny black box out of the pocket of his pants and gets down on one knee. "You're by far the most amazing person I've ever met, Alex. I have to spend the rest of my life with you. Will you marry me?"

Epilogue

Bryce pulls into the driveway in his red SUV first and I follow in my black one.

"What do you guys think of the new house?" I ask the kids.

"Pretty," Jana says.

"I like it." Eli agrees.

"Yeah? You guys wanna go inside?"

"Yes!" they cheer.

I turn off my car and Eli unbuckles himself before helping Jana next.

"You're such a good big brother." I smile.

Bryce meets us in the driveway with Liam. I peek into the carrier and look at his bright blue eyes and chubby cheeks. He looks so much like Eli did at that age.

"Ready to go inside?" Bryce asks.

"I guess so." I look up at our house and smile. It's a small ranch style with tan siding and dark brown shutters. Dark brown brick that matches the walkway frames the front door. "It's so pretty."

"It is," Bryce says. "And it's ours."

"This is so crazy. We have a house. We're twenty-two years old and we have a house. Four and a half years ago we were bringing Eli home from the hospital and calling a crib in the basement an apartment and now we have a house. Together. We have a house together."

"I know." He smiles. "Can we go inside now and see if we like it as much as we did when we put the offer in?"

"Hold on, I don't think I've stared at the outside long enough." I take another couple seconds to take in the way the colors of the house stand out against the green grass and orange leaves. "Okay, now I'm ready."

"Let's go."

I hold Bryce's left hand as he carries Liam in his right and we meet Eli and Jana on the front steps.

"You guys ready?" Bryce asks them as I unlock the front door.

"Yes!" Eli says. "Can I pick my room?"

"Absolutely not." I laugh. "Your father and I will decide who gets which room." I open the front door and the kids run in.

"The moving truck should be here any minute," Bryce says.

"So should our moms and my grandma."

"I'll keep an eye out."

I follow the kids inside and I look through the doorway on the right. The living room is small but large enough for a couch, coffee table, and TV. A fireplace sits on the wall opposite of me. I walk through the living room and into the dining room. It'll fit a table for six but not much more. I go through the doorway that leads to the kitchen and look over the light brown wooden cabinets and granite countertop that I fell in love with the first time I saw it.

"No, that's mine!" Eli yells.

"No fighting in the new house!" I yell back. I take a look down the hallway and see the kids darting in and out of the bedrooms.

"I want this room!" Eli points to the door on the right. The master.

"Your father and I will decide today."

"No! I'm running away!" He runs down the hall and I roll my eyes.

Another one of Eli's attempts to get his way by forcing an ultimatum: give him what he wants or he's out.

"You're gonna have to run a lot faster than that if you don't want your dad to catch you again!" I yell as he runs out the front door toward Bryce. "Speed up! Come on, Eli, run faster!"

Okay, I'll admit it. This is not my best parenting moment.

I watch Bryce scoop up Eli before he even makes it to the driveway.

"You lost one." Bryce laughs as he brings Eli up the front steps.

"Yeah and unfortunately you found him." I roll my eyes.

Bryce sends Eli back inside and wraps his arm around me, grazing my scar with his fingers.

I pull away from him and he glances toward my shoulder. "You okay?"

I nod. "I just don't like knowing you can feel it."

"Alex, you were shot. Your scar is normal."

"I know, but still."

"I think you should see a therapist."

"I'm fine. It's been over a year."

"Yeah, and you still have nightmares."

"My psychotic ex broke into our house and shot me. I think nightmares are normal."

"They are. But going to therapy after something like that is also normal."

"I don't need therapy."

"Okay, then let's talk about his sentencing. It's today."

"I know. Cassie's there."

"Yeah, and you told her you don't want details. You should want to know how much time he's gonna serve."

"Well, I don't."

"Alex."

"Can you just drop it? I'm fine. I'm alive."

"You're not you."

"Would you be yourself after getting shot?"

"Can you just think about it? Please."

"I don't need therapy. I'm fine. Let it go." I look down at Liam. "Fourteen weeks already." I smile.

Bryce lets out a sigh. "He's getting big."

"The time goes so fast."

"Way too fast." Bryce shakes his head. "I know this isn't the best time to bring it up, but do you think you want more?"

"What?" I ask, just slightly caught off guard considering I had my first ultrasound this morning.

"Do you want more kids? I'm not asking for a formal conversation about it, just an idea."

Well, I'm pregnant so there's that.

"Do you?" I ask.

"I think so."

"You think so?"

"Yeah, I think so."

"But is that a yes or a no?"

"I'd like more but it's not just my decision. It takes two people to make the baby."

"But if it were up to you, we'd have more?"

"Yeah."

"When?"

"When?"

"Yeah, when?"

"Well, soon, I guess."

"How soon?"

"I don't know." He shrugs. "Why are you being so weird about this?"

"Would you want one now?"

"Now?" He raises his eyebrows. "Alex, what are you not telling me? Are you pregnant?"

"I found out this morning."

"Really?"

I nod. "I was gonna wait until we were settled in the new house to tell you."

"Why?" He laughs and pulls me in for a hug.

"I didn't want to stress you out."

"Alex, all you do is stress me out. Since the day we met, you've been doing nothing but making my head hurt."

"Thanks." I laugh.

"It's a good thing. That's why I put that ring on your finger when you finally let me."

"I only turned down two proposals." I laugh. "The third time really was the charm for you."

"Speaking of saying yes, happy anniversary."

"What?"

"Our anniversary is today."

I think about today's date. October twelfth. Shit.

"Oh my gosh, how did I forget?"

"We've been busy."

"Yeah, but I forgot our first wedding anniversary."

"You also forgot to mention the tiny human you're growing."

"I only got a positive test a couple days ago. And I just had my first ultrasound today."

"You went for an ultrasound? You told me you were going out to breakfast with your mom."

"I wanted to make sure the test I took at home was accurate before I told you."

"Do you have pictures from the ultrasound?"

I nod. "I'll go grab them." I walk back to my car and pull the envelope out of the center console.

"Let me see," Bryce says and holds his hand out.

I hand him the envelope and he pulls out its contents. I look down at the first sonogram and smile at the thought of another tiny baby in me.

"So tiny." Bryce smiles. "Number four."

"Number four."

"Now the mood swings make sense." He laughs.

"Shut up!" I swat his arm.

"How far along are you?"

"They guessed six or seven weeks."

"Wow. Still early."

"Yeah. It's a good thing I decided to start testing regularly because apparently breastfeeding is not the birth control everyone thinks it is."

"Clearly. I love you." He leans in and kisses me.

"I love you more. We better pick out bedrooms before Eli tries to escape again."

"Yeah. We should label the doors with sticky notes so it's easier to get all the boxes in when the moving truck gets here."

"That's a good idea."

"Does anybody know you're pregnant yet?"

"Just you."

"You wanna tape the sonogram to a bedroom door and let them find out that way?"

"I love that." I smile. "Let's go assign bedrooms."

Bryce grabs a stack of sticky notes, a marker, and a roll of tape from his car and leads us inside and down the hallway. "I was thinking."

"About?"

"Why don't we make downstairs our bedroom and use the three upstairs rooms for the kids?"

"That's a good idea. We should make the front bedroom Jana's and the corner room Eli's."

"I think Liam's crib and everything should go in our room for now. You're still breastfeeding in the middle of the night and you're not gonna want to go all the way upstairs and back down."

"I definitely won't. So what do we do with the master?"

"Save it for when Liam needs his own room. We could use that bathroom to bathe the kids this way the one in the hallway can stay somewhat put together."

"That's a good idea, too."

"Let's get the sticky notes up." He writes 'Eli' on the first sticky note and hands it to me. I stick it on Eli's door and do the same with the one for Jana next.

"Can I have a piece of tape?" I ask.

Bryce pulls the roll of tape out of his packet and tears a piece off for me. I take it from him and tape a sonogram to the door of the master bedroom. I look down at Liam and pick him up.

"Grab that." I point to his carrier.

"Why do you pick him up when he's perfectly quiet?"

"Because he's cute and I want to hold him. It's not like I woke him up." I walk into what's gonna be Jana's room and look out the front window. "He really is such a good baby."

I see my mom's car pull up and park on the side of the road and Maggie pulls up behind her.

"Guess our sitter is here," Bryce says.

"Thank goodness. The moving truck showing up might be nice."

We head outside and wait on the front steps.

"The house is beautiful!" Mom says as she and Grandma walk up the walkway. "The pictures online don't do it justice."

"I know." I smile. "The inside definitely needs some work though."

"That's okay. You guys have plenty of time to get it all done. And based on the photos, the kitchen is already gorgeous and I think that's the most important part."

"The nice kitchen really drove the price up," Bryce says.

"Would you stop?" I laugh. "A house in this neighborhood, at this price, is still a steal."

"The house looks incredible!" Maggie says.

"It's so pretty." Layla agrees.

"Thanks. You guys wanna go see inside?" I ask.

"Of course."

I lead them inside and show them the living room first.

"This fireplace is gorgeous," Grandma says.

"Where are the other two kids?" Maggie asks.

"They're probably downstairs fighting over everything imaginable. Eli! Jana! Come say hi!"

Eli runs up the stairs and Jana climbs up behind him.

"Grandma!" He runs over to Maggie and jumps into her arms.

"Hello! My goodness you're getting so big." She smiles. "We are gonna have so much fun today!"

"Do you guys want to see the rest of the house?" I ask.

"Definitely," Maggie says.

I lead everyone through the dining room and into the kitchen.

"Oh my gosh, these countertops." Grandma smiles.

"Aren't they gorgeous?" Mom agrees.

"They are hands down my favorite part of the kitchen," I say.

"Okay, what else?" Maggie asks.

"Let's go down the hallway." I lead everyone down the hall and point to the first door on the right. "Here's the bathroom. It needs some updating."

"Wait, you don't like the pink tile on the walls?" Bryce asks. "Babe, that was my favorite part of the whole damn house. Why am I just now finding this out?"

"Well, it's a good thing I wear the pants in this relationship." I laugh.

"You've got lots of time for updates," Maggie says.

"That's what I told her," Mom says. "This girl just wants everything done at the snap of her fingers. I'm glad she's your problem now, Bryce."

I roll my eyes and keep walking down the hallway. I point to Jana's room. "I think you can read the sticky note on the door to figure out whose room this is gonna be."

"It's a nice size," Grandma says.

"It is. We can definitely make it work for her." Bryce agrees.

"Oh, and here's Eli's." Mom continues to the next bedroom.

My heart thumps against the wall of my chest as we get closer to the door with the sonogram.

Why are you nervous, Alex? You're on kid number four and you're twenty-two years old. And you're married to the father of all four kids. You have a house. Your life is very much together.

"And the master, what's this?" Mom notices the sonogram. "Is this Liam's?"

"Not quite," I say.

"You're pregnant?" Maggie asks.

"We are." I smile.

"You're having another baby?" Layla asks.

"We are," I repeat.

"Congratulations!" Mom pulls me in for a hug.

"Boy or girl?" Grandma asks.

"We don't know yet." I shrug.

"Well, what's your hunch? You had a hunch with every kid and you were right with each one."

"I'm kind of thinking girl." I admit.

"Then we're going with girl!" Grandma cheers.

My phone buzzes in my back pocket and I pull it out and see Cassie's name on the screen. I excuse myself and answer the call. "Hey."

"Hey. I know you said you don't want updates on today, but it's over with."

"Okay."

"He got the maximum sentence for attempted murder."

"Good. How's school going?"

"Oh, it's good."

"You graduate in two months, right?"

"Yeah."

"You're so lucky. I still can't believe I'm gonna graduate an entire year late."

"I'm graduating with a piece of paper, you're graduating with a piece of paper, three kids, a husband, and now a house. You win here, Alex."

I can't help but laugh. "How long are you home for?"

"I have to go back on Sunday."

"You should come over today, we're waiting for the moving truck to get here and we could use more hands. And I have something to tell you."

"Sure. I'm on my way. Can I find out over the phone or does this need to be disclosed in person?"

"Definitely in person."

"Great. See you soon."

"Bye." I hang up my phone and look out the front window just in time to see the moving truck finally backing into the driveway. "It's here!" I yell down the hallway.

Everyone comes into the living room and Maggie grabs the diaper bag off the floor. "We can always keep them overnight if you need."

"I know." I smile. "Thanks. I just know I'll miss them if I'm not with them tonight."

"I know. But if you're busy unpacking or too tired, I can keep them."

"Thanks, Mom." Bryce smiles. "You have the car seats?"

"I do. We'll see you later," Maggie says.

"Bye, Layla," I say.

We follow them out and I watch her get the kids in her car before I join the others at the back of the moving truck.

"Okay, the kids' bedrooms are labeled. Anything that says 'master bedroom' is going downstairs. Miscellaneous can just get dumped in the dining room for now. Everything else is self explanatory," I say.

Everyone grabs a box or two and heads inside. My box is labeled 'kitchen' so I set it on the kitchen floor in the corner while the movers bring the refrigerator in.

"I still find it so odd that they left the oven but took the fridge, microwave, and dishwasher." Mom shakes her head.

"Right?" I agree. "Who disconnects the dishwasher to take it with them?"

"What's your favorite part of the house?" she asks.

"Definitely that fireplace."

"I'm so jealous that you have one of those."

"It's definitely gonna be nice in the winter."

"Very."

I watch the boxes pour in and take a look around.

"I'm proud of you," Mom says. "You're twenty-two years old, you have three kids, one on the way, you're still going to college to get your degree in teaching even though you're married to an electrician who makes enough to support your family. Not to mention the attack."

"Can you not mention it, then?" I groan. "I'm so tired of people bringing that up."

"Alex, you've overcome so much in the last four years. You haven't let a single thing break you. Not very many people can say they made it through half of what you have and came out stronger."

"Knock, knock," Cassie says. "I brought backup."

I look at the front door and see Cassie with Maya and Amanda, each carrying a box in.

"Oh my gosh, you guys are here!" I smile and run to hug them.

"There was no way we were gonna miss Johnny's sentenc-ing," Maya says. "I hope it's okay we came with Cassie."

"Of course. Thanks for being willing to help."

"What's your big news?" Cassie asks.

"Can we maybe put these boxes down first?" Amanda asks. "Eli's stuff is heavy."

"What are the other two boxes labeled?" I ask.

"I also have Eli," Cassie says.

"Mine says Jana."

"Okay, those all go down the hallway." I lead the way and stand to the side so they can get into the bedrooms.

"These are a nice size," Cassie says when their boxes are down.

"That seems to be the consensus." I nod. "How are you guys? How's school going?"

"It's good." Amanda smiles. "I forgot what Fall is supposed to look like."

"Florida isn't as pretty as New York in October?" I laugh.

"Not even close."

"At least you have warmth." Maya laughs. "Maine is feeling more like Alaska every damn day."

"You wanna trade Maine for spit up?" I offer.

"That depends. Does the world's hottest baby daddy come with it?"

"Absolutely not." I laugh.

"What's your news?" Cassie asks. "I'm dying over here."

"Okay, well, this bedroom is Jana's and this one is Eli's." I point to each room. "And Bryce and I are making downstairs our bedroom."

"So the third is Liam's?" Maya asks.

"Not quite." I step out of the way so they can see the sonogram taped to the door.

"You're having another?" Cassie asks.

"Yeah."

"Four damn kids?" Amanda asks.

"Seriously, Bryce!" Maya yells down the hallway. "Get a hobby that lets you keep your pants on!"

I can't help but laugh as I catch Bryce struggling to get the couch angled toward the living room through the front doorway.

"Can I maybe get the couch to the living room before you start harassing my dick?" he groans.

"I can't believe you're having another," Cassie says.

"I know. I'm out of potential godmothers."

"You'll find someone."

"Do you still talk to Alyssa much? Bryce's friend."

"Yeah, but she lives in Maryland again. She graduated in May and went back down."

"Oh, she hasn't told you?" Cassie asks.

"Told me what?"

"Her and Nick are moving up here after his graduation."

"They're still together?" I ask.

"Two years strong."

"Well, that solves that problem." I laugh.

"I'm so happy for you guys," Amanda says.

"Thanks."

"How crazy is it that one of us has a house?" Maya smiles.

"Not as crazy as the fact that we kept in touch after high school, especially with Alex ditching us for the second half of senior year." Cassie laughs.

"So sorry for graduating early to have my baby." I roll my eyes. "I'm really glad we all got close senior year."

"I'm really glad Eli didn't turn out to be Johnny's," Maya says.

"Amen to that." I nod.

"Talking shit?" Bryce asks as he wraps his arms around me from behind.

"About you?" I smirk. "Always."

"How sweet of you."

"We're gonna go grab more boxes," Cassie says. "We don't need to see number five being made."

"That's not how that works." I laugh as they walk away.

"We have a house," Bryce says.

"I know."

"I love you so much."

"I love you more. Could you imagine if your mom never asked me to babysit Layla?"

"What do you mean?"

"If she didn't ask me to babysit, I don't think our moms would've gotten so close, which means we wouldn't have gotten so close. And my mom wouldn't have been praying for us to date."

"I think we still would've ended up together."

"Why's that?"

"I knew the second I met you that you were by far the prettiest girl in the world. And I knew the second I caught a glimpse of Johnny that he did not deserve you. I would've found a way into your life regardless of our mothers' interference."

"I hope so."

"I'm glad it worked out this way, though."

"Why?"

"We're twenty-two and three and a half kids into this thing. We'd be behind if it didn't go this way."

"That's true."

"And you know what else happens because of things going how they did?"

"What?"

"I get to love you longer." He leans in and kisses me.

"I like it this way."

"So do I."

"Just promise me one thing."

"Anything."

"You're not gonna fall for any more babysitters."

He gives me a smirk before kissing me again. "Deal."